Lovers of the African Night

Other books by William Duggan:

THE GREAT THIRST

Lovers of the African Night

WILLIAM DUGGAN

Delacorte Press/New York

Published by
Delacorte Press
1 Dag Hammarskjold Plaza
New York, N.Y.   10017

Manufactured in the United States of America
First printing

Library of Congress Cataloging in Publication Data

Duggan, William.
Lovers of the African night.

I. Title.
PS3554.U396L6   1987   813'.54   87-5221
ISBN 0-385-29540-5

For Lynn Ellsworth

Naring

THE BATTLE OF THE POTS

The first trainload of men arrived from South Africa. They crossed into Kalahariland and stepped off the train at Lorole Station. The BaNare among them climbed onto the bus for Naring.

The bus was enormous, yellow and old, with bars in the windows instead of glass. The driver refused to stop along the way for any reason, so the men peed through the bars. They argued and sang and fought. Some looked out at the fields along the plain, more than half-abandoned since the men had gone away. Others watched the sky, white with clouds then clearing far ahead above Naring, the last and only stop. Naring was the farthest a man could travel on wheels, for beyond it lay the endless Kalahari.

They had not been home in years, since the English army arrived to take away all the men they could find to help them fight the Second World War. The BaNare, who had been off in South Africa mining gold at the time, refused to come back, for fear that the English would sign them up too. So they spent the war in the mines.

Now on the bus, the men watching the sky saw the Naring hills appear. Soon the bus was in the canyon, rocking over stones. On the other side, at the edge of Naring, little girls stood in line at the well. They were naked except for strings of beads and leather fringe around their waists. Metal buckets perched against their hips. The men waved their arms through the window bars of the bus.

"Ladies!" they called. "We are here!"

The girls cried out and dropped their buckets.

"They are here!" they shouted, running behind the battered bus.

"They are here!"

But the bus left them far behind, and then the rest of Naring heard it too. Boys in loincloths waved both arms and shouted. Old men came out to wave and cry out the names of sons they hoped were among this first busload back. But the bus drove on, up the paths between the mud walls and grass roofs to the center of Naring and into the mine office compound. The men jumped down and pushed into the bluewashed buildings to collect their pay.

Year after year, throughout the war, Naring had longed for its men. Without their strength, their company and wages, the world was a lonely, hungry place. BaNare women stopped using money and paid each other in corn and cattle, in labor and milk. They called these years Ke-Tsoga-Nosi, meaning "I-Wake-Alone."

When the BaNare heard that the war was over, women had begun to set up their pots at the gate of the mine office compound. They expected the men to come back hungry and rich, willing to pay any price for a good familiar meal. One by one the women came, until the line of pots stretched deep into Naring. Suddenly everyone was a cook. The women at the end of the line gave up and took their pots home. Days passed and the line grew shorter, then longer, then shorter again, as opinions changed about just how hungry and just how rich the men would be.

At the head of the line of pots stood Ata Three and her daughter, Ata Four. The child was only six years old, too young to remember men. She knew of them only through stories, songs, and the listless sighs of women who remembered them all too well. The married ones slept late every morning, and those who were not went wandering naked at night through the village. Ata Four would wake to watch them, stealing out of her bed to hide in the shadows, creeping close to hear them mumbling magic phrases to make the men appear.

Ata Four watched the men climb down from the bus and vanish into the compound buildings. Then she bent down to adjust the logs under one of her mother's pots. The pots were black, round, and full, low to the ground and of various sizes. Bent double, face close to the ground, Ata Four took this opportunity to take her first good look at the other cooks in line, her mother's competition. The girl peered out between her legs. There she saw them, upside down, very close, and many.

They all had worn their best clothes and brought along their eldest daughters. These girls did very little cooking. They stood behind the pots in tight dresses that stopped above their knees and showed the world the tops of their breasts. Some wore earrings, bracelets, red on their lips, and shoes with tall heels that made their hips look beautiful.

Ata Three was almost as young as the eldest of these daughters, but she wore nothing fancy at all, just a plain blue dress, long and loose, hiding her arms and legs and womanly curves. A gray scarf covered her hair and most of her face, and a gray cloth hung from her waist as an apron. Ata Four was the only daughter there without breasts or hips. Her mother had dressed her the same as herself.

She was only a little girl, but she saw what the other cooks intended. She knew what women said about men, how they set out to win them, as she herself already looked forward to doing. For years on end these miners and soldiers had lived without women. Surely they would come out the gate, hurry past plain Ata Three, and crowd before these shapely beauties beckoning them with spoons.

Ata Three saw her daughter watching the other cooks from between her legs and then rightside up as she added more oil to the pot. She bent down to whisper in Ata Four's ear.

"You work so hard," she said. "Mothers dream of daughters like you."

And then the men came out. They were handsome and strong, shoving, shouting, kicking up dust with their heavy black boots, their pockets bulging with coins. Ata Four grabbed the dented miner's helmet her mother had saved for this day. She clutched it against her curveless chest, struck dumb at the marvelous sight of men. Her mother grabbed a plate, waved her spoon, and cleared her throat. She and the other cooks and daughters cried out at once:

"Time to eat!"

"Meat for you!"

"Porridge!"

"What a journey!"

"Listen to your stomach!"

"Time to eat!"

For only a moment the miners and soldiers halted. Then all together they moved as one man toward the Ata pots. The first fried cakes were ready and the meat was still bloody but brown enough, so Ata Three filled a plate and the first man took it. She filled another, calling for the next customer, and that plate disappeared too. Coins rained into Ata Four's helmet. She looked down at them, the first she had ever seen. Then she looked up at the men. They stood there eating, staring down at the food and then up at Naring around them.

Ata Four's heart jumped each time a miner or soldier reached for her mother's plate. She watched him raise the spoon to his mouth and step back. Her eyes moved from their deep-voiced throats to their heavy shoes to the scarred hands that reached for the plates. The men waiting yelled and punched and sometimes wrestled each other to the ground. At first she was frightened, dry in the throat, but then she saw them laugh and she laughed too. She leaned forward to smell them through the smoke of the logs, the steam of the porridge and the crackling oil. It was a wonderful smell, overpowering, and she sneezed into the helmet. She kept her face down in it and whispered to herself.

"So these are men," she said.

A miner eating overheard her.

"That's right," he said, smiling down. "How lucky for you we are back."

The other cooks watched, disbelieving, irate, as all the men crowded before Ata Three, who filled plates as fast as she could, hurrying to serve them all. Half the men gave up waiting and drifted down to the other cooks. The women shook their heads as they filled their plates, muttering in dismay.

Ata Four watched her mother, the center of attention, the most beautiful woman in the world. Ata Three's face burned with success, with the eyes of men and heat from the pots. Her mother loved men too, and here they were loving her back.

The rest of the BaNare hurried up to the mine office gate, discussing the number of men on the bus, what they would buy with their pay, who they would marry, the names of the babies, the length of the fields they would plow, the height and breadth of Naring's good fortune to have their men come home. By the time they arrived on the scene, the Battle of the Pots was over. They saw the men crowding before Ata Three, and wondered why it was so.

The question became a debate, lasting into the night and for days on end. Some called it luck, the easiest answer of all. Others claimed that the men had felt sorry for a woman and child in such dowdy clothes. They asked the miners and soldiers themselves, who replied that they did not even know who Ata Three was. They remembered only the food, a woman in plain clothes, and a little girl dressed the same way.

Weeks passed and still there was no answer. At last they asked Ata Three herself, who only smiled and offered them something to eat. The BaNare hated mysteries, so they refused to let the matter drop until they figured it out. And in the end they did.

Back in the barracks, during the long years away from Naring, the miners and soldiers had tossed every night on their bunks. After the noise of the day, the roaring machines, shouting to be heard above them, the commotion of the barracks yard where men pushed ahead in line and dueled with sharpened spoons—sometimes the quiet of night came as a terrible shock.

The men would lie on their backs, listening, eyes open.

Above them the metal roof cooled and creaked. The bunks were too close together for the men to rest with their legs bent up at the knees. They would turn to press their cheeks against the concrete wall, moist from warm breath in the windowless barracks. Staring out in the dark, each man would see the shapes and curves and the smooth soft skin of a distant cousin with breasts of shining black. He was alone in the pasture, herding, until she came into it, carrying water. They lay in the grass while the cattle wandered away.

The other cooks had guessed exactly right about the men's nights. They had dressed up their daughters for that. But the men came back by day, and only Ata Three was ready.

They came through the gate, squinting under the brims of their hats, and saw the line of pots and the line of women behind it. They liked the sight, the eldest daughters beckoning. But most of all they liked Ata Four, the only child among the women, and the woman beside her, Ata Three, who looked to them most like home.

By day they had missed their mothers and sisters, an aunt stepping into the compound with a sleeping child on her back, infants crawling on the compound floor. They watched Ata Four press against her mother's side, eyes wide, fearful of the bustle. Something rose in their bellies and throats. Knowing no other name, they called it hunger, and reached out for a plate.

2
NO-MAN'S-LAND

Who loves children, any child?
Who else but Ata One
Who loves men, any man?
Who else but Ata Two
Who serves beer, any beer?
Who else but Ata Three
Who cooks food, any food?
Who else but Ata Four
Who has no husband, any husband?
Who else but Ata Five
Who works by day, any day?
Who else but Ata Six
Who loves by night, any night?
Who else but Ata Seven . . .

This is a song BaNare children sang as they danced in circles, the girls inside, the boys around them, clapping and kicking up dust. They liked the song because it had no end. They added verses and Atas as high as the eldest among them could count. To children the Atas were infinite, endless, a fixture like the moon they danced to or the night sky that excited them, so far away, like the unknown years to come.

In truth, the Atas had a beginning, and at the time the men came back from the war their numbers had reached only as high as Ata Four. She was the eldest daughter of Ata Three, who was the eldest daughter of Ata Two, who was the eldest daughter of Ata One. There were many more Atas than this, for each Ata mother bore daughters with other names, who also bore daughters, and so on. The BaNare called them all Atas, although only four answered to the name.

The Atas lived in a sprawling, fenceless compound between Naring and the ridge of hills to the east. A stream that children leapt over in summer and walked through in winter wound around the village and through a canyon cut in the ridge. After heavy rains the stream flooded the land between Naring and the Atas, except for a few high spots where Boers lived. The rest of the land between Naring and the Atas remained empty and overgrown.

The Naring Boers dated from an earlier age, when the BaNare fought off invaders who ventured to the edge of the Kalahari spoiling for a fight. Luckily for the BaNare, few bothered to come so far out of the way. As South Africa fell to wave after wave of Zulu, Boer, and English hordes, the BaNare held on to Naring. Refugees learned of their luck and arrived to join them. It was a sign of how wild and hard were those times that among these refugees numbered some Boers.

One of these Boers, named Roodie, lost his wife at the very moment she gave birth to a son. He hired a BaNare girl named Ata to nurse the infant. She bore him children of her own, beginning with Ata Two, of various colors depending on the time of day the child was conceived.

The Boers never asked to settle in Naring itself. They liked the feeling of space, of the empty brush at their door. They built their compounds far apart and never fenced them in. Their houses were made of brick and mud, round and square, widely spaced and facing every which way, with roofs pointed and flat, of grass, hammered metal, and mud. The BaNare fenced their compounds and kept them completely clear of grass and weeds, while the Boers kept theirs overgrown with weeds and brush and strewn with every kind of junk. Goats grazed among the mess and sometimes wandered into the houses. It was the way the Boers liked it, and not at all like Naring.

Roodie was a blacksmith. He fixed BaNare plows and wagons from a forge behind his compound, which the Atas kept as neat as a BaNare compound, though they never built a fence. Around the cookfire the Atas sold beer to men in dry gourds cut in half. They brewed the beer in a clay pot too big to fit through a door, so they built a house around it. As more Atas came along, they built more houses, so the compound came to resemble a smaller village outside Naring.

Aside from beer, the Atas specialized in children and men. Their customers sat drinking and joking with them, and soon enough some moved in, but never for very long. Each time a man moved out, the other Atas consoled the jilted girl with tales of their own disappointments. This only made them all feel worse. Then another man came along, fresh from the mines with dresses and shoes for his mother and sisters. Sometimes he stopped at the Atas' first. Sometimes he moved in. The Atas loved the dresses but never wore the shoes.

Every child that these men left to the Atas came out of their bellies a girl. There were no Ata boys. The name Ata meant "Increase," and that is what they did. By the time Ata Four appeared, the Atas had borne the children of countless BaNare, many Boers, and several Indians. Not a single child knew even the name of her father. When an Ata bore an Indian child, the father's family offered to take the baby and raise her to work in the family shop. The Ata mother always refused.

When Roodie died, the Atas buried him under his forge and then gave it away to other Boers along with the junk around it. This was soon after the war began, when the men disappeared and the Atas had to look for other ways to make a living. They took any job they could find, washing clothes, gathering thatching grass and firewood, patching walls, pounding corn into flour, tending goats and children. Ata Four learned to walk and took her place beside her mother among the Atas discussing men as they worked. The little girl listened, wishing them home. This was an unusual time in Naring, for the entire village was as manless as the Atas. There was no other subject of conversation. No wonder Ata

Four would be so ready to love men, to give herself completely and happily to them. When at last they came, miners and soldiers bursting out the gate, many ended up at the Ata compound. The soldiers named it No-Man's-Land.

Even after she won the Battle of the Pots, it was many years before the BaNare noticed Ata Four again. They excused themselves by explaining that those were the days when they were caught between ages, without heroes for the first time ever, beyond the reach of great men and fortunate twists of fate. While children sang of the Atas, adult songs recounted the lives of noble BaNare warriors, saints, makers of rain, who had saved them time and time again from dangers great and greater. The BaNare did not yet see that times had changed, the past was ended, that they needed a new kind of hero. It took them years to realize that her name was Ata Four.

3

WASHING AWAY THE NIGHT

The last BaNare soldier came back to Naring many months after the other men, long after the clouds of summer had given way to a clear winter sky. He alone came back by night.

He was Boko Tladi, last in a long line of famous Tladis, Naring's second family as far back as the BaNare existed. The Potsos were the BaNare's first family, for they were always the chiefs. But the Tladis gave Naring its heroes, from the original Tladi, evil but undeniably great, who killed the reigning Potso and conquered the Kalahari, to Mojamaje, beloved Eater of Rocks, who saved the BaNare from themselves, to Jacob the Ox-Killer, a Tladi by marriage, a giant and protector of all small things, which to him included every single BaNare.

Boko had left Naring the day he turned sixteen, and quickly became the youngest foreman's assistant the South African mines had ever known. In the barracks he made the BaNare eat and sleep together. Underground, he worked them to collapse. But when fights broke out, the BaNare were never blamed. Once they fought a band of Imitation Zulu behind the barracks, at night. The mine fired all the Imitations and not a single BaNare. The next day one of the Imitation Zulu slipped back underground and lunged with a knife at Boko's back.

All witnesses told the same story, over and over, in mine after mine for years to come. Boko felt the motion behind him, swung his pickaxe, and pierced the assassin's chest.

To the BaNare he was a fierce young man, courageous but wild. They knew of his mining reputation and had witnessed themselves his own father, Jacob the Ox-Killer, striking Boko square on the head with a pump handle. Boko had been wearing his miner's helmet, and thus survived the blow. All Naring heard the helmet ring, the sound of a father doing his best to knock some sense into his son.

Boko had been home on leave from the mines when the war broke out, and he signed up even before the English came hunting for recruits. His grandfather, Mojamaje, had taught him English, so he became the only BaNare sergeant-major. He helped the English recruit, train, and direct the Kalahariland troops in Egypt. Instead of sending the African troops fully armed into battle, the English gave them odd jobs up and down the front. Even so, Boko won a name as a warrior, clearing minefields that no one else would dare to enter, unloading drums of fuel from burning trucks, crawling deep into forward trenches to set off smokescreens, burying the most horrible dead that no one else would touch.

Back in Kalahariland, Boko stepped off the train at Lorole Station and waited for the Naring mine office bus. He leaned against the brick wall of the station, hands deep in his army overcoat, looking out across the plain to the distant line of the Naring hills. For half his life, all of his years as a man, he had lived among miners and soldiers, waiting in long lines before steaming cauldrons of food with a metal plate in his hand, a world of tough talk and fistfights that had been his only home. He had loved the nights in Egypt, the great tents, songs rising from fires scattered across the desert, the stars in the sky upside down. The hills away in the distance now looked very small, and Naring behind them he knew to be smaller still.

He knew the BaNare thought him wild and dangerous. He deeply believed them wrong. His father's blow had indeed knocked some sense into Boko's head. From that day on, Boko had set out to change himself. But the war came and the BaNare had no chance to see the difference. He was not at all wild in the war, just serious, hardworking, and, when necessary, brave.

The time had come to make a choice, to settle down in Naring, marry, and farm, or to live among men forever, or at least as long as his arms held up to the work. Settling down would give him family and friends, the mines would give him excitement and money. Some men tried to do both, to farm one year, go mining the next, but this never worked for long. When back in Naring they hated having no money, and when back in the mines they hated the hard, womanless, childless life. For Boko it could only be one or the other.

And the Tladis needed him. One of the very few pieces of news to reach the BaNare soldiers in Egypt was that Boko's father had disappeared while herding cattle in the Kalahari. After a mining accident years before, the Ox-Killer sometimes forgot his own name or chopped wood with the wrong end of the ax. Some said that even his famous blow against Boko had come as an instinct rather than as a thought. And now, one day like any other, he had taken a herd of cattle out to pasture and wandered away. The Ox-Killer's disappearance left Boko head of the Tladi family, and this burden now awaited him in Naring.

Boko watched the sky over the plain, as dark clouds moved to cover the sun and chill the air beneath them. A soldier who had also arrived on the train came up to him and spoke.

"You are Boko Tladi," he said. "I served beneath you."

Boko smiled and shook the stranger's hand. There was a deep scar on the man's cheek, just below one eye.

"I should know you," said Boko, "if not from your face then from your voice. I can tell you are from Northwest District."

"Yes, and it is too far away to go back. I have no family left there, no reason to travel a distance like that."

"Too far away for me to find someone who knows you and ask your name?"

"Timela Timela," the man said.

The name meant "Stray" in BaNare.

"Many strays end up in Naring," said Boko. "Come with

me there. The women will like your foreign voice and that scar beneath your eye. My family is short of men."

Timela looked out at the plain and the distant Naring hills, brown and bare from a rainless winter.

"All right," he said. "I stayed on with the English as long as they let me. I am lucky to meet you like this. We told stories about you in Egypt. I am sure you are even larger among the BaNare."

"In Naring," said Boko, "the large and small change places overnight. A mysterious sickness wipes out one herd, in another all the cows give birth to female calves. One man's sons run away to the mines, the sons of another come back after years underground and give him a sack of coins. I promise you, by the time our first grandchildren arrive, you will be rich and I will come begging at your door."

Timela laughed, but at once he wanted it all to be true.

"So you will stay in Naring," he said.

"What do you mean?" said Boko.

"I just thought," said Timela, retreating, "that a man of your reputation might find Naring small after all these years."

"Where else can I go? The mines? Or slip across the South African border and seek my fortune some other way? The fortunes there are for Boers and English."

"On the other hand," said Timela, "a man like you must have much at stake in Naring."

"But we are no longer like them," said Boko, changing directions again. "Those who have never seen South Africa or Egypt. We will be restless among them."

"You are too far ahead of me," said Timela. "Let me build up a herd, plow fields, have a family, and then I will join you complaining of boredom in tiny Naring."

Boko laughed, relaxing, pushing the worry of settling down back into the future. This day was his last as a man on his own, and he might as well enjoy it.

The Naring mine bus arrived, and Timela and Boko boarded it. They were alone on the bus, and sat in the back

discussing the war. Now and then as Timela spoke he raised a
hand to touch the scar. Boko saw through the barred window
the sun gone but the sky bright with lightning among the
clouds, a freak winter storm. The air was cold and moving.
Arrows of rain drove across the plain and crashed against the
bus. The two men turned to face the windows, shouting,
washing the dust from their skin. Then the sky cleared and
the world turned dark and silent outside the bus.

The moon came out as the bus rolled into the Naring mine
office compound. Timela and Boko came out through the
gate, shoulder to shoulder, two young men, restless and on
their own, facing the night and their lives beginning anew.

"Hungry, soldiers?" said Ata Three.

The men stopped and peered through the shadows. They
saw a woman, three pots, and a little girl. Boko and Timela
came over. Boko leaned forward, over the pot.

"What have you got?" he said.

He had not been this close to a woman for a very long
time.

"Fried cake," she said, leaning forward too. "Porridge.
Meat. Lucky for you this time you do not have to wait in
line."

Boko saw past her loose dress, the scarf, the child, to her
high, wide cheeks, her full lips, her eyes intent on his own,
her voice young and intimate in the moonlight. Timela
laughed softly and backed away, vanishing into the night,
leaving Boko fixed before the pots. Boko did not see him go.
He saw only the woman before him.

"Good business today?" he said.

Ata Three gave no reply. Instead she smiled, inquiring
with her eyes. Ata Four watched. Perhaps her mother had not
heard the question.

"This morning was good," the little girl explained. "The
other cooks left after that. The bus driver said he might bring
more."

"Yes," said Ata Three. "This little girl waited all day for
you."

"I'm sorry, I'm just not hungry," he said. "I wish very much I were."

Ata Three turned away now, kicking sand onto the last of the fire beneath her pots. There was no flame. The pots were almost cool. As she bent down to pull the logs from the fire, Boko bent down to help. They arranged them in one long bundle. Ata Four packed up, too, all the time watching her mother and the soldier speaking softly with faces close together.

"Welcome home," said Ata Three. "Even if you are not hungry."

"I do not understand it," he said. "In the army I was always hungry. Before that in the mines. Can you explain it?"

"You are excited. At coming home."

"You think so?"

"Truly," she said.

"Will I ever eat again?"

He smelled her skin. Her mouth was close. He tasted her breath.

"These things never last," she said. "Believe me. Maybe you will eat tomorrow."

Ata Four listened. None of it made any sense.

Boko helped Ata Three lift the firewood onto her head. He carried the bucket of leftovers. Each of them took a pot, Boko the largest, Ata Four the smallest, and set off through the village.

Ata Four watched the pale sand before her, winding among the dark compounds. The air was cool, except when she stepped between the soldier and her mother. There the air was hot.

Boko watched the pointed roofs against the night and the woman moving through the shadows. She raised an arm to steady the wood on her head. He caught his breath at the line of her arm and breasts, down to her hips and the legs hidden beneath the dress. His last day as a man on his own was over, but now would come his last night.

Ata Three kept her eyes ahead. They passed compounds

with cookfires glowing deep within them. She heard him, felt him beside her, his eyes on her face and moving along her each time she raised her arm to steady the wood. They reached the edge of the village. Boko looked down at the roofs of the Boer and Ata houses reflecting the moon.

He realized at last that the girl and the woman were Atas.

Suddenly she was no longer an unknown woman at night, but someone whose story he knew, not hers alone but all her family's. The dark around them was no longer empty. He recognized Naring.

Boko stumbled on rocks, following the mother and daughter down to No-Man's-Land. On the edge of the compound he stopped. Ata Three turned around.

"After all that work," she said, "surely you are hungry now. Come eat. There is also beer and tea. And hot water for washing."

Ata Four looked up at the soldier. He stood very straight, unmoving, caught between the day past and tomorrow.

"I must think about it first," he said.

Ata Three laughed.

"Think?" she said. "You are the first man on earth to say that. Men do not think about these things. They do them."

The little girl reached out and touched his trousers, tugging him gently forward. He followed them into the compound. At the center, in a clearing among the houses facing every which way, he saw the glow of the dying cookfire and the shape of the logs around it, where men drank beer by day. Ata Three went into a house and brought out a bundle of blankets.

"Sleep with your grandmother," she whispered to Ata Four, handing the girl the blankets. Then she and the soldier disappeared into the house.

Ata Four stood watching the shadows for a long time, happy for her mother. For months now there had been soldiers and miners spending nights with Atas, but never with Ata Three. She saw how the Atas warmed as the sun went down, speaking more quickly, laughing at anything, unable to stay seated in any one place. The Ata children could not help feeling it, too, each daughter glad to see her mother so happy to have a man for her own.

Ata Four wrapped herself in the blankets and sat on a log before the dying cookfire embers. Already she loved the night. Day could be hard, especially that morning when he woke up quiet, cool, impatient. The daughter felt it as much as her mother. He washed, pulled on his shirt, and never came back. Ata Four herself had only seen this happen. Her mother had waited, choosy, patient, and now had found the one man she wanted. Ata Four rose, pulled the blankets tighter against the cold, and entered her grandmother's house.

Boko Tladi woke with his arms around Ata Three. Her bed was a neat stack of blankets and skins on the smooth mud floor of her tiny house. He opened his eyes to absolute dark and unfolded her from his arms. She made no sound as he rose to his feet, pulled a blanket over his shoulders, and went outside.

A single ember still glowed in the cookfire. He sat on a log and watched it. He tucked his face into the blanket and smelled her there, everywhere on his skin. He looked up at the ridge, then the other way, for a very long time, up at Naring. Now and then he heard a sound from an Ata house. A wind rose, carrying dust, and he closed his eyes against it.

When the wind died he opened his eyes. A streak of gray slipped over the Naring ridge.

An Ata came out.

She wore a blanket around her waist and nothing else. Her breasts were long and came to points, sweeping up and away. She stretched and yawned, raising her arms and rising high on her toes. Boko watched her hang a dress on the branch of a bush and dip a basin into a barrel. He knew those barrels from the war. He had unloaded thousands, lifting them off the truck, rolling them over the sand.

Another Ata came out, young and unclothed like the first. She dropped her dress on a bush and dipped a bowl into the barrel. One by one the Atas came out. They filled their basins and bowls and formed a circle around the barrel. Bushes grew dark with the shadows of dresses.

The sky brightened as Boko watched. They spoke to each other, softly, washing each other's back, rinsing each other's hair, Atas of all ages with gleaming breasts of every color and shape. Each Ata placed one foot and then the other into her basin. She drew water up each leg, parting the blanket up to her hip.

The youngest girls with the least to wash finished first. They pulled the blanket from their waist and slipped their dresses over their heads. For the moment between they wore nothing at all. These young Atas filled kettles and pots with water and set them down before Boko, on the wood of yesterday's fire. He watched them crouch to blow against the whitened ends of the logs. Red sparks glowed. The girls pressed twigs and grass against them.

Boko looked up. The rest of the Atas finished washing and pulled off their blankets. They slipped on their dresses. Boko looked down. The twigs flamed, and the girls added slivers of bark. Soon the fire glowed with heat. Boko pulled his hands from under the blanket and held them out to the fire.

Gray spread across the sky. Men came out, in trousers and bare chests. They stretched and grunted and rubbed their eyes with their palms. Each little girl took a basin of warm water to her mother's latest love. Boko saw the water shine against the men's skins, their strong arms and miners' chests.

The little girls brought them their shirts, then porridge and tea. Hungry and clean, the men sat down on the logs around Boko. There was sugar in both the porridge and tea. Ata Four, late to wake, ran to Boko with a basin filled with hot water. The sun rose above the ridge. Boko rose to wash.

4

BLUE THORN

"Where were you?" said Boko's mother.

She met him at the gate of the Tladi compound, where not an hour before a neighbor had reported seeing her son among the men waking up in No-Man's-Land.

Boko embraced his mother, known as Ma-Boko, and greeted the other Tladis as they heard his voice and came rushing out. There was his unmarried aunt Naledi, his sister Nea, Nea's husband Philip, and their three children whom Boko had never seen. They sat him down and fed him, asking questions that soldiers returning before him had already answered for them, but they wanted to hear it from Boko's own lips. Philip especially never tired of the stories, for he had been sick with flu when the English came recruiting. He tried to rise from the bed, but his wife Nea pushed him back down.

The Tladis in turn told Boko about their life without him, the birth of Nea's children, his father's disappearance, how often they had spoken of Boko and wished him safely back.

"And then your first night home," said his mother, "you spend at the Atas' instead of here."

She said this not as a complaint but as a fact, wondering at the variety of disappointments available in the world.

Just then Timela Timela appeared at the gate. Boko invited him in and introduced him. Nea went away and came back with a bowl of sour milk. As Timela drank, Ma-Boko rose to prepare another bed beside her son's in one of the Tladi houses. Nea's eldest child climbed into Timela's lap.

"Welcome to Naring," said Philip. "After a war you will find it tame."

"Thank you," said Timela. "It looks just fine to me."

Boko introduced him to the many BaNare neighbors who came to the compound to welcome Boko back to Naring. There were childhood friends, distant cousins, friends of the family, children born while he was away at war, soldiers who had served under him in Egypt, miners he had led in the mines, and herders of Tladi cattle. Like most BaNare the Tladis gave part of their herd to others. The first calf born belonged to the herder, the second to the Tladis, the third to the herder, the fourth to the Tladis, and so on. In this way the Tladi herd continued to grow and the herder built up a herd of his own. There were enough Tladi cattle for Boko to give Timela some to herd, to give him a start on his own.

That night, Timela and Boko shared a Tladi house. As soon as the compound outside fell quiet, Boko rose and dressed. Timela spoke from the dark.

"The soldiers and miners admire you," he said. "The others seem to fear you."

"And you?" said Boko.

"I want to think we are not so different."

Boko stood still in the dark.

"I wish I had another sister," he said. "You could marry her right away."

"So they all would come to me and leave you alone."

"I guess that's right," said Boko, and he went out into the night.

The next morning, Ma-Boko met him again at the Tladi gate.

"Please," she said. "Go over and see Monosi."

Boko kissed her and passed into the Tladi compound. Later that day, unmarried women came to see him, to shake his hand and arrange themselves in womanly poses before him. The rush of men back to Naring put marriage on all their minds, and what better catch than Boko Tladi? They knew that these Ata things never lasted, and each one hoped that soon enough he would marry her.

The Tladis lived in the oldest circle of compounds in all

Naring, directly across from the Potsos, the family of the chief. In the clearing between, against the wall of the chief's compound, stood a wild fig tree with branches long and thick with shade. The chief's council met beneath it, and after the death of Mojamaje, Boko's famous grandfather, the BaNare had hung his long, famous knife from the tree, to beat when announcing important meetings. It rang with a solid, ancient sound. The BaNare had always expected Boko to marry Monosi Potso, daughter of Puo, the present chief. She had grown up with Boko's sister Nea, and thus with Boko himself. When he tired of the Atas, as all men eventually did, he and Monosi would marry.

Monosi did not join the stream of BaNare passing through the Tladi compound to welcome Boko home, and Boko did not come over to greet Monosi. All those years while Boko had been away in the mines, she too had expected him to come back and marry her. She was exactly the proper age when the war broke out and Boko disappeared again. That was many years ago. Now she watched from across the clearing the young women coming and going from the Tladi compound. She envied them their boldness and youth. Had she once been like that, all flesh and desire, all senses and empty of sense? Time and again she tried to cross the clearing but found that she could not. She had waited too long. She had dreamed of him every night. Now he was back, in the arms of an Ata instead of her own.

Monosi leaned on the wall of the Potso compound clearing, staring across at the Tladis, running one hand along her arm, under the sleeveless dress to lay her palm on the smooth knob of her shoulder. A man came up to speak to her. She saw a deep scar beneath one of his eyes.

"Why does he ignore you?" he said. "I know that I could not."

Monosi stood up straight, facing him over the compound wall.

"You are the stranger, Timela. And now I know why the

Tladis took you in. They like their porridge with plenty of sugar."

Timela rested a hand on the wall between them.

"And you," he said, "daughter of the chief?"

"I like mine plain."

Timela raised himself up to sit on the wall, facing across the clearing with Monosi behind him.

"He will come to you soon."

"Did he tell you that?" she said.

"No, but I have seen you watching. Up close I can see that you are a woman who chooses men, not one who is chosen. You have your pick of us all. No man can hold out long against you."

This time Monosi believed that he meant it. From the back he resembled Boko, even a bit from the front, and he spoke with strength and sincerity.

"Then why does he go to the Atas?" she said. "Do you?"

"I am new here. Until I know more about Naring, I must take very careful steps. Maybe some men risk nothing by going to the Atas, and maybe some risk all. I do not want to go and find out later that I number among the lucky."

"You want to marry here," said Monosi.

"Once I have a herd of my own."

"Do you have anyone in mind?"

He turned to face her.

"Who would have me now?" he said. "I am no one to Naring."

"Many would have you."

"Would you?"

"I do not know you," she said. "I would need some time."

Timela reached out to touch her arm.

"Forgive me," he said. "I should not be envious, he has earned his name and all he has. But to see you waiting, day after day, makes me wish you were waiting for me."

When he left her, Monosi rubbed her arm where Timela's hand had rested. It was the first time in years a man had so much as touched her. This thought gave way to worry, but then she replaced it with anger. If Boko could wake up each morning in No-Man's-Land, why should she resist Timela?

Again that night, Boko slipped out of the Tladi compound and down to No-Man's-Land. This time Timela let him go without a word. The next morning Ma-Boko again met her son at the gate.

"What is wrong with you?" she said. "There are plenty of men in Naring these days. Do you think Monosi will wait forever?"

Again a stream of young women came to see him, as he continued discussing the state of the Tladi cattle with the BaNare who herded them. Timela crossed the clearing again to find Monosi leaning on the wall. He moved close to face her across it.

"He is afraid of you," he said. "Once he crosses this clearing to see you, the decision is made. He will settle down and marry, stay in Naring, give up his life of adventure. A decision like that requires careful thought."

"Is that what he does at the Atas," she said "—think?"

"You will have to ask him."

"So," said Monosi, "have you picked her out?"

"Who?"

"The lucky girl you will marry as soon as you become rich."

"You laugh, but with cattle one never knows. The rich become poor and the poor become rich overnight."

"Overnight?"

"So they tell me," said Timela, smiling now too.

This time they both sat up on the wall, changing the subject. Timela told her all about where he spent his childhood, how he lost his family, his hopes for a life in Naring.

That night as Boko rose to head down to No-Man's-Land, he spoke to Timela.

"How is Monosi?"

"Fine."

Boko opened the door, and Timela saw moonlight through it.

"I have known her all my life," said Boko.

"I have known her two days."

On the way to the Ata compound Boko felt his step slowing and his neck aching, a tiredness overcoming him. When he reached the arms of Ata Three, she tasted of something strange, a flavor new to his lips, the first pungent hint of regret.

The next morning, as Ata Four brought him hot water for washing, she set the basin down, looked into his face, and raised her hands to her mouth.

"My mother loves you," she said. "You are the best one of all."

He looked away. He was quiet among the other men washing. When she brought him porridge and tea, his eyes still avoided her own. Her mother had finished washing herself and was back in the house when Ata Four came for Boko's shirt. She tried to hide her eyes from her mother, but Ata Three saw them and cried out, throwing herself at the wall, pressing her face against it.

Ata Four ran out with the shirt. Boko was there on the log, drinking his tea among the other men, a world away from their conversation. Ata Four held his shirt over her mouth and spoke into his ear.

"Please," she said, "oh, please stay just another night. You are not like other men. You must not go. My mother loves you. No one else can ever love you as much. You like it here, I know it. Please, oh, please . . ."

Boko rose, tugged his shirt from her hands, and left her without a word. As he walked back up to Naring, he admitted his mistake. He had allowed his own weakness to harm another, this Ata who already loved him. The daughter was of an age when she lived for only her mother, and he perhaps had harmed her even more.

This time it was Monosi, not his mother, waiting for him at the Tladi gate.

"Remember me?" she said.

Boko stopped before her, his head pounding and his gaze

unsteady. Here was someone else his weakness had certainly harmed, Monosi who once had loved him long ago.

"Of course I remember you," he said.

"Say my name."

"Monosi."

"Thank you," she said.

Behind him she saw the BaNare beauties coming toward the Tladi compound. His eyes were cold and empty on her. She shivered.

"Your admirers are here," she said.

"It is over," he said.

"What is?"

He lowered his eyes to the ground, shaking his head, and moved past her into the Tladi compound.

Monosi walked away, holding her arms around herself to keep from falling. What was over? This Ata thing or his by-gone love for her?

Timela came to see her again, but her thoughts wandered away from him. When he left her, she went to bed and slept through the afternoon. That night Timela lay awake, waiting for Boko to leave for No-Man's-Land. When he finally did, Timela saw through the open door the first streak of daylight in the sky.

When the sun came up, Monosi rose to look out across the clearing. She saw Boko coming back again from No-Man's-Land.

"Thieves," she said aloud, watching him disappear into the Tladi compound.

She made her way down through Naring to the Atas', to plead with them to give Boko back to her. A girl stood at the end of the path, picking her teeth with a reed.

"Who serves Boko Tladi?" Monosi said.

The girl led her to Ata Four, who knelt behind a black goat tied by the neck to a bush. A leather strap bound its hind legs. The other Ata went away. Monosi stood above Ata Four and the goat.

"You serve Boko Tladi," Monosi said.

The little girl held a blue enamel bowl in one hand. The other hand tugged at the udder, squirting milk into the bowl. Ata Four looked up at Monosi. The goat tried to look as well, but the rope held its neck too tight.

"You are tall and beautiful," said Ata.

Monosi smiled.

"Not as beautiful as you will be," she said.

Ata looked down at the goat. Its snout and slender demon's tongue reached toward a purple berry on the bush. Ata slapped its head.

"But I will not be tall," she said.

Monosi knelt, her back straight and long, on one knee behind the goat. Ata milked. Spurts of milk rang against the bowl.

"He is sad," said Ata.

"I thought he comes here to be happy."

The goat suddenly hated giving milk. Its forelegs jittered. The bush swayed as the goat tugged on the tether. Monosi pressed her hands against the flanks, steadying the goat as Ata milked.

"I know who you are," said Ata. "I know what they say."

"What do they say?" said Monosi.

"They say he loves my mother."

Ata let go the udder. She sat back on her knees, licking the hot milk from her fingers.

"You loved him when you were small like me," said Ata. "You wanted to marry him years ago. Then you would have a child almost as old as me. But he went to war instead."

Monosi peered into the little girl's face. Her cheekbones were high, her eyes were large and unswerving from Monosi's gaze.

"How do you know this?" said Monosi.

"Everyone knows."

"So everyone knows everything."

"No," said Ata. "There is a secret."

Monosi let go the goat. It tried to turn its head to look at them, but the tether held it.

With both hands Ata held up the bowl.

"Drink," she said. "You helped me work."

Monosi drank, peering over the edge of the upraised bowl. Ata told her the secret.

"At first he came to love her, at night. Today he came in the early morning, before the sun, to sit on a log and be sad. Everyone washed. I gave him porridge and tea. He went away."

Monosi lowered the bowl.

"That is all?" she said.

Ata sighed, deeply for such a little girl.

"I wished very much for more," she said.

Monosi handed the bowl to Ata, leaning forward to kiss her.

"How can I thank you?" she said.

"You cannot," said Ata, rising.

Monosi untied the back legs as Ata released the tether. The goat leapt away, but only a step. It turned back to watch them with slit eyes narrow and mean. Ata watched Monosi hurry back to Naring, but the truth remained solid, bitter against her tongue. She had not believed it would happen to her mother, a love of the night turning cold by day. All Naring would soon learn that Boko Tladi no longer loved Ata Three. The sooner the better. Then other men would want her. And one of these would turn out to be the kind of man who stayed.

Back up in Naring, Monosi knew that priceless news was a weapon, not a shield, and the sight of her shapely rivals coming and going from the Tladi compound drove her back across the clearing to her own empty bed. She lay atop it, practicing what to say, beautiful speeches lost in the dark. Her competition had nothing to lose. They had not invested their lives in him. He had already broken an Ata heart. Maybe he was afraid of breaking her own. By visiting No-Man's-Land, if only in the morning, he was not just refusing to settle down. He was refusing to settle down with her. He himself had no idea what he wanted.

Rain fell, the sky warmed, and old men asked Boko how many fields he would plow that year. He answered them with evasions, confusing the askers but not the soldiers and miners who overheard. They too felt lost, unused to mothers reaching into their pockets to remove their pay, women they hardly knew hounding them into marriage. Their families readied the wagons for the journey out to the fields to plow, but the unmarried men waited for Boko to make his decision, back to the mines or out to plow, to flee or marry into this foreign place they once had called home.

Monosi lay in her bed all afternoon and into the night, summoning the courage to face him again. She heard Timela calling her name in the compound outside, but she did not answer. There was no time to lose. Her rivals would soon discover the secret. Some bold little temptress would hide in the shadows, waiting for Boko to pass on his way to the Ata compound. Wearing only a blanket, she would leap from the bushes, holding the blanket out like vulture wings, showing him all of her bare curves glowing with moonlight. She would wrap the blanket around them both, pressing his face against her high exquisite breasts, his nose between them, breathing in the glorious scent of her skin.

Monosi sat up. Her eyes opened wide in the dark. She ran her hands along her breasts, feeling her heart racing beneath them. Blood rushed between her ears, to the tips of her fingers, between her legs.

She rose from the bed, drew the blanket around herself, and slipped out into the night. She made her way down toward the Ata compound. She found a dark shadowy mass back from the path, walked into it, and crouched down among the silent bushes. Her bare chest rested on her bare thighs beneath the blanket. The night was cold. She pulled the blanket closed around her, leaving only a space to peer out at the moonlit path.

"This is ridiculous," she whispered.

Cocks crowed far away in Naring, dogs joined in, and

something rustled in the bushes behind her. She heard her breath and heart beneath the blanket, and closed her eyes.

The sun rose, and the Atas again found Boko around their fire. But this time Ata Three came over to him instead of her daughter.

"Come here," she said.

Boko followed her into her house.

"Stop this," she said, her voice thin and searching for force. "You are punishing my daughter each time she sees you. Go away and do not ever come back."

After Boko left and the other men wandered away, the Atas went to work. Ata Four kept so close to her mother they stumbled over each other's feet.

"He will come back to you," said Ata Four, scrubbing a pot. "I will make him come back."

"There is no need," said Ata Three, her voice calm. "To me he is already forgotten."

"He wants to come back. Truly. He cannot go. See how he comes in the morning. Soon he will come again at night."

"These things happen," said Ata Three. "You will see."

Ata Four pressed her face closer to the pot, then inside it, alone in the dark.

"No," she whispered, hearing her voice from all sides. "It will never happen to me."

At last some Atas found Monosi asleep in the thicket. She woke as they tried to lift her, then she followed them into the compound. Ata Four came up to her, pointing to one of the logs around the fire.

"He sits here," the little girl said.

Monosi sat down on the spot. The fire before her was smoking and red with flames invisible in the sunlight. She held open her blanket to wave hot air inside it.

"I am still cold from the night," she said.

Ata Four brought her porridge and tea. Then Monosi washed, tying the blanket around her waist to bare her breasts and back to the water. Ata Four washed Monosi's back and rinsed her hair. She brushed a bee from the blanket.

"They are so slow in winter," said Ata Four. "Like Boko Tladi. He must make up his mind."

She went away and came back with a dress for Monosi. The blanket came off, the dress went on, and Monosi sat down on the log again. Ata Four sat down beside her.

"I told them about you," the little girl said. "They say that they will help."

One by one the Atas came out of their houses, or stood up from patching a wall, or stopped chopping wood or washing an infant with warm water glistening with soap. One by one they came up to Monosi, reaching out one hand for Monosi to shake, placing the other hand over the forearm extended, knees slightly bending, warming Monosi twice as fast as the fire or the sun.

They sat down around her, filling the logs.

"Lungroot will do it," one Ata said.

"Too strong," said another.

"She just wants to marry him, not kill him."

"At least it always works."

"No roots or barks or berries."

"We can give it to her."

"A cure for the shyness."

"She is not shy," said a younger Ata, "except with him. Are you shy?"

She looked at Monosi, who shook her head no.

"See? She is not shy at all. She is only in love."

"I can cure that."

"She does not want to cure it."

"She wants him to love her back."

As each Ata spoke, Monosi moved her eyes from face to face, wondering which one was the little girl's mother.

"You loved him first," said another Ata.

"You alone deserve him."

"No one else."

The little girl sat beside Monosi, digging her toes into the warm sand around the fire. At last she spoke, without looking up, watching her buried toes.

"Blue thorn," said Ata Four.

The Atas fell silent.

"Of course!"

"Smart girl!"

"The perfect thing!"

"Of course!"

"What is it?" said Monosi. "What is blue thorn?"

An older Ata stood up to shoo the younger Ata sitting on Monosi's other side. She sat down in her place. Her face was lined and lovely with a pointed chin and narrow eyes. Her name, Gaolatlhe, meant "Do-Not-Throw-Away."

"Listen," she said to Monosi. "Blue thorn is what you need. Herd boys know it. They grow up and tell us. No one else knows."

The Atas stared at Monosi. She looked from face to face, young to old to young. She took a sip of tea. The Atas stared. She took another.

At last Monosi said, "The secret is safe with me."

"We know we can trust you," Gaolatlhe said, pressing her face close to Monosi's. "Herd boys lie in the grass."

"All day," said another Ata.

"On their backs."

"They watch the shapes of clouds."

"Sometimes they lie on their bellies."

"They bend their knees."

"Their feet wave in the air."

"They chew grass."

"Like goats and cows."

"But sometimes," said Gaolatlhe, "they look for blue thorn."

"A very small vine."

Gaolatlhe reached over Monosi to grab the hand of Ata Four. She pulled it across Monosi's lap, seized a finger, and waved it in Monosi's face.

"As small as the finger of this little girl," she said.

Then she dropped the hand in Monosi's lap. Ata Four withdrew it, watching her mother across the fire. Ata Three stared at Monosi, defeated.

"To see blue thorn," said Gaolatlhe, "you must press your face to the ground. Light-blue leaves and pale-blue thorns the size of the tiniest ant. The vine grows against the clumps of grass, not in between. Once you know where to look it will take you less than a day to collect enough from the pasture just behind Naring. Be careful. Once you break off the thorns, the smell does not last long. But while it does . . ."

She closed her eyes, smiling, breathing in. The other Atas closed their eyes and sniffed too.

Monosi waited politely. Then she could wait no more.

"The smell?" she said.

The Atas opened their eyes.

"There is nothing like it."

"In all the world."

"Like flowers."

"Like rain."

"Like the sweetest wild fruit."

"Like the smell of a woman in love."

Gaolatlhe leaned to Monosi.

"We have a song," she said. "We change the words for every occasion."

The Atas conferred quickly, composing in whispers the proper lines, and then began the song. Gaolatlhe sang one line, the other Atas the next, verse by verse to the end:

> *Blue thorn*
> *The smell of falling rain*
> *Blue thorn*
> *Cows dream of tender grass*
> *Blue thorn*
> *The wind blows in the trees*
> *This life is full of waiting days*
> *Let this at least be true*
> *If Boko Tladi will not love us*
> *Let him at least love you*

An Ata stood up and hurried away. Monosi caught only the curve of her back disappearing into a house. Ata Four rose and followed. The other Atas fell quiet, gazing into Monosi's face.

"I am so sorry," she said.

"It is better this way," said Gaolatlhe, waving a hand. "She hardly knew him at all."

That night, as Boko and Timela lay down to sleep, each listened to the other breathing.

"Did you tell Monosi?" Boko said at last.

"No."

"So she thinks I still sleep at the Atas."

"You will have to ask her."

"Why not tell her?" said Boko. "You seem to have become the best of friends."

"Maybe I want her for myself."

For the first time Timela's voice was hard, almost bitter, and Boko knew he deserved it.

A knock on the door shocked them both to their feet. At the second knock Boko opened the door. A small girl he did not know stood in the moonlight.

"Boko Tladi," the child said, "come quick. Chief Puo calls you."

"Why?" said Boko.

"I am too small to know. You must come quick. Chief Puo calls you."

So Boko followed the girl across the clearing. The night was cool, and the last drafts of cookfire smoke touched his face. Low mud walls cut up the Potso compound, with round houses close together among them. The houses were dark except for a small one far at the back. The child led him to it. Light glowed around the door and under the grass eave. The girl disappeared. He opened the door and went in.

There at the height of his head, hovering in the air, was a gently waving haze of blue. Fire glowed and blue smoke rose from an iron pot on the floor. On the windowsill there were candles flickering yellow and soothing his eyes. He remembered the look in Monosi's eye when he left for the mines, not at all the eyes of a girl of twelve, the same eyes that looked up at him now from the bed across the room.

She lay naked and still on the bed. The air was warm and dry and Boko remembered, only a leather loincloth between his skin and the grass and sand. Slowly he unbuttoned his khaki shirt. He was back in the fields, a boy of sixteen, carrying Monosi on his back. She laughed in his ear. He pulled off the soldier shirt, then his boots and trousers, and lay on the sand on his herdboy belly, swollen with milk from the herd. He opened his eyes. There they were, on a string around Monosi's neck.

He sniffed the air, then between her breasts where the delicate necklace of blue thorns lay against her skin, warm and soft like the sand. He sniffed again.

Now she moved, raising her arms to press him against her. He lay atop her, lost in the scent of childhood, the memory of youth, years in the long, sweet grass of wild Kalahari pastures, enfolding the lovely Monosi of that very same time.

He murmured, lips against her skin, "Do all women know?"

She gave no reply, no clue to the secret inside her. He heard only her breath, her heart, and only cared that she was the woman he loved.

5

STRANGERS

Monosi invited the Atas to the wedding, the first they ever attended. They worked very hard, filling gourds and plates, cooking the porridge, taking over the roasting pits from the men. The day was hot, a fine summer day, so as they worked the Atas unbuttoned the tops of their dresses. The tasks they performed required much leaning over. Their glistening breasts were everywhere. It was a marvelous wedding. Men especially had a wonderful time.

Monosi found Ata Four stirring porridge.

"Thank you," Monosi said.

Ata shrugged, stirring on. The huge black pot came up to her waist. The heat from the sun, the pot, and the stirring soaked her skin with sweat. Her dress was unbuttoned, too, showing the bosomless chest of a child. Her headscarf almost covered her eyes.

"I never asked your name," said Monosi.

The little girl answered without looking up.

"My name is Ata Roodie."

"And your mother?" said Monosi.

"Ata Roodie."

Monosi laughed gently, kindly.

"Not all of us have that name," said the girl.

"I know," said Monosi.

Another Ata called out for more porridge. Ata Four picked up a large enamel bowl. Monosi took it from her. She held it while Ata spooned out porridge.

"I never met your mother," Monosi said.

"She is not here."

"She did not want to come?"

Ata raised the back of her hand that held the spoon to wipe a pool of sweat from her eyes.

"She is happy for you," said Ata Four. "We are always happy when someone marries."

She finished spooning and took the bowl from Monosi.

"You are always helping me," said the little girl.

When Monosi left her, Ata Four watched the BaNare in celebration, and for the first time she regretted being an Ata. She wanted to be a wife, like Monosi. During the war all Naring had been as manless as the Atas, but now, with the men back, she finally saw the difference. The Atas were manless forever, except, she now vowed, for her mother and for herself. She would grow up and find a man who would have a father in need of a wife. Father and son would marry Ata Four and her mother.

Following Boko, miner after miner, soldier after soldier, took a BaNare wife. Soon these wives bore children. The men held them clumsily in their arms. So many babies born all at once—the BaNare made up a song:

> *Hands that tore rock*
> *BaNare hands!*
> *Hands that tore apart enemy guns*
> *The hands of men!*
> *Hands that tear up the earth with plows*
> *Be careful with that baby*

They also made up a song about Boko Tladi, but this one they sang late at night after all the children had gone to bed:

> *Who loves the mines, any mines?*
> *Who else but Boko Tladi*
> *Who loves war, any war?*
> *Who else but Boko Tladi*
> *Who loves Monosi, only Monosi?*
> *Who else but Boko Tladi*

Who loves Atas, any Ata?
Only time will tell

To the Atas' disappointment, Ata Three's belly failed to
swell with Boko Tladi's child. He was a man all women admired, and they would have loved to raise his child. As for
Ata Three, she was distracted and quiet for weeks, until a
young man stood at her pots, buying plate after plate of her
food and giving away each one to children who gathered to
watch. When her pots were empty, he helped her carry them
home.

But Monosi could not escape the thought that only chance
had prevented Ata Three from bearing Boko's child. How
was he different from the other men who left children behind
in No-Man's-Land? This subject was a sore one for Monosi,
for she had grown up with the worst of men like that, her
father the chief.

Winter was the season for court cases, weddings, council
meetings, funerals and feasts, when all the BaNare were back
from their fields and eager for the company of Naring. The
oldest among them refused to die in summer, alone in their
fields with no one there. If they felt death coming on, they
would sit down to conserve their remaining breath until winter, when they could die in Naring with everyone watching.

Although Boko now ranked as the head of the Tladis, he
was too young to join the chief's council. But any BaNare
was free to come and offer opinions. When Monosi heard
that the case of Sia Bajaki was coming up, she and Boko
crossed the clearing to attend it.

The chief's councillors were all very old, the oldest
BaNare in trousers. They sat in the shade of the wild fig tree
against the wall of the Potso compound, slouching, on low
wooden chairs with laced leather seats, holding worn
knobbed canes between their knees, in broad-brimmed hats
pulled over their eyes, and shoes without laces or socks. Rope
belts held up their trousers. They drew with their canes in the
sand as they talked, tracing the shapes of horns or the out-

lines of old men's dreams. One was blind, two had no teeth, and three were always asleep.

The councillors had spent their lifetime building up herds of cattle. Now they worried only about keeping out of the sun. When the shade of the tree moved to leave an elder squinting and hot, he waved his cane to halt the debate. He struggled out of his chair, dragged it across the dust, and set it down in the shade again. He sat down and waved his cane. Debate resumed. One by one they did this, as the shade of the tree moved through the day. Every time, without fail, they all forgot where the discussion left off, except for Blind Kgetse, who always sat close to the trunk of the tree and so never lost the shade. He repeated the debate up to the interruption, pointing his cane at the elder who made each point. But now they were all in different places, so each one disclaimed the words Blind Kgetse put in his mouth.

Monosi and Boko came up to stand at the edge of the council circle. Chief Puo was there, in a blue suit too small for his chiefly belly, a bright yellow shirt, and a wide green tie. His heir, Vincent, Monosi's brother, sprawled on a chair beside him. Vincent wore black miner's overalls and a shiny orange helmet, far too large for the boy inside.

Chief Puo spoke, spreading his soft, fat hands before his face.

"And so, cherished elders," he said, "grandfathers to us all, I must leave you. Yes. The son of the niece of my mother's brother's daughter is sick in bed on the far side of Naring. Very sick. We Potsos are very close. Vincent and I must go visit. Good-bye. I love you all."

Puo and Vincent hurried away, through the gate of the Potso compound. They rode back out on bicycles, across the clearing, down the winding paths of Naring. Puo grinned and bounced on the seat.

The councillors called the next case, the reason for Puo and Vincent's hasty departure. Sia Bajaki entered the circle, dragging her son by the arm. The boy's father was Chief Puo. She had no husband.

She was there to collect the boy's *mpe.* This word meant "belly," where children come from, and also "give-me." A husbandless mother asked the council to order the father to give her money to raise the child. The council demanded witnesses, careful study of the baby's face, testimony from family and friends that the woman had touched no other man. No Ata had ever claimed *mpe.* The council would only laugh.

Sia had long ago won her case against Puo, but the chief had failed to pay. She waited and waited, in vain. Now she was back to complain to the council, to make Puo pay. She argued her case again while the boy, Elias, squirmed in her grip and glared at the elders. He hated standing there in the circle, a fatherless child on display, begging for money.

Finally Monosi stepped forward.

"Cherished elders," she said, "grandfathers to us all. It is just as our chief said. We Potsos are very close. Tell to me the legal amount. By the law of *mpe,* if a child's father refuses to give, the mother is free to take."

The councillors watched Monosi speak, except for Blind Kgetse.

"Who is that?" he said.

"A daughter ashamed," said Monosi.

And she led Sia into her former family compound. Boko followed and came out with a narrow English bed on his back. Monosi and Sia carried pots and a kerosene lamp. The boy Elias refused to touch a thing.

The council examined every item. They argued over the value of each, the total, the size of the *mpe* award. Elias slipped out of the circle and leaned against the tree. Handsome, strong, but still a boy, he quivered with venom and loathing.

"Die," he hissed, under his breath. "All of you, die."

Blind Kgetse had very good ears. He turned his sightless eyes on the boy.

"The money pays for food and clothes," the old man said. "You yourself are priceless."

After Sia Bajaki had taken her *mpe* payment home, after she spent the afternoon crying into her blankets, she came out into the setting sun to hear the news that her son Elias had stolen aboard the mine office bus and vanished from Naring. He was too young for the mines, but old enough to slip over the South African border and look for other work.

That night, as Monosi and Boko lay together in their house in the Tladi compound, children danced in the clearing, singing:

> Mpe *this*
> How much is that?
> Mpe *that*
> How much is this?
> Instead of a father he gets a bed
> Instead of a husband she gets a lamp
> To light the lonely night

Monosi rose, pulling a blanket around her. She went outside and called to the children.

"Sing something else," she said.

As she lay down again, she heard the children begin another song:

> The chief had a daughter
> Kgo-kgetse
> Who had a husband
> Kgo-kgetse
> Who had an Ata
> Kgo-kgetse
> Who had no husband and never will
> Kge-kgotso-tlhatse-kgo. . . .

The case of Sia Bajaki made Monosi decide to take some responsibility upon herself and her husband for the child of the woman he once had loved. The following summer, after the birth of her own first child, Monosi invited Ata Four, the only child of Ata Three, to come with the Tladis to plow their fields. When the BaNare plowed, everyone working marked out a part of each field as their own, and owned the harvest from it. The Atas owned no fields, and had never worked on the fields of others. Ata Four would be the first.

Children loved to farm, for they spent part of each day running through the brush, chasing down sand hares, hunting wild berries, and following hawks with enormous wings to their distant, hidden nests. They scooped out honey from fallen trees and begged milk from herdboys. The children lay on their backs beneath the udder and the herdboys aimed the milk into their mouths.

"I will be gone only half the year," Ata Four explained to her mother. "I will still belong to you."

Ata Three laughed.

"Of course," she said. "And you will bring us corn, sweet melons, and honey."

"I will."

"They are kind to ask you. With them you will live like the other BaNare."

"No," said the girl. "I will still be just like you."

"Children grow fast on all the milk out there. You will come back too big to lift."

"You lift the pots. I will never be bigger than that."

Ata Four regarded her mother, imagining spending so much time away from her, from all the Atas, among the real BaNare.

"He should have married you," said Ata Four.

Ata Three laughed, almost crying, already missing her daughter.

"To me he is already forgotten," she said, gathering the girl into her arms. "Now go. I have work to do."

Ata Four rode in the Tladi wagon, through the canyon out to the Naring plain. During the war the BaNare had plowed only part of each field, so bushes and weeds grew up on the rest. Now that the men were back, they spent a part of each summer reclaiming the fields for the plow. Ata Four joined the Tladis cutting down brush, leaving the grass for the plow to turn up. Boko, Monosi, Nea, and Philip used axes against the larger bushes, while Ma-Boko and her sister Naledi led the children in felling the smaller with hatchets.

Ata Four left the children and came up to work between Monosi and Boko. When they paused to eat, lying on the grass, Monosi put her infant to her breast, Boko ate beside her, and Ata Four came up between. In the field she kept one eye on her work, in the grass she kept one eye on her food, and the other she kept on Monosi. With her dress unbuttoned and torn from branches, thorns and spiny leaves, showing her chest and recently flattened belly, with her skin glowing with sweat from the work and sun, Monosi looked just like an Ata. She talked like an Ata, too, laughing and telling stories. A baby tugged at her breast.

But everyone knew the difference, and Ata Four felt it there between them, like a spider's web across her face, the invisible cord tying Monosi and Boko together. This was what she wanted, a man all her own, a man like Boko. She saw how he ate quickly, listening to the conversation but seldom joining in. He finished eating and folded his hands, strong and thick with work, clenching them, relaxing, again and again. They ached for the ax. But he waited for everyone else to finish too. There he was, Boko Tladi, the wild and reckless leader of men, a farmer at last like everyone else. Ata Four finished eating and folded her hands like his, squeezing, relaxing, then squeezing again. Their eyes met and they laughed silently to each other, Boko and this serious little girl.

Ata Four saw the world in circles then, like a full moon, like Naring. A mud circle made a house, a circle of houses made a compound, a circle of compounds enclosed a clearing, the circles of compounds formed a circle around the center of Naring. The Atas lived outside the village, not in circles at all, but Ata Four was here with the Tladis to become more like the BaNare up in Naring. She saw a circle around Monosi, Boko, and herself. Another circle surrounded the

Tladis, another took in the BaNare, another enclosed the sky and all the world.

Then someone called her name.

"Ata!"

No other child had that name. It returned Ata Four to her mother, who owned it too. The moon shifted, encircling Ata Four and her mother.

When the harvest was over, they loaded the Tladi wagon with corn and returned to Naring. Ata Four rode atop the sacks, singing with the Tladi children, laughing and chewing sweet reed stalks. When they reached the center of the village, Ata Four jumped down, ran to the mine office gate, and leapt into her mother's arms.

"You are so big!" said Ata Three, laughing and crying, clasping her daughter against her breast. "Where is my little girl?"

"Here I am!" cried Ata Four. "I am your little girl!"

That night, back home, Ata Four found another man in her mother's bed. In the morning Ata Four brought him hot water for washing, porridge, tea, and his shirt. She helped her mother carry pots to the mine office gate to meet the weekly bus. She worked beside her, and together they carried back the pots. The Tladis seemed very far away. The Atas asked her all about farming, and she tried to tell them all about it, except for the part about feeling less of an Ata.

6

WHAT LOVERS DO

It was a rule of the Tladi family that adults taught children to read and write and speak English, while the Potsos sent their children to school in Naring. It met only in winter, in a small brick room behind the brick church at the far end of the village. The fees were very high, so few BaNare could afford it, least of all the Atas. Out at the fields Monosi taught the children of Boko's sister, and now Ata Four as well. She was the first Ata to learn to read and write, let alone speak any English.

Each year that the Tladis went out to plow, Boko grew more restless and quiet. He no longer waited for everyone else to finish eating, but leapt up to get back to work. At night he woke to grab his ax and go out to enlarge the fields beyond their size when the war began, lighting a fire to help him see and to keep away hyenas and jackals. Each time Monosi woke up to find him gone a bolt of fear ran through her chest until she remembered where he was.

One night she rose, grabbed her own ax, and followed him out to the fields. She came up behind him and raised her ax. They swung together, she at a bush, he at a tree, without a word between.

After a long time clearing in silence, Monosi spoke.

"You are impatient," she said.

Boko glanced over, swinging at a tree.

"The bigger the fields, the better."

Boko's blade caught in the trunk of the tree. He worked it out.

"You should be in bed," she said, "with your wife."

They swung at the same time. Their blades flashed in the

light of the fire behind. Boko said nothing, his eyes watching his work. Monosi matched him, blow for blow.

"So this is life with Boko Tladi," she said, keeping time with his ax. "Endless mystery, ceaseless wonder. The life of a farmer is not for him. Hard work and worse, the same thing year after year, unexciting and empty of surprises. He might at any moment decide to leave me, to return to the mines or the arms of another woman. A farmer's life is not for him. Naring is too small. He has seen the world and conquered it. How can he settle down in Naring with a typical wife like me?"

Boko continued to slice away at the tree.

"Another woman?" he said at last.

Boko hit the tree one last time, cracking it through. The branches caught in the bush around it. The tree dropped slowly into the shadows. Monosi's dress caught on a thorny bush. She yanked it free, adding another rip.

"Each night," she said, "when I wake up to find you gone, I think you went back to her."

Boko stepped up to the next bush.

"And what of Timela?" he said.

Monosi sliced away a bush, absorbing the question, this first indication that Boko had noticed.

"It is not the same thing," she said.

"No," said Boko, swinging, "it is worse. Every man has an Ata in his life. From his youth, the time before marriage, fields, children."

"And every wife regrets it," said Monosi. "All her life."

"So do I," he said. "But Timela is something else. He is always there, and always will be, waiting for his chance."

"He will marry."

"And nothing will change."

"You did not even come over to greet me," she said. "If another man looked at me, you have only yourself to blame."

She stepped forward to swing at another bush, breathing hard now from the work and the conversation. Thorns caught her dress. She yanked it free and it pulled away, exposing most of her back. Boko lowered his ax and turned to her, watching her lift her own, moving his eyes along the line of her upraised arms, her breasts and belly reflecting the fire.

Back in bed, Ata Four woke to pee. She went outside to crouch in the brush around the compound. As she stood up straight again, she noticed the glow in the distant field.

She walked across the fields, through shadows sighing with breezes, until she saw the fire, and then Monosi and Boko. She stopped and held her breath, invisible in the dark, as they dropped their axes and lowered themselves to the sand, pulling off their clothes.

Ata watched from the shadows, holding her hands to her mouth, overwhelmed at the revelation. It was her first time to see what men and women did together at night. The Ata children talked about it, but none had actually seen it. There were noises, movement, and it lasted a very long time. Monosi and Boko looked wonderful in the firelight, and Ata felt a new sensation of warmth and excitement rushing along her skin and between her legs to become an urgent longing.

When they finally fell quiet, entwined on the sand, Ata crept away and returned to her blankets. From that night on, when the sun set and adults went off together into the dark, the feeling returned to Ata Four. She lay in her blankets imagining them there, then herself and a face unclear and unnamed against her own, his arms around her, their legs together and moving. This eagerness lived easily inside her, sharing the place with her vow to love no more than one man, forever. They would eventually have to fight it out, when Ata changed shape, her dreams became decisions, and her life as a woman began.

7

WILLOUGHBY

As for Timela, he took his Tladi cattle out to Loang, the only well in the Kalahari. Before the war the Tladis and many others had kept their cattle all year round at Loang. When the men disappeared, the BaNare abandoned the well. Now some BaNare took their cattle back there, reopening the well and grazing them on the grass around it. Timela did his best to forget Monosi and the man he was not, Boko Tladi. But in the Kalahari, herding cattle alone, there was plenty of time to think.

The Kalahari was a dangerous place, a sea of sand scattered with grass, thorny trees, and lonely herders thinking too much, without a single river, stream, or even spring, nowhere at all to drink without digging a hole in the sand. And holes in the sand had a habit of drying up. When rain fell in summer, leaving pools of water everywhere for cattle to drink, many BaNare drove their herds into the Kalahari to eat the new-grown grass. They were careful not to take them out too far, for when winter came and the pools dried, it did not take long to die of thirst.

The BaNare had always taken the Kalahari for granted, until the English posted a new District Commissioner to Naring. At first the BaNare ignored him, assuming he was like all the other District Commissioners, harmless and seldom seen, spending time collecting the tax, issuing passes for miners to enter South Africa, judging serious cases like murder whenever they arose, which was never, and writing reports that no one ever read.

The District Commissioner lived in a big house in the center of Naring, behind a fence of tall white gum trees with cane growing between. A new one arrived every few years, but the BaNare remembered the first one best of all. His name was Willoughby. They called the ones that came after him Willoughby, too, for very few BaNare spoke English and they thought that Willoughby meant "District Commissioner." When a wifeless Willoughby lived in the house, the cane surrounding it dried back completely, leaving gaping holes in the fence. When a wife lived there, she watered the cane through the rainless winter to keep it full and green. Once a Willoughby arrived with a wife but after a month the cane turned brown. The BaNare knew she had left him.

The new District Commissioner arrived the year that breasts and hips began to rise from the body of Ata Four. He met with Chief Puo and revealed to him a plan. There were so many English soldiers back from the war unable to find a job that England was looking for somewhere else for them to go, such as Kalahariland. Since the BaNare hardly used the Kalahari, the English would pay for drilling wells, erecting fences, and buying cattle to settle English soldiers there, as ranchers. The English would pay the BaNare for the land, and the settlers would hire BaNare for everything. Even if the ranches failed, the BaNare would make money, with no risk at all.

Chief Puo informed the BaNare of this English proposal, and argued in its favor. He explained that this was not at all the same as the old days, when invaders came to steal cattle, women, and land. This time the English were asking beforehand and offering to pay for a desert the BaNare never used. Since all the BaNare owned the Kalahari together, the English would pay the chief for the land. Puo, of course, would spend the money to benefit all Naring.

"Believe me," said Puo. "Not even a fool would turn down an offer like this."

Boko Tladi argued firmly against Chief Puo. The BaNare used the Kalahari for herding in summer, for hunting, and they grazed their cattle around Loang throughout the year. The English ranches could never fill the Kalahari, but they would take away the best parts, the ones the BaNare used. Boko presented it also as a matter of principle, that the BaNare should farm their own land themselves. If they saved up their money, little by little they could pay for wells of their own.

Naring discussed the offer for many days and nights, each BaNare arguing one way when the sun came up and the other when the sun went down. Never before had they faced a question like this. They knew the world to change of its own accord, something new every generation, be it Boers, money, rifles, mirrors, or wheels. The thought that they themselves might have some say in the matter drove the BaNare to indecision. The English were much like the Kalahari: useful at times, but mostly something to fear. Should they trade one threat for another?

Around and around Naring the debate circled without conclusion, until finally landing on Boko Tladi. When the BaNare could not resolve an argument, they judged the arguers instead, in this case their beloved chief and the reckless young man come home to stir up trouble. It was fine for a Tladi, rich with cattle, to speak of saving up money to drill wells, but others could never afford it. He was married now, but who believed it would last? And why did he take in the child of the Ata he had kissed before his own mother when he first came back from the war? Who was the little girl's father?

And so, in the end, Mojamaje's knife rang to gather the BaNare before the council tree. They soundly endorsed Chief Puo's point of view. Afterwards, Puo embraced Boko with two fat arms.

"Cheer up," said Puo. "My people love me. When you finally calm down you will love me too."

But Boko refused to give up. What would it take to convince the BaNare that he was settled once and for all, serious and sober?

"Gray hair and a limp," Monosi replied. "But that will be too late. Go see the new Willoughby yourself."

And so he did.

Boko found the Englishman outside the cane-and-gum fence, peering into the engine of a long green armored car. He wore army khakis, like Boko, left over from the war. The car looked left over, too, stripped down, topless, and broken.

"Ko Roodie can fix it," said Boko in English. "He fixed them in the war."

The man turned around to face him. He was dark for an Englishman, with olive skin, wavy black hair and a moustache to match, short and trim with rimless eyeglasses and a long flaring nose. Boko saw maps, a ruler, and pencils on the seat of the car. The Englishman saw a former soldier like himself, looking him straight in the eye.

"I will send for him," said the Englishman.

"He is Boer," said Boko. "He will never come. We must take the car to him. I will bring oxen to pull it. They are grazing around the village, so we need people to gather them."

"All right. Let's go."

They walked together through the village.

"Frank Scott," said Willoughby, reaching to shake Boko's hand, "Naring District Commissioner."

"Boko Tladi," came the reply, "BaNare farmer."

Children ran up to the men, calling out, "Willoughby!" and "Boko Tladi!," delighted to see the two men in identical uniforms side by side in Naring. Very few Willoughbys had ever walked through the village.

"I saw maps in your car," said Boko, clasping his hands behind his back. "You are going out in search of sites for the new wells. I should go with you. I know the Kalahari."

Scott clasped his hands the same way, and then the children behind did the same, marching in step with the two men.

"I know your name," said Scott. "Chief Puo says you want the Kalahari all to yourself and your twenty wives."

Boko kicked a stone in the path.

"Do you believe it?" he said.

Scott unclasped his hands behind his back. Boko did so too, and then the children did the same.

"The map is empty," said Scott, "except for Loang. A man who knows the Kalahari will be a tremendous help."

The children grew tired of marching like the men, so they jumped around them again, crying, "Willoughby!" and "Boko Tladi!"

There were more children at the Tladi compound, and Monosi among the adults with another child at her breast. The adults shook the Englishman's hand with vigor, saying in English, "Hello, Willoughby. Good morning, sir." Dogs sniffed his legs. He nodded politely, smiling, replying, "Good morning," to each greeting, accepting the chicken leg offered to him. It was good to escape the solitude of his office and house. This was not at all how he had expected them to treat their District Commissioner, and he liked it.

Boko pulled Monosi aside.

"Can you spare some blankets and food?" he said, switching from English. "We are going to map the Kalahari wells. I will keep him out there until I convince him the BaNare can use the wells themselves."

Monosi watched Boko hurry away with the Englishman. He had known many men like this in the war, while she was to have just this glimpse. She envied him the breadth of a man's life, away from a home that was always there when he wanted it. And now he would vanish again with this Englishman, not very far, but still to a place where women never go.

Scott helped gather the oxen from around the village, attracting helpers and children calling out "Willoughby!" until a curious, noisy crowd had the oxen yoked to the District Commissioner's car. They laughed at the sight and he laughed, too, mixing among the BaNare and the stubborn cattle. A child came too close to the oxen and he picked her up. She was very light so he carried her, walking alongside the moving car. She smiled in his face and said, "Willoughby!"

The crowd escorted them to the compound of Ko Roodie,

eldest grandson of the original Roodie who long ago had first hired Ata One. When they reached it, Scott put down the child and Boko called out, "Ko Roodie! An Englishman needs you!"

The Boer came out.

He too wore English army khakis, faded and stained, and a battered khaki hat. His face was enormous and red. He shook Boko's hand but ignored the Englishman. He looked under the hood, then turned to shout into his compound, in Boer. Boer boys came running out, all ages and sizes, barefoot and dirty, with wrenches and saws in their hands. Whooping and shouting, they dived under the car. They scrambled back up and carried away pieces of metal.

Ko leaned back against the car, smiling now to the Englishman. Gold sparked from two of the Boer's front teeth.

"My boys," he said in English.

Ko followed his boys to the forge. Boko and Scott remained at the car. Children stood in the distance, watching, and then began a game, dancing in and out of a moving line. Some made circles over their eyes, like Scott's glasses, some swung their arms like Boko digging for gold in the mines, some hammered like Ko at his forge. They made up a song:

> *One soldier*
> *Boko*
> *BaNare!*
> *Two soldiers*
> *Roodie*
> *Boer!*
> *Three soldiers*
> *Willoughby*
> *English!*
> *How can we tell them apart?*

Scott turned to watch the children.

"What are they saying?" he said.

"It is a begging song," said Boko. "They beg the English

not to take away the Kalahari. In time the BaNare can pay for wells of their own."

Ko and his boys returned and put the car back together. Scott counted out notes and coins into the Boer's scarred palm.

"Taking an Englishman's money," said Boko, "is the dream of every Boer."

Scott raised a finger to touch his front teeth.

"Where did you get them?" he said, nodding at Ko.

The Boer raised his wrench to tap his gold teeth. The sound was a gentle clink.

"Egypt," he said.

Scott and Boko drove away, stopped at the Tladi compound to collect the blankets and food that Monosi had prepared, and soon were out in the Kalahari, along the faint track worn by cattle to the Loang well. The car rocked gently back and forth over the sand.

"It is like the sea," said Boko.

"I remember you BaNare," said Scott, eyes fixed on the swerving road. "The worst sentries in the history of warfare. Every night, from guardpost to guardpost, you shouted across the dark."

"That was us," said Boko. "All alone in a strange desert, at night, surrounded by enemies. Did you understand what we said?"

"Not a word."

"We talked about eating," said Boko. "Roasting sparrows when we were boys. We skewered them, roasted them black, and ate them whole, beak, feathers, and feet."

For a while now Boko watched the empty brush roll by, searching for words to keep the English out of the Kalahari. At last he spoke the first of them.

"BaNare have grazed their cattle here since before the English knew it existed, before the Boers or even the Zulu, before District Commissioners or English soldiers with nothing better to do."

Scott was ready for him.

"We are building a slaughterhouse," the Englishman replied. "At Lorole Station. The mines will take all the meat Kalahariland can produce. If the BaNare do not want to try it themselves, what can I do?"

"Chief Puo did not tell us about a slaughterhouse. That changes everything."

They drove on in silence. After a while Scott spoke again.

"So the English are no better than the Zulu or the Boers?"

"If we did not have the English here," Boko replied, "the Boers would have taken our land. We would be part of South Africa now. I know that. You and I wear the same uniform, we speak the same language, we fought the same war, but I know this country and even though you do not, you are high above even the chief. . . ."

Scott smiled at the road ahead.

"You want my job," he said.

"I want you to serve the BaNare," said Boko. "And nothing more."

But as he spoke the words felt false. Perhaps he did want the job.

"How can I serve the BaNare?" said Scott.

"By keeping the soldiers out of the Kalahari."

"How?"

"You are District Commissioner," said Boko. "It is you who should be able to tell me."

"All right," said Scott. "We could map the sites quickly, so the drilling can start in this district. The settlers would not come to Kalahariland until all the districts are done. Once Naring District is finished, and the drilling moves to the other districts, we could tell the BaNare about the slaughterhouse and they can move their cattle out to settle around the wells."

Boko leaned his arms on the metal ledge before him. Scott began to hum. A bird bounced off the windshield.

"I was right," said Boko. "I knew you could think of something."

Boko saw the plan unfolding, the work it would take and

the life he would lead while they did it. He was back in the world of men.

He directed the car off the road, deep into trackless brush. The car crept around trees, over bushes, following Boko's pointing arm to a clearing where summer rain collected in a shallow pool. Pools like this sometimes lasted into the winter before drying up completely. Herders watered cattle there. They would be very good places to drill for wells. This one was dry now and empty of cattle, but Scott marked it down on the map. They camped that night by the clearing, eating quickly and lying down between their cookfire and the car as the night closed in around them. They lay back on their blankets for a long time, staring up into the black sky and stars.

"Do you hunt?" said Scott at last.

"On foot, with dogs," said Boko. "You can come along anytime."

Jackals called from the darkness and the grass moved with wind.

"You are a lucky man," said Scott, rising on one elbow to look at the fire. "To have the Kalahari all to yourself and Naring whenever you want it."

Boko leaned toward the fire, tossing on more wood.

"They say you have no wife," he said.

"She is in England. Doctors are taking a look at her. Nothing serious."

"Children?"

"No."

They were quiet now, and soon Scott heard Boko's breathing slow to that of sleep. The mention of his wife took him out of the Kalahari and back to England, to a doctor's waiting room and her face as she came through the door. A bat flew through the light of the fire and the brush rustled behind the car. He smelled the fire and the warm sand close to his face on this, his first Kalahari night.

8

MARRIED MEN

When they saw Boko Tladi helping the new Willoughby map and then drill the new wells, the BaNare were more than a little suspicious. At first they thought he had changed his mind about the English settlers, but then they decided that he simply hated to be where the action was not. If he could not stop the English plan, he would at least have the pleasure of making it work.

As for Scott himself, the BaNare did not know what to make of him. After they guided the team of drillers to a new site, he and Boko hunted for food while they drilled. When they came back to Naring for supplies, Scott slept in his own house but ate at the Tladi compound. He began to learn to speak BaNare, to brush his teeth with a stick, to argue with old men, and to eat porridge with his hands.

Some BaNare were pleased to see an Englishman among them like this, but others thought it could only lead to trouble. Monosi fed him, often on antelope meat that he and Boko brought back from the Kalahari. At first they spoke English together, but more and more he tried out on her his new BaNare phrases. Mostly he and Boko talked about the wells, and the rest of the Tladis listened. They were gone for weeks at a time.

Boko confided to Monosi alone the scheme that Scott had proposed, the true reason he was helping him drill the wells. Boko had feared at first that Scott might change his mind as soon as the drilling was done, calling in English settlers right away before the BaNare could occupy the wells. It took some time for Boko to trust him, for the space between them to close enough for Boko to judge that the Englishman meant what he said.

The BaNare doubters grew fewer and fewer, until there were none at all. If the English settlers turned out as friendly as Scott, Naring would be lucky indeed. And then there came an event that everyone should have foreseen, that swept all the BaNare with one gust back into the ranks of the disbelievers. Scott met the Atas.

It was all because of Ata Four. Now that she brought home part of the Tladi harvest as her own, her family had the right to dance at Maru-a-Kgosi. Rain clouds, and thus the crop they yielded, belonged to the chief, and Maru-a-Kgosi meant "Clouds-of-the-Chief." After every harvest each BaNare woman and girl was supposed to carry a basket of grain to the chief's compound, set it down outside his gate, and dance. His wife came out to sing:

All you grow belongs to my husband
Your great Chief!
This will do
Your glorious Chief!
But next year bring me more

Then she ordered half the grain made into beer for a feast. The other half went into her own storehouse.

Long ago, when BaNare farmed with hoes, this storehouse fed Naring if the next harvest failed. But when the BaNare began to use plows, there was so much grain that most BaNare were able to feed themselves even in bad years. The South African mines began then, too, so those unable to feed themselves sent out a husband or son to earn enough money to feed them instead. Fewer and fewer women came to Maru-a-Kgosi. Those who did carried smaller and smaller baskets and danced in store-bought dresses instead of furs and skins.

Without fields the Atas had never danced at Maru-a-Kgosi. Now Ata Four gave them the chance. Every Ata pulled off her dress, tied skins around her waist, and painted ocher lines on her face. Some hung furs across their breasts, but others left them naked. The little girls wore leather fringes around their waists, and rattles made of dried cocoons with pebbles inside from ankle to knee and elbow to wrist. Half the Atas filled baskets of grain and balanced them on their heads. The other half did the same with pots of beer. They formed a line and headed up to the village.

All Naring heard them singing. Children ran to see and their elders followed, shading their eyes with their hands, catching a glimpse of the Atas snaking up along the winding paths. By the time the Atas reached the clearing between the Potso and Tladi compounds, a crowd was there to meet them. Three Atas set their smallest baskets down before the Potso gate, and sang:

> *All we grow belongs to your husband*
> *Our great Chief!*
> *But remember*
> *Our glorious Chief!*
> *Your daughter gave us the field*

The BaNare laughed, shouting out, and began to clap along with the song. Puo's wife refused to come out. The Atas danced over to the Tladi compound and laid the rest of the corn at the gate and passed the pots of beer to the BaNare.

The crowd stepped back, forming a circle around the Atas. They whistled and clapped as the Atas formed a circle of their own. A tall Ata with light skin and dark freckles, young but a woman everywhere, jumped into the center. Her feet kicked up dust, her arms waved and snapped. The jackal fur across her shoulders flew up to reveal her perfect freckled breasts, then flopped back down to cover them. Up, down, up, down. Now she spun, the jackal fur held out by the spin, her breasts rising beneath them and pointing to each BaNare in turn. Men cried out from the crowd.

Now a little Ata danced out, all skinny arms and legs, half

covered with rattling cocoons. She began the fastest dance the BaNare had ever seen. Her feet rose and stamped the ground too fast for the sharpest eye to see, for the strongest heart to bear. The clapping and singing rose to follow her, sweat rose to soak her bare skin. The crowd moaned, calling out for her to stop, such a skinny thing, her belly too small to fuel such a dance as this.

Another Ata jumped out. A stuffed baboon danced on her back. Its legs were tied around her waist, its arms around her neck. She jumped, the baboon jumped, frolicking on her back. A miner jumped out from the crowd. He landed before the freckled Ata, one heel tucked beneath him, the other leg stretched out along the ground. He froze before her, staring at the ground, then rose slowly and danced.

Ata One emerged from the crowd. She was very old, completely covered in golden antelope skins. Her feet moved hardly at all, sliding in tiny steps across the ground. She held up her hands and a dead snake between them, waving it over her head. She sang an ancient song with words that only the oldest BaNare understood. An old man tore off his shirt and danced out to join her, slowly, on creaking limbs, answering her line by line.

More men jumped out from the crowd, then women and children. Scott heard the commotion and came down to the clearing to watch. Some BaNare noticed him now, and then Ata Three, who grabbed Ata Four and pulled her over to the Englishman. A few BaNare moved close to hear.

"Speak English," she said, smiling proudly at her daughter.

Ata Four buried her face in her hands. Some BaNare around them laughed, but others were watching Scott's face and his eyes on Ata Three. Mother and daughter wore skins and furs like the other dancers, with plenty of Ata exposed.

"Say something," Ata Three urged.

From behind her hands, Ata Four tried out her English.

"I am so glad to meet you, fine sir."

Scott laughed and spoke in BaNare.

"Tell me how to say this in English: My sister is very beautiful."

"She is my mother," said Ata Four, lowering her hands.

Dancers came past, forcing themselves between Scott and the two Atas, separating them with swirling bodies and dust. Scott watched the mother and daughter disappear. Someone pushed a gourdful of beer into his hand. He drank it slowly, watching the dancing, and then went back to his house.

The BaNare waited for Scott to find his way down to No-Man's-Land, but months went by and he did not. And then one afternoon he and Boko drove past the mine office gate just as Ata Four and her mother were packing up their pots.

"I know them," said Scott. "We can give them a lift. Those pots look heavy."

"They are very strong," said Boko. "I am sure they can manage on their own."

But Scott stopped the car, and Boko helped him pile up the pots and firewood into the back of the long green car. The Atas sat in the backseat, and the car rolled away.

"What do you do with the pots?" said Scott in BaNare, turning his head from the wheel to glance behind at Ata Three, who turned her head to look out at Naring.

"We are cooks," said Ata Four in English, narrowing her eyes.

"Good idea," said Scott, still in BaNare. "You speak English and I speak BaNare."

"You speak well," said Ata Three to Scott. "If I close my eyes I forget that you are an Englishman."

Boko sat with his arm over the back of the seat, looking from mother to daughter, remembering those nights when he had awakened with this woman and her daughter had served him. Ata Three was lovely still, and he felt the lowering of her voice, directed this time at Scott instead of himself.

As the car bounced down to No-Man's-Land, Ata Three and Scott continued talking as Boko and Ata Four kept silent. Everyone knew that Willoughby was married, Boko had told them, but his wife was far away.

Scott took the Atas home and then drove Boko up to the Tladi compound. Boko waited to see which direction Scott would take now, but the car headed up to the Willoughby house instead of back to No-Man's-Land. News of the two men in the car with the Atas had already reached Monosi. She met him at the Tladi gate.

"How is she?" said Monosi.

"How is who?" Boko replied.

BaNare in neighboring compounds or walking past wandered closer to overhear. Monosi waited.

"Fine," said Boko at last. "She looks fine. I think she likes Willoughby."

"He is married. Like you."

Boko shrugged.

"All the same, I think she likes him."

Ata Four wanted to warn her mother, but found that she could not. Only when an Ata gave up hope of finding a husband did she find a married man. She knew he would soon go back to his wife, and he always did. The next one would be married, too, and the one after that. It freed her daughter to look for a man not for her mother but for herself.

Scott and Boko continued working, drilling wells. Boko warned him about the Atas, but Scott only laughed.

"I can take care of myself," he said.

"We all say that," said Boko, "and never once is it true."

Nothing happened for months on end. Then Scott received a letter from his wife. She was on her way to Naring.

"Very good," said Boko warily. "We all have missed her. As soon as she comes you must bring her down to eat with us. We will have a feast to welcome her."

"Not right away," said Scott. "She will need some time to get used to Naring. It is not like England. And I have changed."

"All right," said Boko.

"She will need a maid. It's a big house and she'll need help. She can get to know this girl, and then her family, and then the rest of Naring. That girl we once picked up with her mother, with all the pots—she speaks English, she cooks. How about her?"

"I will tell her," said Boko. "She will be very glad to have such a good job."

"I must speak to her mother first," said Scott. "To ask her permission."

Boko shook his head. It was not up to him to argue against what Scott was about to do. This was how the Atas lived.

"No!" said Monosi when Boko told her about it. "You must stop him."

"What can I do?" said Boko.

"Wrestle him to the ground. Twist his arm behind his back. All those things men do to each other to make a point."

The Atas were sad that Ata Three would give up hope of finding a husband, but they were not at all surprised. For Ata Four they felt nothing but joy.

"An English Ata!" they said.

"The first English Ata!"

Scott walked down to No-Man's-Land to talk to Ata Three about her daughter. He started out truly believing that this was all he would do. He had grown used to Naring, so far away from England and his wife. He did miss her, and now she would arrive and begin to bring him back, to her, to England.

He sat drinking beer with the other men on the logs around the Ata cookfire. There was no mine bus due back that day, so Ata Three was free to sit beside him. Next morning, when Scott came out of her mother's house, Ata Four brought him hot water for washing, porridge, tea, and his shirt.

9

THE JACKAL

Ata Four loved the English house, the smell of wax on the wooden floors, and the quiet, even in the rain, cool and dark with covered verandahs shading the windows and curtains covering half the glass. The wax clung to her knees as she polished the floors. She dusted shelves, scrubbed walls, scraped mosquitoes and moths from the screens, washed and ironed clothes, polished Willoughby's boots, even the soles, and his eyeglasses every morning. His wife took care of the cane in the fence, watering it daily, using a can with a long nose and spray at the end, like sneezing.

Willoughby called her "Anne," and Ata called her "Madame." Her hair was dark, pulled away from her face, and her eyes were dark and wide. Her skin was pale but smooth, glowing, and her lips were thin, especially when she held a smile as she spoke. She wore trim dresses with wide belts and read books in a padded armchair with a high, straight back.

Ata lived in the maid's quarters out back, to be close whenever Anne wanted her, and visited No-Man's-Land late each afternoon. She had two small rooms and a toilet in between, behind a swinging door. Ata pulled the chain whenever she passed it, to hear the rush of water. A younger Ata came up to take care of these quarters while Ata Four took care of the English house. Once a month the Scotts drove to South Africa for a long weekend, and Ata took the girl into the house and told her the name of every English thing. The girl touched each one, repeating its name. Her own name was Loa, meaning both "Thicken" and "Bewitch."

Anne taught Ata to use an oven, something the BaNare had never known before. She did many chores in the house, but this new skill made Ata begin to think of herself as a cook. All women cooked, but already twice in her life she was paid for it, and still while she was a girl.

She liked the cakes, the breads not so much, and loved the meat pies. She watched as Anne cut out the circles of dough with a porcelain knife.

"I know something about your family," said Anne, cutting.

Ata pretended she did not hear it, and bent down to push more firewood into the stove.

"My husband says they have babies without husbands and sell beer to men. But you will be different. You will learn to be a proper wife, no men coming and going, no beer. For your own good, if I catch you with a man you will have to leave. Here you have a chance to make something of yourself."

"Thank you, Madame."

"Put these in now, Ata."

The BaNare felt sorry for Willoughby's wife. She did not possess the usual means of learning that her husband loved an Ata. She never waited on line at the well, a cousin never came by to return a borrowed pot, children did not compose songs outside her house at night. Ata Four refused to take her to No-Man's-Land, and Anne, aware of the Ata reputation, never asked to go.

Boko and Monosi came to visit, to speak English with Anne, but she asked too many questions about his travels with her husband, drilling wells in the Kalahari. When she mentioned specific nights, Boko rose to go, for often Scott slept not under the Kalahari stars but in the arms of Ata Three. Monosi invited her to the Tladi compound, where everyone treated her like an invalid, smiling at her every word as if it were the last ever to come from her lips.

The BaNare waited for Willoughby to give up the Ata. Everyone knew these Ata things never lasted. But this one did, month upon month. And it only strengthened Ata Four's resolve to do precisely as the Englishwoman urged—to make something of herself and find the perfect husband. She prac-

ticed her English, learned to cook English food, kept a perfect English house, and stayed away from boys.

"Don't get me wrong," Anne said to Ata as they worked.
"I love children. So does Frank. But nothing ruins a woman
like a fatherless child."

"Madame," said Ata, changing the subject, "why did you
take so long to come to Naring?"

"I was taking medicine, in England."

"Did it work?"

"Open the oven."

Scott spent less and less time at home. Anne knew that
something was wrong. He refused to discuss returning to
England, and sometimes he came home smelling of some-
thing she could not name and did not want to. She liked
Naring, but she was more than a little lonely. She sought out
Ata and worked beside her, chatting through all her chores.
A hundred times Ata wanted to tell her. BaNare women had
family and friends to cushion the blow of such news, but
Anne did not. In fact, distant relations and casual acquain-
tances usually flocked from nowhere to hear the details. Anne
Scott was alone, except for Ata Four.

Day after day, the BaNare discussed the situation.

"He is welcome to all Naring, except for the women."

"It is different when we BaNare spend the night at the
Atas."

This was the men talking. The women had something else
to say.

"He is no better or worse than all of you."

"Which is not very good at all."

The men defended themselves.

"When he has his fill of the Atas, he will go back to England."

"When we have our fill, we stay in Naring."

Scott felt the BaNare turning against him. Sometimes as he
talked with Anne over dinner he dropped hints and watched
Ata's face as she served them, daring her to react, to break
the secret to Anne and rescue him from Naring. That was the

only way it could end, for his wife to drag him back to England.

"How is your mother?" he said.

"She is very well," said Ata.

"I must meet her sometime," said Anne, not meaning it.

"I think she's very busy," said Scott. "Isn't she, Ata?"

"Yes."

"Why is she so busy?" he said. "Does she have many friends?"

No one foresaw that the solution would come in the person of Elias Bajaki, *mpe* child of Chief Potso, half-brother to Vincent his heir and Monosi his daughter. After working on South African farms, Elias was old enough to sign up for the mines. He hated Naring, the BaNare, all Kalahariland, and vowed never to return. He was two months older than Vincent but had no hope of becoming chief. But once in the mines he saw that a life underground had no future at all.

Elias also hated his name and never used it. He called himself the Jackal. From BaNare miners he heard that Ata Four had become the maid of Willoughby's wife while her mother slept with the husband. As he rode the mine bus back to Naring, he decided to pay Ata Four a visit, to see inside the English house and everything they owned, everything he wanted. From the mine labor office he demanded payment in paper banknotes.

"Those heavy coins make the others feel rich," he said. "But nobody fools the Jackal."

And so as the Jackal came out the gate no coins jingled in his pocket, he made no sound as he bounced. He saw Ata Three behind her pots, but did not join the other men crowding before them. He sniffed the air, smiling slyly, taking in the smell of the food and smoke. Her daughter was waiting to give him some English food, an English bath, and a night in an English bed.

The Jackal's suit was clean and hardly wrinkled. His shirt was new and gleaming white, his shoes were pointed and shiny. He headed up to the English house and circled behind, listening for dogs. He pushed his way through the fence.

Ata's quarters stood before him. He opened one door, looked inside, and sniffed. The room was empty but clean. He opened the swinging door and sniffed. The toilet gleamed. Baring his teeth in a Jackal grin, he opened his pants, aimed, and peed all over the seat. He opened the door to the other room and sniffed again. He saw the bed, the smooth white sheets and pillow. Color pictures from magazines hung on the wall. There was a wooden crate beside the bed, covered with a white cloth, and a lamp, candles, and matches atop it. White curtains hung from two small windows.

The Jackal hopped onto the bed. He arranged the pillows and leaned back to wait. The girl Loa came in, looked at him, and ran out. Very soon Ata came in.

"Who are you?" she said, holding her hands, dripping wet, out and away from her dress.

The Jackal smiled.

"Everyone knows me," he said. "I am like you, a fatherless child, but the father I lack is chief of this miserable place. Come back with me to South Africa. Naring is less than nowhere. The BaNare despise us both and we of course feel the same about them. Let them have their kingdom of dust and sand and mindless gossip. We will have South Africa, enormous cities with houses like this one all in a row. We will have one all to ourselves and never part. . . ."

He lay there, smiling up at her, speaking through handsome lips, with laughing tender eyes and elegant shoes, shiny and black against the white of the bed. Miners and even Willoughby always wore boots. Her hands still hung in the air between them. She liked his voice, young but tough with experience underground. By the time he finished his speech her hands were almost dry.

"I have work to do," she said. "I can meet you later down in Naring. . . ."

"Where are the English?"

"South Africa. They come back tomorrow night. You can hear the car from far away."

The Jackal rose from the bed, and Ata lowered her hands. He came close to her. She saw his perfect teeth and smooth skin. She liked his voice.

"I need an English bath," he said. "And English food. And you."

She led him into the English house. Loa stoked the stove, heating the oven to make meat pies and a tank of water for his bath. The Jackal took off his clothes and stepped into the tub. Loa brought him a towel and soap and he reached out for her arm. She screamed, giggled, and jumped away. She liked him.

Ata rolled out the dough, thinking about him. His suit was so clean, his shirt so white, his cheekbones high and wide, his eyelashes long and thick. She cut out the dough and spooned on the meat. He seemed intelligent, handsome, and kind. Very much like Boko Tladi. He was Monosi's half-brother. When the Willoughbys returned, she would ask if they needed a gardener.

When the pies were done, she carried them in to him on a plate. He sat in the tub, waving his knees above the soapy water. She watched the muscles across his shoulders, smooth and gleaming wet. She handed him a pie.

"English food," she said.

He held it lightly in one hand, admiring the crust. Then he ate it.

"Marry me," he said.

"All right," said Ata.

He splashed his face, cleaned out his ears with his fingers, ducked his head underwater, and rose to his feet. Ata handed him the towel. He dried himself and wandered naked through the English house. A generator behind the house made current for all the machines. He touched the toaster, the lamps, the freezer, the phonograph. Ata watched him. Loa peeked around corners.

"In South Africa," he said, "I too will have these things."

When he reached the bedroom, Ata closed the door behind them, pulled off her dress, and lay on the English bed. The Jackal lay down beside her.

"We cannot do the last thing," she said. "I cannot have a baby now."

"Have you ever done it before?"

"Never."

"Then you are safe," he said. "The first time only opens things up. The second time makes the baby."

Now Ata had heard this many times. Some girls swore they had babies after only once, but others accused them of lying. The Atas themselves were divided on the issue. And even if it was not true, no one could predict when a baby would happen or not. Her own mother had lain with many men but had only borne one child, herself, Ata Four.

She thought it all through, her heart racing, there on the bed, the Jackal's arms around her. He pressed his lips to her breast.

What harm was there in opening things up?

She closed her eyes. His lashes brushed her cheek like a fly landing. His hands touched her everywhere, then the rest of his skin. Everywhere. He made noises. This one was different —clean, loyal, and strong. She was just for him.

She moved beneath him and wrapped her arms around his back. She opened her eyes but the world disappeared. She was in the air, in the dark, on the sand with fire around her, no longer Monosi and Boko but she herself and this man inside her. At first she was frightened and clutched his back at the pain. But in the end, after all, she was sure that nothing was better than this.

She slept the night beside him, waking often to look at him in the dark. When at last the room began to fill with light, they awoke together. He smiled and nodded and talked with a laugh, but his eyes moved away from her own.

She stood still, and then pulled on her dress.

"Loa will bring you water for washing," she said. "And porridge and tea."

"I washed last night," he said.

Loa appeared without asking, with all three things, but the Jackal was dressed and out the door. He sniffed the morning air. Ata followed him, stopping on the back steps.

"When the English are here," she said, "come only at night."

Without replying or even turning around the Jackal disappeared through the fence.

Later that day, Ata sent Loa into the village for news of him. The girl came back to report that the Jackal was gone. He had taken the bus back to the mines. She stared at the girl for a long time until Loa flew away, crying for yet another broken Ata heart.

That night Ata lay with her hands between her legs, weeping without tears or sound. She had hoped to be the first Ata to marry, to love one man forever. She had been so sure he was the perfect man. Instead he turned out to be worse than all the others. She had ended up with the shortest romance in Ata history. One night. The other Atas came up to console her with stories of their own lost loves. This only made them all feel worse.

In the English house Ata no longer talked English, and worked without seeing. She dropped plates. Anne repeated things many times, in simpler and simpler English, before Ata understood. Months went by, Ata wore looser and looser dresses, until at last Anne guessed the truth.

She gasped, turned away from the kitchen, and marched into the parlor. She sat down in the dark green armchair and folded her hands in her lap.

"Ata," she called. "Come in here, please."

Ata came in, but she did not sit. She stood before her, hands folded over her belly, smoothing the dress against the swelling skin.

"Ata," said Anne. "Ata, Ata. Ata."

She brushed a strand of hair from her eyes. Her English fingers were soft and long.

"I thought we were friends," she said. "I trusted you."

She lowered her head, closing her eyes. Ata waited. Silence surrounded them. Ata looked up at the copper ceiling, out through the curtained windows, then down again at Mrs. Scott. She smelled the wax that she herself had rubbed on the floors, and her own cakes baking.

Anne looked up again.

"You were such a nice girl," she said. "I thought you liked it here."

Ata turned away her head. She did not like the look in the woman's eye. Her breath came faster now. Her heart was in pieces, she was trapped but she would not squirm. It was the end of her life, the one that had begun when she saw for the first time from behind her mother's pots the men come through the gate. She would not have the strength to begin another.

"Anything," said Anne. "Anything but this. You did not even bother to tell me. You know I must let you go."

Ata looked back into her eyes. There was the look again, not scorn exactly, and Ata tried to name it. Anne's thin English lips were pale and trembling. One hand rose from her lap. She closed her eyes. Her face lost its English beauty and turned to ash.

The English hand rose and drifted through empty air to rest against Ata's belly. Ata pulled her own hands away and raised them to her mouth. The other English hand moved to flatten against her own flat English belly, the source of her pain, the reason she had taken so long to come to Naring, why her husband came home smelling of another woman, why she would now drive Ata away.

Willoughby's wife sat in silence, pressing one palm against her own belly and the other against Ata's swollen skin above the unborn child. She hated and loved and cursed Ata's simple power to have what all the doctors in England could never give to her.

The sight of Ata nursing a child, oh, the sight—it would stop her jealous heart dead.

Taung

1

WHERE RICH MEN BEG

Ata Four lay in her mother's house, on the night her child came out, listening to children outside the compound dancing, clapping, and singing:

> *Lover of pots*
> *Lover of pans*
> *Lover of every gold-digging man*
> *Different is as different can*
> *Now she is the same*
> *English dreams*
> *English lives*
> *English maids and English wives*
> *She opened her legs and out came Five*
> *The Jackal is to blame. . . .*

The child was a girl, and everyone called her Ata Five. Ata Three took the infant into her arms, and the other Atas reached out to touch her.

"I am a grandmother now," said Ata Three. "I am getting old."

Ata Four spoke softly from her blankets.

"I wanted so much to love only one man, forever."

The other Atas looked to Ata Three, who smiled down at her daughter.

"When I was your age," she said, "I thought the very same thing."

And so, after life among the real BaNare, and then among the English, Ata Four ended up an Ata after all. She recovered from the birth and rose to pace the Ata compound, as the Atas passed the baby from arm to arm, breast to breast. Her love for the infant came without joy or pride and with a cold and wary edge. She wanted to give her child the world, beginning with a father. Her very own, the Jackal.

Ata Four paced and paced and finally kept going, out of the compound and up to Naring. She wandered the winding paths, reviewing the twists her own short life had already taken. She passed No-Man's-Land and ended up at Ko Roodie's forge. The Boer hammered and swore at a plow. Ata stood watching. He spoke to her without looking up.

"What do you need?" he said. "Besides a husband. It must be metal or wood."

Ata shrugged.

"Tell me about South Africa," she said. "I want to go find him, to leave this place and make myself into something else."

The Boer hammered and swore some more. Then he stood up and kicked the plow.

"South Africa," he said. "There is a place I will never go. The hard Boers came to Kalahariland. The soft ones stayed behind. They are worse than the English now. They never work. Here you can still be a man."

He bent down to hammer again. Ata stood with her hands in her pockets, watching this Boer who shared with her the Roodie name.

"There is an English pan," she said. "With a flat bottom, deep sides, a long handle, a high lid, and no legs."

Ko shook his head. She saw the red jowls flutter.

"Who told you that?" he said.

"I cooked with one."

"Who told you it was English? That is a Boer pan. The English stole it from us."

He left the plow and searched among the junk in his compound yard. He found a wagon spring and heated, sawed, shaped, and pounded it into a Boer pan. Into the bottom he carved ATA 4 ROODIE. He handed her the pan, smiling to show his gold teeth.

"This was invented for cooking outside," he said. "When did the English ever do that?"

Ata hefted the pan with two hands and then balanced it on her head. It was very heavy and just right.

"If you find him," said Ko, "the very best thing you could possibly do is hit him over the head with that."

"It will leave my name on his forehead."

"So everyone will know who did it."

"And offer congratulations," she said, smiling now, thawing.

"The South African Roodies still have a farm," said Ko. "Near Taung. If you meet any, give them a kiss for me."

And he slapped his own backside, chuckling and winking at Ata Four.

"Do not forget to come back," he added. "You will see at once why I never go there. Even if you find him, even if he marries you, South Africa will turn you into a beast. Like him."

She took the pan home, secure in its weight. An armed cook had nothing to fear in South Africa. Men went there all the time. She would cook her way across the country if she had to, all the way to the mines. There she would find the Jackal, grab him by his charming neck, and drag him back to Naring, or maybe somewhere else. Perhaps they would stay in South Africa.

Ata Four went up to the Tladi compound to say good-bye. Everyone else retreated, leaving Monosi and Boko alone with her around their cookfire.

"I can press an *mpe* case for you," said Boko. "If he is gone, then his father must pay. The BaNare know you are not like—"

Boko stopped himself, but Ata Four replied to the thought.

"But I am," she said, her head high and her voice raw. "I am just another Ata, with a child and no husband. You tried to be kind, but look at me now."

"You are leaving Naring," said Monosi.

"Yes."

"Forever?"

The word was a strong one and Ata bowed to it, lowering her head and raising her hands to her face. Monosi embraced her.

"The BaNare laugh," said Monosi, "but I love you as my daughter. If you never come back, I ask you, please, remember me."

The Atas said good-bye in a very different way, excited at her journey, certain that she would be back very soon, crushed and despairing, to tell them her sad but exciting tale of the Jackal refusing even to meet her eyes. Never before had an Ata chased a man. Men came to them, and left when they wished. The Atas knew better than to beg them to stay. Once a romance died, nothing could bring it back to life.

Ata Four wrapped her Boer pan in a blanket, raised the bundle onto her head, and kissed each Ata in turn, last of all her own Ata Five. Her mother walked with her out along the path, to the mouth of the canyon through the Naring ridge.

"Perhaps it was a mistake," said Ata Three, "to send you among the Tladis and then their English friends. You desire to make yourself more than an Ata, and I fear for you. It makes me fear that this sadness I see in you now will never have an end."

Ata Four made her way through the canyon, stumbling into rocks and trees and wiping her eyes with each step. At last she reached the other side, the Naring plain, with the sky clear and the road dark with recent rain.

She kept one hand on her bundle, and the other rubbed her recently flattened belly. Away from the soggy road, oxen pulled plows through red and rolling fields. Women scattered seeds before them. Ata was too far away to see the seeds, so it looked as if the women were shooing crows. She remembered doing the same herself, so long ago among the Tladis.

Behind her on the narrow road Ata heard an engine. She stepped off the road and moved behind a tree. A white truck splattered with red mud, with bundles and boxes piled up on the open back, swerved along the road and stopped beside her.

"Get in!" cried an old man's high, Indian voice. "Get inside this truck I am driving! Get in!"

Ata stared at him, unmoving.

"Get in!" the Indian shouted again.

Ata climbed in, pushing her bundle onto the floor between her legs as the truck drove on.

The Indian sat behind the wheel, in a white robe embroidered with shiny blue thread. A white, wispy beard swung from his chin. His hands and cheeks were bony and pale. His feet were bare except for stringy sandals, with red circles painted around his ankles.

"So!" he said. "Who are you? Why do you deserve a lift in this truck? I am a too too busy man. I tell you truly I cannot just stop for who knows who knows who. Driving is very lonely. The road, the sky, this wheel . . ."

He pounded the steering wheel.

". . . do not know how to talk. Do you?"

Ata stared at him. The cab smelled of a smoke she could not name.

"Yes," she said. "I can talk."

"So talk!" he said. "Who are you? Tell me your story. Your deepest desire. Tell me. Surely you know who I am. I know you do. Armah. Yes, me! Armah Trading. The biggest shop in all Kalahariland except for one or two others here and there. Where are you going?"

"Lorole Station," said Ata.

"You know my shop! Right there across from the train itself. The biggest in Kalahariland. You are taking the train I know it. Where are you taking this train to go to see a boy I know it."

"Johannesburg mines," she said.

Armah tugged on his beard.

"Which one?" he said.

"Which one?" said Ata.

Armah drove very slowly, peering out ahead as if fearing attack.

"Exactly the words I spoke to you not more or less than a moment ago," he said. "Which one? The mines are very very many, my lovely dear. Here and there. Mines all over. Some a hundred miles apart."

He glanced at Ata catching her breath from the shock.

"I see this news I tell you cracks your heart," he said. "Forget this man you chase. Whoever he is. Whoever you are. Do you know who I am?"

"Armah," whispered Ata, turning her head away.

"You know my shop?"

She breathed deeply, struggling to think of what to do. She did not know which mine to go to. She was a fool not to have asked Boko Tladi about the mines, or any of the men who woke up with Atas. The Indian talked on as she sat, defeated already, no farther than the Naring plain.

"Even so," said Armah, "you are very smart to think on your own this wise idea to leave that place. Indians? Them? Not anymore. They make me come all the way out here just to take back what they ordered so long ago without paying or selling or dusting. Children as black as you, my lovely girl almost crying."

Ata sat very straight, watching the countryside rolling by. She thought about this latest twist and yes, it was a fortunate mistake. He was not at all worth it. She would never find him now. He had destroyed in one night what for years she had worked to attain, among the English, with Monosi and Boko, working beside her mother at the mine office gates. All in all, he had ruined her life.

"Cheer up," said Armah. "They gave me tea not even warm. I drank it closing my eyes. Their daughters bake cakes that taste like cows. Everything smells like cows. They neglect the shop. Instead they buy cows. Cows! Instead of a nice clean Lorole shop with a train every day and shelves tidy and everything there just so."

The name startled her back to hope. Lorole Station. She

was certain a miner on his way back from South Africa would know where he was. She could wait at Lorole and ask the miners passing through.

"Cakes?" she said. "What kind of cakes?"

Armah licked his lips and wiped them with his beard.

"Indian cakes, but not like those black Indians make them. Honey smelling of ginger all over is just the right way. Not honey smelling of cows. Their daughters too they smell of cows. . . ."

"Do you have daughters?" said Ata. "Do they make cakes?"

"Daughters!" Armah cried, gripping the wheel. "They know nothing of cooking or anything else you can think to name. They starve me to kill me to get the shop. My wife passed on from this earthly world without taking them with her. Do they dirty their feet in the garden? Everything died. They only wear silk—so loose you see them all over everywhere and silk you know it melts too near the stove. Bracelets so long they drop in the pot. Every finger they paint to a beautiful work of art. Rich men beg at their feet. My daughters laugh at them. Yes! Laugh! Do you know their names? The names I call my daughters?"

He paused, waiting.

"No," said Ata.

"One is Stupid," said Armah. "The other is Lazy. But even these names are so very far above them the clouds seem low from so high. You look at me anytime. I am very hungry. Right now the sun is straight up but they sleep for beauty they tell me. . . ."

Ata pulled the Boer pan from the blanket between her legs.

"I am a cook," she said. "I have this pan with my name on the bottom. All the best cooks do that."

She turned it over to show the Indian. He looked at the name, then out again at the road. He was very quiet now, peering over the wheel.

"This is a Boer pan," she said. "So of course I know how

to cook Boer. I worked for the English in Naring, so I can cook English too. You can ask them except they will tell you they fired me for having a baby without a husband. I am chasing him now."

Armah began to nod, and then to smile to himself.

"I come from Naring," said Ata. "So of course I can cook BaNare. You think I am young but I started to cook ten years ago. For someone like me it is nothing to learn to cook Indian too."

Armah stared ahead at the red road and the oxen pulling away in the fields beside it. At last he spoke.

"I prayed and prayed with my mind in the air," he said. "Each time I spit out my daughters' food, I pray and then I spit. I spit and then I pray."

"Also I can wash clothes," said Ata, "and clean the house and work in the shop."

They drove into Lorole Station, past the train yard and up to the shop. It was huge, green-painted brick with a wide verandah. The house behind was of yellow brick and its roof was yellow tile. Armah led Ata around to the rear porch and then inside. This was the kitchen, stretching the width of the house. There were screens on the windows and a cool breeze moving through them.

Armah sat watching while Ata found what she needed. There were shelves along the walls, stuffed with colored bottles, jars, and tin boxes. Dried spices and herbs with tiny leaves hung from the ceiling. Ata sniffed the air, but smelled only dust. There was a freezer and a good stove hooked to a generator outside. Ata heard the hum of the motor.

"This time," she said as she worked, "I am cooking English. For Indian I must practice first."

An open doorway led from the kitchen to the rest of the darkened house. Ata looked up as she cooked, hoping to catch a glimpse of an Indian daughter. The Naring Indians were nothing like Armah or the daughters he had described. Their shops and houses were not at all grand. They dressed and talked like the BaNare. Their children, as Armah decried, looked very much like BaNare too.

Armah ate without speaking, eyes closed, murmuring praises to Ata and the food itself. She watched him closely, and then suddenly heard singing. Armah did not look up from his plate.

She swung her eyes again to the door. The singing was high, lovely, and sweet, strange, in long phrases climbing and falling, breathless, a hymn.

Armah's daughter came through the door. Her eyes were heavy with sleep and orange powder smeared across the lids. Her lips were sharp and fine at the edges, turned down in a pout as she sang. Her thick black hair rolled down one shoulder, across one breast to her knees. She stretched her arms, bare and slim, and rose up onto her toes. Ata looked down at her feet. They were powdered and painted, a thick gold chain around one ankle and silver around the other.

Ata smelled her, the fragrant oil and pungent lotions. She stared at the crimson silk twisting and rippling around her, parting, revealing the brown skin of a smooth, flat belly. Ata saw in her deep, round navel a sparkling lavender jewel.

2

TWENTY-TWO

Ata Four departed Naring just as the last of the Kalahari wells went in. Monosi told her neighbors that the English were building a slaughterhouse at Lorole Station. It would buy all the cattle Kalahariland could sell. That same afternoon, BaNare from all over Naring descended on Chief Puo's compound to ask whether what Monosi had said was true. Under his breath Puo cursed the Tladis, realizing now why Boko had worked so hard to drill the wells, and then he raised his chiefly voice for all the BaNare to hear.

"My people," he said, "now you see my plan for you. The wells are in. I urge you now to drive your cattle out to claim them. What if I had told you before? You would have refused the English offer. This way the English pay for the wells and we the BaNare use them. Who do they think they are? The Kalahari belongs to us. It serves them right to lose these things they paid for. People so loose with money deserve a lesson like this."

All that night the BaNare sang songs in praise of their chief, roasting goats and swallowing beer. The Tladis joined in. Monosi wanted to announce that it was Boko, not her father, who had saved the Kalahari. But they had decided to protect Scott, whose superiors must never know what he and Boko had planned. BaNare came up to Boko and waved their beer in his face.

"Your English friend is in for a surprise."

"This will finally knock him back to England."

"Are there Atas in England?"

"So where are they?"

"Where are what?" said Boko.

"The wells."

"Where are the wells?"

"How do we find them?"

The other BaNare nearby stopped to listen to the questions, then the praise-songs to Puo died and a crowd formed around Boko.

"Tell us."

"Where are they?"

"How do we find them?"

Boko said nothing, returning the stares of the gathering, worried BaNare.

"All right," he said at last. "I will take you there."

It took many days for BaNare owners of cattle to pack up their wagons and collect their herds from the Naring plain. Not everyone had enough cattle to take to the Kalahari, for they still had to plow their fields on the plain. Boko explained that only Loang was close enough for herders to visit Naring often, so many families loaded up all their belongings to move out to the wells to live by their men. Boko led the cattle and wagons over the sand slope behind the village, into the Kalahari.

The English settlers never came. The slaughterhouse went up at Lorole Station, and the BaNare sold there the cattle that they raised on the wild pasture around the new wells. Timela Timela turned over his Tladi cattle to other herders around Loang and took his share of the offspring out to the farthest of the new wells. Word reached Naring that he married there. Other men married there, too, and children began to grow up without ever seeing Naring. Hyenas and lions came to the wells to eat the cattle, and the BaNare shot them with rifles.

The new wells were deep and reliable, with an engine atop each one. Puo appointed one man at each well to serve as pumper, to fill the engine with diesel and oil, to run the pump that filled the tank, to collect a fee from each BaNare for every head of cattle watered there. In return the pumper's cattle drank for free. The diesel and oil for the pumps cost

much less than the fees the pumpers collected. The chief kept
the extra money, to spend in the name of all the BaNare. So
in the end Puo profited after all. He bought a motorcar, long
and red, and a white truck with an open back for Vincent, his
son. They made a driveway by cutting a hole in the Potso
compound wall.

As for Scott, he came to the Tladi compound to tell Boko
he was leaving Naring. They stood at the gate, face to face
across it.

"When?" said Boko.

"Today."

"You have served the BaNare well."

"I made a mess."

Boko looked into his face, and there in the center of Naring he saw Scott retreating from him, back to his English
wife, perhaps all the way to England. There was a world of
English ties that Boko could not see.

"She knew all along," said Scott.

"About Ata Three?"

"Yes."

"You are right to take her away from here."

Scott turned to go, without shaking hands or bidding fare-
well. Then he stopped.

"I should not tell you this," he said. "I will not be replaced. We are pulling out of Kalahariland. We're giving up
countries one by one to let them run themselves, except for
this one. It does not even have a city. We are turning it over
to South Africa."

Boko stood in the sun, absorbing the shock of this news.
His body stiffened.

"Does Chief Puo know?" he said.

"Yes."

"We must stop the English from doing this."

Scott laughed, sharply, in a way that Boko had never heard
before.

"I am the English," he said.

That evening Monosi and Boko decided that Boko should

talk to the council before alerting the BaNare. So the next day he crossed the clearing to the shade of the fig tree before the Potso compound, beneath his grandfather's famous knife.

He arrived at the council circle just as a young Ata stepped inside it, carrying a white enamel bucket and a stack of yellow gourds. Boko moved to the center to help her. The councillors spoke on as the Ata knelt filling gourds with beer from the bucket, and Boko handed them out to the men. Her name was Ellen, but she called herself Cooking-Oil. When each old man held a gourd, they paused to take the first sip and Boko spoke.

"Cherished elders," he said. "Grandfathers to us all. I know you discuss important business, but here I am to mention something grave. What does Chief Puo propose to do about saving us all from South Africa?"

The old men peered across the tops of their gourds. Why ruin a calm afternoon, the sun behind the clouds and beer waiting beneath their noses?

Toothless Monyi spoke for them all.

"Behave yourself," he said to Boko. "Our glorious chief has left Naring on a vital mission with the other Kalahariland chiefs, to England. To demand that Kalahariland rule itself."

"Beloved councillors," said Boko calmly, "he is not the man to do it. You know it yourselves. The English will take one look at Puo and know they were right, that Kalahariland cannot rule itself."

The old men lowered their beer, frowning at Boko with wrinkled faces and foamy lips.

"He is the chief," said Sleeper Thobo, who always woke up when the beer arrived. "Only the chief can speak for all the BaNare."

The others nodded solemnly, drinking.

"Wise and elderly BaNare," said Boko, "it has been that way in the past. But you the council must send someone else. Times change, we must change too. Or South Africa will come and change us forever."

His mouth went dry from concentration, from choosing his

words carefully. The Ata saw this and pressed a gourdful of beer into his hand. He wet his lips with the beer.

"You want to weaken the chief," said Moabi-Shoeless-but-Rich. "We are his council. If we weaken him, we weaken ourselves."

Boko watched the elders drink, feeling Kalahariland slip away as he argued with old men drinking beer in the shade.

"Noble ancients," he said patiently, "I challenge the chief to explain what he does with the well fees. How did he pay for that motorcar, and a truck for his son? Is this the chief the BaNare want, who steals for himself what belongs to them?"

The elders paused with the gourds at their lips. At last Selepe-One-Eye spoke.

"The wells, the Kalahari, the breath you take, all Naring belongs to the chief."

"Magnificent drinkers-of-beer," said Boko, still crouching, his voice unsteady now. He closed his hands to fists. "You must call a meeting. If you must send the chief, choose a different one. Puo cannot win an argument against himself, let alone against the English. We must choose someone who can."

Bachelor Kang laughed and said, "You ask too much of a chief. Every man has his faults. You yourself are famous for them. That poor unlucky stray with the scar beneath his eye, in love with your wife and rotting away in the Kalahari. That Ata you and Willoughby shared, and of course those countless deeds of your wasted youth. . . ."

Ellen Cooking-Oil watched anger burn up Boko's arms to his neck and jaw. She pushed the gourd in his hand up to his lips to cool them.

"Wizened beings," Boko replied, fixing his gaze on each elder in turn, "you must let the BaNare decide. You can do so without breaking BaNare law. Once the BaNare make their choice, you the council can depose Puo, then Vincent, then each chief in order until you reach the one in line the BaNare want."

"Aha!" said Loke-the-Limp. "So that is what you are up to."

"What number in line are you?" said Moabi.

"You want us to depose and depose," said Selepe.

"Until we get to you," said the Bachelor.

Boko moved his eye from elder to elder, handing the gourd back to Ellen, who pushed it back until Boko dropped it into the bucket. His hands were fists.

"What number in line are you?" the elders chanted, happy again, sipping from their gourds.

"What number in line are you?"

Still coiled in a crouch, Boko replied, "Twenty-two."

The beer washed up the old men's noses. Toothless Monyi rose behind Boko and raised his cane to strike him. Boko felt only the blur of the weapon, the same angle he had sensed deep in the mines when the Imitation Zulu had come at his back with a knife. He spun quickly, faster than anyone saw, up and around to pull the cane from Toothless Monyi's hand.

Monyi fell back in his chair, stunned with terror, gazing up at Boko holding the cane.

"Murderer!" he gasped.

The other elders gasped, too, in horror and fear at the cane in Boko's hands. Ellen rose, pulled it from Boko's grasp, and pressed it back into Monyi's.

"What happened?" said Blind Kgetse. "What happened? What happened?"

By the end of the day all Naring had heard the story, that Boko Tladi had tried to kill Toothless Monyi. Cooking-Oil tried to argue the truth, that Boko had only pulled the cane from the old man's hands, but everyone believed the version the elders told.

That night, as he lay in the dark with Monosi, they heard children outside in the clearing, singing to the moon:

> *If you happen to dig gold underground*
> *Twenty-two*
> *Twenty-two*

If you happen to fight in Egypt too
Twenty-two
Beware
If you happen to love his lovely wife
Twenty-two
Twenty-two
If you happen to be too old to stand
Twenty-two
Beware
If you happen to be BaNare chief
Twenty-two
Twenty-two
If you happen to try to breathe his air
Twenty-two
Beware. . . .

"I will stop them," Monosi said, rising.

Boko held her back.

"Let them sing," he said. "They are right. I raised my hand to an elder."

"You did not," she said. "You disarmed one among many foolish old men. They are far more dangerous than you could ever be."

"Foolish? But they won."

"Not on their own. You handed them victory yourself. You have made my father very popular. Suddenly all the BaNare have never been more loyal to their beloved chief."

"I can only hope," said Boko, "that the other Kalahariland chiefs are better than Puo."

They lay back in silence, and then Boko spoke again.

"Why do they sing of Timela?" he said. "Why did the old men taunt me about him?"

Monosi said nothing.

"Has he been to Naring?"

Still Monosi lay without speaking.

"Well?" said Boko.

"It is simple," she said at last. "They see the possibility for trouble between you and Timela, and they want to make it happen. To give themselves more to gossip about."

"Has he been to Naring?"

"You see?" she replied. "Already their trick is working. Do I ask if you have been down to the Atas again?"

Boko lay back, staring into the dark. The children outside added verses to the song, changing the subject and throwing in nonsense words.

"Now that the wells are in," said Monosi, "and your English friend is gone, you need something to do. If the council thinks you want to be chief, so be it."

"I am a farmer, with children and a wife. That is enough for any man."

"You are different."

"No," said Boko.

"Why deny it?"

They both fell quiet now, and then Monosi spoke again.

"Are you really twenty-two?"

"Who knows?" said Boko. "I made it up on the spot."

"What number are you truly?" she said.

"You are worse than the old men."

They lay back, silent again, as the children finished their song. Dogs barked and a breeze came under the eave of the roof.

Boko rose up on one elbow.

"Twenty-three," he said.

3

THE WRONG PANTS

It was a place of danger, of injustice, of opportunity, mystery, and gold.

Deep in the mines the Jackal had heard the stories. Cities were rich. First Cape Town, then Durban, Johannesburg, Bloemfontein, and last but not least Taung. When the railways came they met at Taung and the explosion produced a city. Then when the Second World War began, a Boer named Roodie sold his farm outside Taung to the English. This made him as rich as the English themselves. He kept a few acres to graze some cattle and bought the Taung Hotel in the city. The farm became factories, replacing those in England that the Germans bombed to rubble.

Boers and English lived in the center of Taung city, on wide, straight streets, in houses of wood and brick. When the Scotts drove to South Africa, leaving Ata Four to spread her legs to the Jackal, they visited doctors on these streets. On the edge of town lived everyone else, in one enormous village with winding paths of every size and houses to match, of mud, tin, brick, of branches and straw. Men who worked in the Taung factories slept in Taung village among women and children, in houses. Lying in the barracks bunks, listening to sound of men sleeping, every miner dreamed of sleeping there too.

Except for the Jackal. He alone dreamed of an English house, like the one he had slept in once. He dreamed of English food, like the pies that Ata Four had cooked, and he dreamed of an English wife, like Ata Four herself. If the English and Boers could get rich, so could he, and in the mines, sweating, dreaming, the Jackal wondered how.

His miner's pass allowed him only to ride the train from Kalahariland to the mines and back, and to sleep in the mining barracks. It expired at the end of his contract. If he tried to sleep anywhere else in South Africa, he risked arrest and maybe a beating from the police. To sleep in Taung he needed a city pass. To qualify for a city pass he first had to find a city job. But no one would hire him without a city pass. It was an endless, impossible circle, but finally the Jackal arrived at a solution. He would steal a city pass.

His contract expired and he rode the train toward Kalahariland. At Taung station he slipped off the train. He dusted off his shiny suit and wiped clean his pointed shoes. Police strolled past. Outside the station he looked down the straight streets to the center of town, shops and the Kalahariland offices, hotels, houses, where Boers and English lived. Then he turned to look the other way, along the tracks to the village. Beyond it he saw the factory smokestacks.

He headed down the track, with the sun low behind his back and the village humming around him. There were children racing, shouting, men on bicycles ringing the bells, donkey wagons, battered trucks, a car without a windshield. Women walked, carried, laughed, talked, pointed, raised their arms, and everywhere caught the Jackal's eye.

The Jackal stepped off the track, into the township twilight, picking out the smell of beer from among the many others. He followed it down the winding paths. There were shops among the houses, mostly Indian. Some were only tiny shacks and some were bigger than Armah's in Lorole. The Jackal followed his nose, turning one way, then the next, until he reached the Diamond Café.

It was a small brick shop with windows that took up half the front. The Jackal read the name of the shop above the window, then looked inside at the men standing, drinking beer from cartons. He moved up to the window. Beside him two men leaned against it, peeing on the wall. The Jackal saw a counter at the back of the shop and three women behind it.

The shelves behind them were empty except for glowing kerosene lamps. Crushed cartons littered the floor.

The Jackal watched the men talking, slapping each other's shoulders, arguing and lifting beer to their lips. He looked for the newest suit, the shiniest shoes, and singled out an enormous man with huge hands and a neck as thick as his head. He was nothing but muscle, even in his face. His size was unnerving, but then the Jackal saw him reach a hand down to tap his trouser pocket, checking that his precious pass was still securely tucked inside.

The Jackal stood at the window, watching, devising a plan to remove the pass from the big man's pocket. He took out his own pass and folded it many times, creasing the photograph, blurring his face. Then he slipped the pass into his jacket pocket and entered the shop.

The Jackal pushed to the back, bought a carton of beer, and moved up to his prey. He watched the big man talking, drinking, and the size of him made the Jackal afraid. It was a dangerous thing he planned to do, and only the yearning to change his fate drove the Jackal on. But for an accident of birth, he would have been taking home an excellent pay to a fine house filled with electric devices, and this unintelligent brute before him would have grown up the unclaimed son of a witless chief in the middle of nowhere. The act he was about to perform was not a theft. It was justice, righting a wrong, securing the Jackal his due.

"You!" the Jackal cried. "Murderer!"

The men around them fell silent. The big man looked quizzically down. The Jackal turned to the crowd.

"My sister! He beat her every day. She died in the end of a broken heart!"

The big man waved his beer.

"You make a mistake," he calmly said. "I never saw you before in my life."

"She was beautiful!" the Jackal cried.

Then he splashed his beer in the big man's face.

The crowd stepped back. They saw the size of the Jackal and the size of the man with the beer dripping from his chin.

"He is mad," someone said from the crowd.

The big man raised a massive hand to wipe his eyes.

"I do not want to hurt you," he said. "You must apologize nicely."

The crowd formed a circle around the fighters. The Jackal dropped his pants. The men hooted and cheered.

"What are you doing?" the big man said, staring at the Jackal's bare legs.

"We must honor our ancestors," the Jackal replied in a solemn voice.

"My ancestors never did that," said the big man. "They had no trousers to drop."

"Exactly," said the Jackal. "They never fought in trousers."

"Do it!" the crowd urged.

So the big man dropped his pants. He placed them on the floor, pointing a muscular finger to the nearest man in the crowd.

"Watch my trousers," he said.

The Jackal dropped his own pants atop the big man's. Then he turned to his prey.

"At last I will have my revenge," he said, twisting his voice and his face to match. "I asked our sorcerer to fill me with a demon. When I die the demon will enter you."

With that he leapt at the big man, whose hands closed around the Jackal's neck.

"Chrghl," said the Jackal.

They fell over, and the Jackal on the bottom did not fight back but simply tore at the big man's sleeve. Their faces almost touched. The big man squeezed. The Jackal's face turned colors. Still he tore at the sleeve.

"It is true," someone said.

"He is possessed."

"Let him go!"

"Do not kill him!"

"The demon will enter you!"

The big man's hands flew away from the Jackal's neck. He stood up, backing away, awaiting the feeling of the demon passing through his skin, tingling, sticky, cold. He stared at the Jackal still on the ground, wishing him back alive. In his motionless hands the Jackal clutched the torn sleeve. Everyone stared at the two fighters, wondering in which the demon now resided.

The Jackal coughed, sputtered, opened his eyes, and jumped to his feet. He dusted himself off with the big man's sleeve.

"Forgive me," the Jackal said. "Just now our faces were very close. I saw you in detail. You are not the man who ruined my sister. He was big like you but his eyes were farther apart. His nose was bigger. . . ."

He talked on, as everyone stared, including the big man, afraid of the demon that might or might not be inside the Jackal. As he rambled on, the Jackal pulled on the big man's trousers. He slipped his own pass into the big man's pocket, and the big man's pass into his own jacket pocket.

Then he held out the waist of the trousers. Two Jackals could fit inside.

"Wrong pants," he said.

When they both wore the right trousers again, the big man tapped the pass in his pocket, not knowing it was only the worthless, expired pass of a miner. The Jackal gave him back his sleeve, pushed into the crowd, and was gone.

Back in the shop the men discussed the event. The big man drank more beer. When he finally left that night, the police followed him from the shadows. A well-dressed man with a city pass had told them that a drunken giant in torn clothes, reeking of beer, had tried to steal his pass.

The big man turned a corner. The police pounced, knocking him down. He stood up, roaring in protest. They knocked him down. He stood up again and knocked them down.

He ended up in jail, bloody and sore. Then they chained

him to six other Kalahariland men caught with expired miner's passes. The prisoners boarded the Kalahariland train. The police chained them to their seats.

"I had him," the big man explained to his fellow prisoners. "Right in these very hands."

He locked his fists together, squeezing the neck of a Jackal demon that only he could see.

4

ATA ON ICE

At first light Ata Four rose from her bed in the Indian kitchen, heated water on the electric stove, wrapped a blanket around her waist, and stepped outside to wash.

She drew the water across her breasts and looked out at Lorole Station, quiet and dark around her. There was a small village against the hills, the slaughterhouse down the tracks, and the station with shops and traders' houses around it. Miners slept against the station-house wall, wrapped in blankets, waiting for the train.

The village was small, but otherwise very much like Naring, with mud walls and grass roofs and winding paths between. Above the village, along the crest of the hills, ran the South African border. Somewhere on the other side the Jackal waited for Ata to win him back.

The village was named Lorole-la-Dinaledi, meaning "Dust-of-the-Stars." When the English built the railway, they shortened the name to Lorole. The people who lived there were Wall-Makers, not BaNare. When Ata arrived, every Wall-Maker woman had worked at least once as Armah's maid. He never gave them a single day off. He spat out whatever they cooked, smashed the plate on the floor, but never fired them. They quit too quickly to give him the chance.

Armah ate everything Ata cooked. She rose, washed, and cooked his breakfast. Then she cleaned the house, washed the clothes, and cooked his lunch. Then she worked in the shop until late afternoon. Then she cooked his supper. After that, from sundown to late at night, she worked for Armah's daughters.

She braided their hair, rubbing in henna and fragrant oil

with every twist. They looked in the mirror, pouted, and told her to do it again. She bathed them together, with a velvet cloth, in a sunken tub of ivory tile. The soap smelled of honey and flowers. She fed them sweets as they soaked, and poured them sugary tea, green and murky with mint, from a shining silver urn. They rose from the steaming bath, glowing with heat from every pore, and drifted naked through the dark house. The cool air dried them off. They ended up in their bedroom, arrayed on the bed in delicate poses, and called for Ata to join them.

The Indian daughters took out their jewels, whispering praises to every gem, to ruby, jade, and gold. They rubbed a yellow ointment on Ata's ears and pierced them through with a silver pin. She felt nothing at all. They hung in her ears their cheapest rings, of brass and scarlet glass, and rubbed the ointment on the side of her nose. This time she felt a stabbing pain. They pinned in her nose a polished stone, round and icy blue. Ata's breasts were still heavy with milk for Ata Five, so the Indian daughters squeezed it out and rubbed it on their own.

Suitors came to beg for marriage. They were ugly and old, but rich. Ata watched through the kitchen door. The girls sat smiling, posing, as the suitors praised their beauty and charm. Then the rich men fell to the floor to beg at their feet. The girls turned their heads away and began to sing, then rose and drifted away, singing, whispering, and touching each other's hands. Their slender hips swayed beneath the silk. The old men moaned with madness.

Armah sat between, raving, insulting his daughters, assuring the suitors the girls deserved no dowry at all. Armah, of course, was the one who would have to pay it.

Young men came to beg, too, none of them rich but all of them dressed to look it. Ata liked them. The Indian daughters gave these men their dreamiest looks, eyes wide, yielding, as the suitors breathed the steamy scents of spices and oil from secret places beneath the twisting silk. The young men leapt to their feet, crying out in despair, babbling in Indian, clutching their hearts. The daughters rose, singing, and drifted away. Armah buried his head in his hands.

Ata studied these daughters, so different from the Atas or anyone else. Did they love men, hate men, or ever think about men at all? They were happy to let suitors look and admire, but not when admiration became desire. The men demanded marriage, to wrench the daughters away from themselves, to have them for their own. That was when the daughters withdrew, to the lavish joy of scented oil and dark perfume, the pride of daily beauty.

Men never begged at Ata feet, nor ever had to. Perhaps men loved best the women who loved them least. If the Atas loved them a little less, men might love them more, and even someday marry them.

This was the lesson Ata Four learned from the Indian daughters. She practiced what she learned behind the counter of Armah's shop. Earrings dangling, jewel in her nose, smelling of cinnamon, Ata leaned her elbows on the wooden counter and tried to love men less.

They came into the shop one by one, stunned by the cool and sudden dark. Bargains hung from the high ceiling, buckets and shovels, dresses on hooks. The shelves were full of candles, blankets, soap, cans of fish from an unknown sea. A Wall-Maker girl worked there too. Armah was sometimes there as well, but the men always came straight for Ata.

Her dress was tight, orange and sleeveless, with bare shoulders and thin straps holding it up. Her scarf was orange as well, enormous and tied at the back in a fancy knot. She fingered one earring and toyed with the knot, watching the men approach. They were Wall-Makers, miners or meat cutters from the slaughterhouse. They came up close, pretending to peer at the shelves behind her, breathing the scent of a woman adorned.

She looked them straight in the eye, smiling wryly, and asked them what they wanted. If the man was a stranger and looked like a miner, she asked him two questions: "Have you been to South Africa? Did you see Elias Bajaki?"

When Wall-Maker women came into the shop, they questioned Ata about her jewelry, the scent of her skin, how she kept her breasts from falling out of the dress when she bent over. When children came in, Ata let them touch the stone in her nose.

BaNare miners came in, with news of Naring and No-Man's-Land. Boko Tladi had raised his hand to an elder, the Scotts had disappeared, and soon afterward Ata Three's belly had swollen with another child. Months later, other miners reported that this child, a girl, came into the world with light brown skin and a full head of straight brown hair. Her mother named her Willoughby Roodie. She was the first English Ata, the very first English BaNare.

This child confirmed all the worst Naring had suspected of Scott's intentions. On hearing the news Ata Four was happy for her mother, as Atas were always happy when another child came into the world. There were always plenty of children around, but Ata Three had only one daughter, Ata Four, until Willoughby Roodie came out. And Ata Four was relieved that the Scotts were gone from Naring, so Anne would never see the child her husband had given to another woman instead of to her.

Each time the BaNare miners told her another tale of Naring, the place seemed much farther away than the hills she saw across the plain whenever she stood at the door of Armah's shop. Even the news of a sister, her first, and from Scott no less, failed to disturb her life as a woman on her own. She had looked for herself among the Atas, the Tladis, the English, and now she did the same among the Indians, and more and more within her own hands, heart, and head.

Then one day in the shop she saw the doorway darken. A man stood there, filling it, blocking the sunlight outside. Slowly he approached her. She saw his missing sleeve, his bruised face and scabs, his enormous arms and filthy clothes. He was a towering, manly mess.

Ata fingered her earring, toyed with her scarf, smiled, and

asked him, "Have you been to South Africa? Did you see Elias Bajaki?"

The big man stopped before the counter. Ata stood up. He reached his hands together, squeezed the air, and Ata fell back against the shelves. When he reached into his pocket, Ata turned to run. But he brought out only a folded square of paper. A pass. He pressed it flat on the counter and looked into Ata's face.

He was very unhappy, and angry, but kind. Ata saw that in his eyes. Then she looked down at the pass. The picture was blurred, but she read the name and her heart stopped.

She closed her eyes and pressed her hands on the counter to hold herself up. Then she made her way around the counter and took his massive arm. He moved, still wordless, with only a gentle tug. She led him out and up to the back of the Indian house. There she brought him water to wash and one of Armah's old Indian robes while she washed his clothes. He ripped a seam pulling it on.

She fed him porridge and meat on the back step, and he began to talk. His name was Jack Vanu, and he told her how the Jackal had stolen his pass. His job at the Taung brewery was written on the pass. The Jackal had certainly stolen that too. With the Jackal's expired mining pass Jack had to go back to Naring and apply for a new one to enter South Africa again.

His anger faded as he talked. He liked the sight, the smell, the sound and eyes of Ata Four upon him. She told him her own Jackal story, but less than the truth, and also more. She said the Jackal was her husband.

"If I find him first," said Jack, "you will have to look for a new one."

Ata sat beside him on the step, patting his arm. She saw that he liked her.

"Go to Naring," she said. "Stay with my family. Ask for the Atas. Everyone knows them. I will go to Taung and bring him back to Naring, where you can wring his neck if you want. But I think you will thank him. Maybe you will want to stay. Naring is the place for a man like you if not for a woman like me."

Jack leaned forward, breathing in strange aromas, pressing his massive face close to her own.

"He is not the man you think," said Jack. "You are too good for him."

"And you?" said Ata.

"It is not polite to speak of myself. If I had friends here, you could ask them. Maybe they would tell you I am someone you can trust."

"Make friends in Naring. I will come back and ask them there."

He agreed to her plan, confident that she would find the Jackal and come to her senses. She would see what kind of a man he really was and come back to Jack, waiting in her very own home. So he told her how to find the brewery and his house in Taung village.

"No doubt he stole that too," said Jack.

They talked until his clothes dried. He put them on and they walked to the station, arm in arm. Ata liked the feel of him, not at all like the Jackal, neither handsome nor charming but as he had said, reliable, solid. She wondered what life would be like with him, and laughed.

"I am such an Ata," she said.

"What?" said Jack.

"Nothing," she said. "There is the Naring bus."

The bus was stuck in the sand before the station. BaNare miners crowded behind it, pushing.

"I will bring him to you," said Ata. "Squeeze his neck or thank him, as you please."

Ata stopped, and Jack took a step toward the bus.

"I will repay you," he said, still moving. "For the food, the wash, my clean clothes, your arm in mine. You will come back and find me waiting."

Now he was running, aiming at the back of the bus. The miners heard him roar, looked behind, and parted to give him room. Jack threw himself against the bus. It rolled free of the sand. The miners cheered, ran to the door, and jumped inside one by one, last of all Jack. Ata waved, first at Jack, then against the billowing dust behind the bus.

She stood there, watching the bus drive away, facing west to Naring and the Kalahari beyond. Then she spun on her heels to face the east, South Africa, and the Jackal.

It was the moment she had waited for, had devoted her life to here in Lorole. She had found him. He was so much closer than she had thought, not underground in a distant mine but just beyond the border. The railway before her now led right to him. She looked down the tracks to the slaughterhouse smokestack, the railcars beside it, and the men in blue overalls scrambling around them, loading meat.

Her memory of him, of his hands everywhere on her, came up from behind to overwhelm her, to push her along the track. She needed a pass to enter South Africa legally, but it was easy enough to slip at night over the border fence along the hills above the Wall-Maker village. It would take three days, maybe four, to walk to Taung. The train would take an afternoon. She could be in his arms tonight.

Ata ran back to Armah's house, grabbed her Boer pan, and hurried along the tracks. She reached the workmen just as the train began to roll, as they walked along beside the cars locking the freezer doors.

"Please," she said, coming up alongside. "I must go to Taung today. I have found Elias Bajaki. He is there. Let me ride inside with the meat."

They all knew Ata from the shop, and they knew her story, her quest for the Jackal. The train moved faster.

"It is very cold," they said, slamming the next door shut.

"If you fall asleep you will ride to Johannesburg."

"You will freeze."

"That dress is not very warm."

"Please," she said. "I will stay awake. When the train stops I will know I am in Taung. I will scream for men like you at the other end to let me out."

So they helped her into the last meat-car, running now.

The world disappeared as they rolled the door shut and locked it behind her. The train gained speed and left them behind.

Ata's open eyes saw nothing. The air was cold, thick with the smell of blood and fat. She shivered, and bumps rose on her skin. Outside, far away, she heard the hum of the cooler motor. Inside, the car was quiet. She heard her breath and racing heart. The car creaked along the rails, and she fell against a swinging carcass, slick with fat, and down to the floor, slippery with blood. She sat up straight, wrapping her arms around her trembling knees. Her dress was very thin and left half her skin completely bare. The car rocked on the rails. Her icy earrings swung against her face.

The cold was like a deep winter night. That was all. Taung could not be far. The dark, the blood and the fat on her dress and skin, the dead cattle creaking above her, swinging on hooks, were all much worse than the cold. She loved the smell of meat but not on herself. Before she fell into the Jackal's arms, she would have to find an Indian shop in Taung, beg for a bath and fragrant oil. She would braid their hair in return, and cook them sweet square Indian cakes soaked with honey and clarified butter.

The cold made her tired. She must stay awake, to hear and feel the train stop at Taung. Her legs tingled, then her arms, deeply, down to the bone. She thought of the Jackal, but even that could not erase the cold. She tried to rise, to pound on the door for someone to come and drag her out, but no one was there to hear and the train was moving, rumbling along the tracks.

She could no longer move but at least she could still think, but there, too, she found no escape. So this was the best she could do, with all she had learned, all her planning, her resolve to change her life. Here she was freezing to death while chasing a man.

The tingling spread through her body, and Ata fell asleep.

5

THE SCENT OF A WOMAN
IN LOVE

In the Taung train yard workmen switched cars from track to track. Suddenly they heard a scream and raised their heads. It was a woman's voice, from one of the cars. She screamed again and again.

They raced along the standing trains, shouting, "All right!" "We are here!" until they found the car. The screams came now without pause. They were terrified and hoarse. The workmen aimed their crowbars at the lock, which swung in its hinge. They all swung at once, hitting each other's bars instead of the lock.

"We are coming!" they shouted, aiming again.

They tore away the lock and rolled open the door. The screaming stopped and they looked up to see Ata Four standing in the sunlight, framed by the door and shaking with cold, with arms raised to shield her eyes from the glare. One shoulder strap had fallen down, revealing a breast stiff with cold. The orange dress and her bare arms, shoulders, and legs were stained with blood and yellow fat.

The men stared, mouths open, still clutching the crowbars. Ata lowered her arms, squinting against the sun. She pulled the dress strap back up to cover her breast.

"South Africa?" she said weakly. "Taung?"

All together, eyes unmoving, the men nodded their heads.

They helped her down and brought her a blanket. She lay in the sun beside the tracks as they hurried back to work. Closing her eyes, feeling the heat return to her skin, Ata breathed the oil and smoke of the train yard, the smell of South Africa, and then her own, that of meat and dried fat.

When she rose, returned the blanket, and thanked the men, she was warm and ripe, sweating now, adding this smell to all the others clinging to her. As she followed Jack's instructions, out of the station, along the tracks to the village, the sun was low behind her, setting into Kalahariland, away to the west where Ata had so recently been. Cookfire smoke rose up to fill her nose. Around her the village came home from work, and she searched the paths for an Indian shop. With a bath, some aromatic oil, a clean dress, she would be ready again to love the Jackal less.

The world darkened. She imagined another woman in the Jackal's house. He was just coming home from work. This stranger, this thief, was cooking the Jackal's supper. The paths wound without pattern or names. It was not hard to follow Jack's instructions, but there was no time to find an Indian shop. She knew the Jackal was just now sitting down to eat. Her rival was stirring the food in the pan.

Ata missed the house by only one. The village was dark now, with the factory lights illuminating the sky behind it. Without pausing for breath or a steady heart, she knocked once on the door.

A woman came out, with a baby on her hip. Ata stepped back.

"I seek Jack Vanu," said Ata.

"Which one?" said the woman, only a shadow in the doorway, against the lantern light. "The police have the real one. His friend is taking his place until Jack gets out of jail."

"The skinny one," Ata said.

"Next door," said the woman, gesturing with one hand.

She went back in and closed the door, leaving Ata in darkness.

This pause, this moment, drained away Ata's courage. She was ready to face him once, not twice. She knew now she never should have come at all. The Jackal had stayed with her only one night, long ago. Certainly since then he had known many other women. He would see her face and remember nothing about it.

She was not Monosi. She would never find a man like Boko. She was an Ata. Her life was a journey from man to man.

She looked around at the village, close and strange, and at the next house, tiny and dark except for a single curtained window. She touched her earrings, the stone in her nose, and sniffed herself for remnants of cinnamon and her former life. There was none left. Lorole was far away, Naring farther still.

Ata moved toward the Jackal's window, to glimpse a life beyond her, beyond all Atas, a life with only one man. She pressed her face to the glass. The room was small and crowded, with two metal tables and two metal chairs. At one of the tables sat the Jackal. A woman stood at the other table, cooking. The Jackal was just as handsome as ever, smiling, sitting very straight in the chair. Ata kept her eyes away from the woman and watched instead the pan in her hands. It moved to the table, then down toward the Jackal's plate.

The door burst open.

The Jackal leapt from his chair, turning to face the police, thinking up lies to explain. They had found him out at last. The woman stepped back from the table with all the food still safely in the pan.

Instead of police the Jackal saw a young woman standing in the doorway, in a tight orange dress that exposed more skin than it covered up. He saw the long earrings, the jewel in her nose, blood and fat smeared everywhere on her.

The Jackal sniffed, moving closer. He remembered the meat pies. English food. The Willoughby house.

"Ata?" he said.

Unable to speak, she watched his perfect lips approach, his smooth skin, his eyes puzzled and drawing her into him. He raised a hand to her cheek. It was hot, rough, familiar. He sat her down at the table, in a chair before the empty plate.

Ata still did not look at the woman, who now began to shout. The Jackal pulled the pan from her hand and dropped it onto the table. He pushed her into the other tiny room of the house. Now she kicked and screamed. Ata looked at the pan, then down to the floor. There was the empty can, with a jumping fish on a label as red as the sauce. A kerosene ring stood beside the can. This woman did not know how to cook.

The Jackal was just the same: intelligent, handsome, brash. She had proved her worth by finding him here, at night, in a tiny house on a winding path in a sprawling village with all South Africa around it.

The woman hit the Jackal twice, but finally she left, with curses, threats, and a suitcase. The Jackal closed the door behind her and came to sit beside Ata Four. He took her hand in his, smiling deeply into her eyes.

"Ata!" he said. "How I missed you! My job is very good. I can buy whatever you need to cook. No one here knows how to cook anything. With a wife I can get a good house. They are building new ones outside Taung. They will not let just anyone in. There will be electricity. We can live like the English in Willoughby's house. . . ."

When she heard the word *wife*, Ata closed her eyes.

He asked her no questions, but spoke on about Taung, his job, their new life together. Ata listened, and felt herself beginning anew, a stranger without a past. Did a place like this have marriage feasts? She imagined an office, signing a paper. It would be her first time writing since Monosi had taught her how. She would tell him tomorrow about their child, Ata Five, and arrange for someone to bring the girl to Taung, or Ata herself could go back and fetch her.

That night, her first in South Africa, Ata washed twice, once for the journey and once for him. The smell of meat and fat came off, along with any doubts about the Jackal. She tossed them outside with the wash water. She had no aromatic Indian potion to smear on her skin, no blue thorn to hang at her neck. The soap smelled strong, rough and clean. She rinsed herself until the smell of the soap vanished too.

He lay in the narrow bed in the narrow room in the dark. The village was noisy outside, voices and dogs, an occasional wagon or truck. Ata lay down beside him. He stirred and touched her. The memory enfolded her. Suddenly he was everywhere on her, above her, his hands beneath her.

She stared out into the dark, listening to the village night. Her legs floated, then her hips, and then she felt the shock. She closed her eyes, and touched his face. He rolled away, panting and smelling of her.

6

HANDLING MEN

Jack Vanu, the real one, told his story to the men on the mine office bus. They were BaNare, so they had tales to tell to him. They explained that Ata Four was not the Jackal's wife. He had left her after only one night. There was a child. There were many Ata children. They told him about No-Man's-Land in Naring, the Atas and the Tladis, and the cook who never missed an arriving bus and bore an Englishman's child. That was Ata Four's mother.

Jack listened, shaking his head. He did not know what to think. But he liked the idea of the Atas, he looked forward to meeting them, and also of Naring, a place to settle down and farm. When he came through the mine office gate and stopped at the first pots, miners already crowded before them. Yet another Ata child worked at Ata Three's side. Her name was Lemang, meaning "Let-Us-Plow."

Jack called over the heads of the men.

"Are you the mother of Ata Roodie?"

Ata Three looked up. She saw his head above the others, then his body through the crowd. He was huge and missing a sleeve.

"Who wants to know?" she said.

So Jack pushed up to the pots and told his tale. Ata Three turned to Lemang beside her.

"Take Jack home," she said. "Then hurry back, or my sadness will have no end."

The girl smiled shyly at Jack. He lifted her onto his shoulders and set off through Naring. He found the Ata compound just as the miners had described it. Children jumped into his lap, onto his back, into his arms as he told the story again. The Atas liked him very much, and he liked them. They gave him porridge and meat to eat, and he chopped wood, carried water, skinned goats, replaced roof poles, dug out the stump of a tree where the Atas wanted to build another house. Ata children tried to help but mostly got in his way.

That night, tired and happy, Jack went to sleep in the house the Atas had built around the enormous pot that cooked their beer. An Ata lying manless woke to creep up to the beerhouse door. Her name, Gaborone, meant "It-Is-Not-Unbecoming." She woke him up and they quietly lay down.

"I must go," she whispered afterward, rising from his arms. "We agreed to stay away from you, to let you choose on your own."

Jack drifted back to sleep, but then another Ata came in. Her name was Ntata, meaning "Loves-Me," and they, too, had a wonderful time. After she left he fell asleep again, but her twin Sentata woke him up. Her name meant "Loves-Me-Not."

By morning Jack had lost all count of the Atas passing through his arms. A dozen daughters fought over bringing him hot water for washing, porridge, tea, and his shirt. That was when the Atas all found out about each other, but no one said a word. Jack sat down among the men on the logs around the fire, greedily swallowing porridge, slowly regaining his strength.

Vincent Potso, chiefly son, came with his friends to drink. More and more they were No-Man's-Land's best customers. Vincent now filled out his black miner's overalls and orange mining helmet, but still he had never been to the mines. They came into the compound shouting and laughing, and paid for a bucket of beer.

The Ata who served it leaned away as she set it down before them. Her name was Winifred, and Vincent grabbed her arm.

The Atas were used to men such as Vincent. As he pulled her onto his knee, Winifred looked at Vincent's friends.

Other Atas stopped to stare, with the same calm as Winifred. Vincent's friends opened their mouths to speak, to tell him to let Winifred go.

But Jack was there, suddenly, hugely, and Vincent rose in the air. He kicked his feet above the ground. Jack held him up by the shoulders of the miner's overalls.

"Do not touch me!" Vincent cried. "Someday I will be chief!"

"You must apologize nicely," said Jack.

Then Vincent did exactly the wrong thing. He spat the vilest possible curse.

"You are your father!" said Vincent.

Jack wrapped his hands around Vincent's neck and squeezed.

"Chrghl," Vincent said.

And now his friends fell on Jack, and the Atas fell on them, until Vincent was free and he and his friends retreated from No-Man's-Land.

"You will pay!" Vincent called out from a safe distance. "You and all these wasted women will pay!"

That night the Atas sat down around Jack, and Ata Three explained to him their trade.

"You will drive away our business," she said. "We know how to handle men."

"I will do it again," said Jack. "How can I see that and sit on my hands?"

The Atas went to sleep worrying. Jack worried, too, wondering what to do, how else to act in a situation like that. At last he fell asleep, snoring, rattling the enormous pot beside him. No Ata came into his arms.

At first light a young Ata girl wrapped a blanket around her waist and came out to wash. The warmth of the bed still clung to her skin. She stretched her arms high, rose up onto her toes, and yawned. Her name was Sira, meaning "Shadow."

She dropped her dress on a bush and filled her basin with

water from the barrel. She poured it over her face and chest before she noticed the smell.

Sira's screams woke everyone up, especially Jack, who roared out to see in the dawn the child covered in blood, arms at her sides, screaming.

Jack pulled her to him, searching all over for open wounds. Then he saw the barrel and the basin, and lifted her into his arms.

The Atas rushed out and then the rest of the men. The children began to rush out, too, but the Atas chased them back inside. They carried the barrel out of the compound, washed Sira clean, and led her to the barrel.

"Watch," said Jack. "It is only blood from something someone dropped in the barrel. Maybe a cat. Maybe a dog. They cut it up and dropped it in. It cannot harm you. Watch."

They turned the barrel over. The watery blood poured out, then the bodies of three large dogs. And then, detached, the heads.

They put Sira back to bed. Without washing first, the men pulled on their shirts. Without eating porridge or drinking tea, they drifted out of the compound.

"Good-bye," said Jack to the Atas. "I am going up to squeeze Vincent's neck. This time nothing will make me let go."

Again the Atas sat down around Jack, and Ata Three explained.

"You are causing trouble between Naring and us," she said. "Vincent may be a fool, but he has many cattle and friends. Let us hope this is the end of it. You must not start another round. The next one might destroy us."

Jack looked confused and forlorn.

"Then what do I do?" he said.

"Go to Loang," said Ata Three. "Boko Tladi is out there with his family herds. You would be glad to meet a man like that. He has been very good to my daughter, who kindly sent you here to us."

Jack rose and shrugged his massive shoulders.

"All right," he said. "But I will be back."

And so he left. There were no customers that day. When at last they went into their houses, the Atas lay awake thinking. All at once, from their separate beds, they realized that this was the very first night since the war had ended that no man slept among them.

7

HOW JACK VANU MET BOKO TLADI

The track through the Kalahari was easy to follow. Cattle hooves had worn it wide and clear of grass, and it did not branch into smaller tracks until Loang, Jack's destination. He carried matches, a flask of water, and a knife. He saw no one along the way, no fields or cattle, just trees and bushes, birds and grass. A jackal loped across the path ahead, and Jack laughed.

It was a wilderness from his dreams. He had grown up on a Boer farm, until the owner bought three new tractors and fired everyone else. Surely the farm he had known as a boy was nothing like the Kalahari around him now, there had been fields everywhere and voices were never far away, but his memory made it vast and wild, like this, the endless Kalahari.

Jack slept at night beside a roaring fire, hungry, with a clean feeling in the fresh, dry air. When he heard the first clang of a cowbell, hidden by brush and trees, he felt sad. The walk through his childhood was over.

He saw the cattle, moving toward Loang, kicking up dust. They filed into the path ahead. Herders appeared, smacking the cattle with sticks, shouting something Jack could not make out above the noise of the cattle lowing and their hooves scraping the sand.

Soon there were cattle everywhere. Jack saw the first compound. Women ran, scooping up children. They all ran in the same direction, through the cattle and brush. The herders began to smack the cattle urgently, shouting out and running too.

The compounds were scattered so far apart that Jack saw

only one at a time. He came to the vast clearing around the Loang well, with the engine pumping away in the center. Cattle filled the clearing. The running BaNare passed the cattle and headed away, forming a crowd as they ran. Jack ran after them.

The crowd swarmed around a compound. Jack pushed his way to the center, where men in khaki clothing stood among women in dusty dresses. One of the men, tall and lean, handsome, was holding an ax. Even when others were talking, the faces of all the BaNare pointed to this one man.

The crowd shouted, wailed, cried out, as Jack pushed up beside the man with the ax. He could not understand what anyone said. There seemed to be a word missing, something no one would say.

An old woman shouted at the man with the ax.

"They ate him!" she cried. "They ate him! They want to eat me!"

"Who are they?" said Jack.

The man with the ax looked up.

"Hyenas," said Boko Tladi.

Jack saw men push through the crowd with rifles and sacks of bullets. Boko dropped the ax as he reached for one of the rifles. No one noticed a huge hand reaching out to grab the falling ax.

"BaNare!" Boko cried out, waving the rifle high in the air. "They killed one herdboy and many cattle. Let us kill enough to scatter them before the sun goes down. We must take the day. If not, they will take the night."

Jack held the ax in his hand as Boko formed the riflemen into a long line. He called each one by name. Jack had never fired a rifle. There had been no guns at all on the farm of his youth. The Boers had long ago taken them away.

"Stay in line!" Boko shouted. "We win if we keep them before us. We lose if we let them surround us."

Jack saw them all twitch, adjusting the sacks on their shoulders, sighting along the rifles, except for Boko, who calmly took the middle and waved them forward into the brush, disappearing. The crowd watched the brush close behind them, now empty and silent, hiding hyenas and men.

Jack had seen not a single hyena on the way from Naring. They came from the west, the deep Kalahari. Over the years, as the BaNare brought more and more cattle out to the new wells, more hyenas came to eat them. Each year the BaNare shot more hyenas, who had always hunted alone, until now. Now the hyenas had banded together to take back the Kalahari. They slipped past the other wells to begin the war at Loang, to cut the road to the rest of the world. After Loang they could move from well to well, tearing apart BaNare.

Suddenly the first shot rang out from the brush. The crowd fell silent, listening. They heard another shot, then many, all at once. Then single shots, one by one, slowly, as if only one man fired them.

The bushes erupted before the crowd. Men came running out. No rifles, no sacks of bullets, just men with their hands waving and feet kicking the sand. One by one they fell at the feet of the crowd, until only Boko Tladi remained in the distant brush, firing at the hyenas.

The crowd cried out and waved their arms. Women ran from man to man, tearing at faces, screaming for them to rejoin the battle. Men wept with shame, raising no hand to block the women's blows, as in the distance Boko fired and fired.

From somewhere among them the crowd heard a roar. They saw an enormous stranger, clutching Boko's ax, stride out to vanish into the brush.

Jack swept his eyes from tree to bush to tree, as the sound of the crowd faded behind him. He did not run, but walked swiftly, listening. A dead cow lay in the grass, half eaten away, and then to his left he saw a blur and swung the ax. Blood spurted over his arms as the hyena's head flew into space. Its quivering body fell at his feet. Jack thought of taking the pieces back to Naring to drop in Vincent Potso's water barrel.

Another hyena came up behind. Jack spun and swung. The

hyena yelped and hit the sand. It limped away on three legs. Jack hurried toward the shots with the ax already red. He passed more cattle, eaten, then a rifle and sack of bullets. He picked them up with one hand. The other swung the ax but the hyena leapt away, untouched. It stood away now, snarling through hideous jaws. The spotted yellow fur rippled with venom. The rounded ears stood stiff upon its head, and the neck was as thick as the head, rising out of the massive chest, high on long, muscular forelegs. The hind legs were short, with a greasy tail drooping between them.

Jack swung the ax again, a warning. The hyena moved off through the brush as another came up from behind. Jack spun and sliced away its jaw.

At last he reached the firing. Boko saw the movement and swung the rifle to aim at Jack. Then he swung it back to kill another hyena.

"Do you want the rifles?" said Jack. "I do not know how to shoot."

"Only the bullets," said Boko.

The brush around them was noisy with snarling and grunting. Jack dropped the rifle and slipped the sack over Boko's shoulder. They moved away, Boko firing, Jack searching the ground for more sacks. Each time he found one he slung it over his shoulder. When Boko emptied the sack on his shoulder, Jack pulled it off and slipped on a full one.

After the fourth sack Boko ran out of bullets before Jack found another. Now Jack swung the ax while Boko searched the ground. They said nothing except "Over there!," pointing, and "Left!" "Right!" "Behind!"

Jack with the ax, and Boko with the rifle, both aimed at only one hyena at a time. The other men had made the mistake of seeing the hyenas all at once, a sight no man could endure. But Jack and Boko looked at only one, swung or fired, then aimed at the next, on and on through the battle.

They found more sacks, so Boko fired again. A hyena leapt from behind. Boko spun and blew a hole through its open jaws, out the back of its head. The mouth fell over the barrel.

The end of the barrel poked out the back of the head. Boko wiped the blood from his eyes and worked the barrel out of the dead hyena's jaws. Two more came at him. Jack missed one but drove it back. He severed the spine of the other.

They were deep among the hyenas. The bushes were hung with glistening streaks of white. This was how the hyenas marked out their territory, lifting their legs to spray from a sac beneath their tails. It stank like nothing else on earth. The white rubbed off on Boko and Jack as they moved past.

They counted the sacks as they found them. When they found the last one, Jack had three full sacks on his shoulder. Boko swung the rifle left, right, behind, then left again, ahead, right, behind.

Nothing. No movement, no sound.

Jack and Boko stood still, catching their breaths, listening, sweeping their eyes through the empty brush.

Then they heard howling, grunting, just ahead, invisible but close. The noise grew, shrieking, barking, louder and louder, hyena voices joining together, massing for a final attack. They would come at the men all at once, too fast and too many for two men to fight.

Boko dropped the rifle and sack.

"Before they come at us," he said, dropping his trousers, "we are going after them. Running. Our clothes will catch on the thorns."

Jack looked at Boko's bare legs, thicker than the Jackal's, then he pulled off his own clothes as well.

Naked, weapons in hand, the two men faced the brush and snarling hyena army. Boko looked up at the sun.

"We do not have much time," he said, shouting above the hyena sound. "We are too far away to get back by sundown. We must kill enough to drive them away. We will have to go back by night."

Jack peered out at the shrieking brush.

"We will do it," he said.

Boko shouted, Jack roared, and they ran at the hyenas.

Back at Loang, the BaNare ringed the Tladi compound

with firewood and set it blazing. Then they sat on the sand inside, trembling, watching the sun fall low and set, listening to the firing fade and then finally vanish. They left a narrow gap in the ring of fire, on the impossible chance that Boko and the enormous stranger might come through the battle alive. Night fell but no one went home or had any suggestion for what to do. The fire burned yellow and high against the Kalahari.

Suddenly someone rose to his feet and cried out, pointing through the gap in the fire.

"There!"

The rest of the crowd rose too, disbelieving, and the two men came through the circle of fire. The BaNare surrounded them, shouting, kissing their faces smeared with dust and sweat, hyena blood, and something sticky white. The two men stank like nothing on earth.

Boko and Jack kept walking, blind to the crowd, deaf to their voices. Their muscles quivered with fear and exhaustion. At last the crowd fell back, puzzled and silent. The two men made their way to the Tladi cookfire, where meat still roasted on the dying coals. There they crouched, and reached for the meat. The BaNare stared as they grunted and growled and tore at the meat, their eyes wide and wild with the sight of foaming hyena jaws and flying hyena blood.

8

THE DREAM OF EVERY COOK

In a noisy office in the center of Taung, Ata Four leaned over
the paper, signing her name in clear, round letters, carefully,
slowly, exactly on the line, as Monosi had taught her, out at
the Tladi fields so very long ago. Now here she was, about to
become the first Ata wife, Mrs. Jack Elias Bajaki Vanu the
Jackal.

When she finished the first word, *Ata.* she paused and
looked up at the Jackal. Then she looked down again at half
her name on the paper, the most important half, and smiled
through the wall before her, out across Taung to Kalahariland. Triuimph welled up inside her, along her throat to burst
out in a single laugh.

The Jackal stared at her, confused and uneasy.

"What is it?" he said.

"Nothing," said Ata, laughing quietly this time, and then
to herself.

She leaned over the paper again, her face close and hot
with the joy of discovery. She had attained the goal all Atas
desired, and from this position of strength looked out at the
world with new eyes. She raised her head again and looked
up at the Jackal, a man she hardly knew, and what she did
know was mostly bad.

"What is it?" he said again, worried now at her distant,
mocking smile.

"I was just thinking," she said.

"Do not think. Write."

As Ata wrote the rest of her name, she knew that the Jackal
did not love her, that marriage was not what she needed. The

Atas had never tasted it, they could not know, but now it was in her mouth and she knew before long she would spit it out.

That night, her first as a wife, she continued to think as the Jackal gently pressed himself between her legs. There were no glistening bodies on the sand, only Ata Four, thinking, and her sweaty husband on a narrow bed in a Taung village house. Monosi and other BaNare chose their husbands, and always with an eye to what their lives would be thereafter. She herself had had no choice, at least in Naring. If she had not set out in pursuit of the Jackal she would never have married at all.

The Jackal finished, rolled over, and fell asleep. Ata thought on. She remembered the feeling of life on her own in Lorole, attracting the eyes of men who knew nothing of the Naring Atas. That was the way for an Ata to find a decent husband, a marriage with a sweeter flavor than the one she herself now held, unswallowed, between her teeth.

As the wife of a man with a city pass and a city job, Ata received a city pass as well. She looked for a job from house to house along the Boer and English streets, still thinking. She reached the center of town, facing an old painted brick building with tall windows on three floors and small arched windows on the fourth. A broken clock faced out from the central arch instead of a window. A verandah shaded the sidewalk. The old sign was painted over, but Ata could still read the raised plaster letters: TAUNG HOTEL. The new sign was painted directly onto the brick: ROODIE HOTEL.

Roodie was her name too. She found the back door and asked for the head cook.

"What is it?" he said impatiently, in English.

He was bald with hollow cheeks, in white trousers, shirt, and apron, and skin the color of winter grass.

"I am a cook," Ata replied, also in English. "And my name is the same as this place."

"So?"

"I have a city pass and I can cook anything. BaNare, Boer, English, Indian."

Just then the front door of the kitchen burst open. A skinny, angry Boer with red hair and huge red freckles everywhere, in khaki farmer clothes and a battered hat, stormed in with a plate of food in his hands. He threw it at the head cook and screamed at him in Boer. Ata heard him call the cook "Vlei" and other names she could not understand. Then he stormed back out.

Shaking with fear, covered with onions and a watery red sauce, the cook grabbed Ata by the shoulders, shaking her too.

"Cook something," he said. "Your very best dish. Make it good or he will kill me."

So Ata baked meat pies. There was only goat on hand, so she used that with honey and mustard to stuff inside, talking to the cook as she worked.

"Your name is Vlei," she said.

"Yes, yes. Hurry up."

"I really am a Roodie."

"Wonderful. Why so much mustard?"

"To balance the honey," said Ata.

"Hurry and mix in the meat."

"Not yet. The meat must boil until it is tender. To cook right you must take your time."

Vlei paced behind her, scratching his elbows.

"Why do you speak English here?" she said.

He stopped and drew up straight.

"This may be a Boer hotel," he said, "but this is Dani Vlei's kitchen."

Roodie loved the meat pies. Ata was hired.

She rose each morning before first light, cooked the Jackal's breakfast and left it on the stove, walked through the waking village, and arrived at the hotel in time to cook breakfast for Boers. Lunch was the biggest meal, and after supper she walked home to cook again for the Jackal. She washed herself as he ate, then he crawled atop her as Ata continued to think.

She asked Dani Vlei if he knew the story of Mojamaje's

cloak. As a very young man, Boko Tladi's grandfather, Mojamaje, had worked on a farm near Taung, which was owned by a Roodie and run by a foreman named Vlei.

"My grandfather," said Dani the cook.

Mojamaje had brought along a magnificent cloak sewn from thirty Kalahari jackals, and one complicated night he exchanged it for Vlei's knife, which ended up in Roodie's chest. Mojamaje later recovered the knife, and the BaNare hung it from the council tree when he died.

"Mojamaje's cloak, Vlei's knife, Roodie's chest," said Ata. "Every BaNare knows the story."

"That was long ago," said Dani. "It is no longer so easy to kill a Boer."

She had one day off a month, a Sunday, and when this day came she slept until the Jackal woke her.

"Time to eat," he said, smiling with his charming teeth, touching her cheek with a gentle hand.

Ata rose and began to cook. He sat down at the table to watch.

"I think you should give me your wages," he said.

Ata stood stirring porridge, missing not a single beat. She added salt, trying to name the feeling inside herself now. It was stronger than relief. Perhaps it was freedom.

"Why?" she said at last.

"To buy things," he said, sincerely, kindly. "Lamps, radios, toasters, phonographs, stoves, telephones, freezers. Sharpetown will have electricity. When it comes, the shops will raise the prices of all these things, and so will we. Everyone will buy them and we can make a good profit."

"Maybe I do not want to go to Sharpetown."

"You say that because you have not seen it. The houses are beautiful, all in neat rows on wide, quiet streets. Not like this noisy village mess. You must go out and see it."

"I like the village," said Ata, not arguing at all, simply measuring the distance between them. "The winding paths and the Indian shops, the Diamond Café and the others, everyone all together. Sharpetown sounds lonely."

"You have not seen it. And anyway, they will tear down the village. We will have to go there."

Ata turned to look at him, at his face as handsome as ever, at his contentment with himself.

"We can go to Kalahariland," she said.

"That dry place?" He laughed. "There I was nothing, the *mpe* child of a worthless chief. Here I am a man. If we plan carefully, if we save and work hard, we can start out small in one of the last rows of Sharpetown and work our way up to the bigger houses in the better rows. Some day you will have a maid of your own. With both of us working, and no children, I know we can do it."

"We already have a child."

"Of course," said the Jackal.

"And maybe I will have more."

"We can send them to the same place, your family compound where no one notices another child."

"I will miss them there," she said. "I already miss my little Ata."

She was toying with him now, for she knew what he would say before he said it. She enjoyed this small power of finally seeing the Jackal clearly.

"Ata dear," he said, "we cannot have everything. We must give up some things to have some others. That is life. Go out and see Sharpetown. You will see that I am right."

"My wise husband," she said, setting his breakfast before him. "I am the luckiest woman in the world."

The tone of her voice confused him, but then he took the first bite of the sauce atop the porridge. It was wonderful.

"What is this?" he said.

"Goat meat with honey and mustard. Boers love it."

That afternoon, after the Jackal rolled off her and fell asleep, Ata dressed and went out to look at Sharpetown. It lay beyond the factories, far from Taung village and city. She was hot and thirsty by the time it came into sight, rows of empty houses stretched across the plain as far as her eye could see, up a rise and down the other side.

The English and Boers of South Africa did not like Taung village at all, so they planned to destroy it and move everyone into Sharpetown. A few like the Jackal were eager to go, but mostly they despaired. In the village they could own their own houses or rent them out, or brew beer and sell it, or run a shop, instead of working for English or Boers. Only those with Boer or English jobs would be allowed in Sharpetown, with the number of the house recorded on the pass beside the number of the job. Everyone else would have to leave Taung.

Ata reached the rows of houses and walked in among them. The streets were of gravel and dirt, treeless, empty, dusty, and wide. The first rows of houses were concrete block, unpainted, on large square lots fenced in. A maid's quarters stood behind each house, like Ata's in Naring. The next rows of houses were smaller, on smaller lots, without maid's quarters. The next rows were gray asbestos, small and square on tiny lots. The houses grew smaller, row by row, and then grew larger again, divided in half with an outside door to each room. Each row now had longer houses, with more outside doors. At last, at the very end, Ata came to long gray windowless barracks, each with only one outside door. Here men would sleep alone, as they did in the mines.

She stopped and turned around, to look back on the full length of Sharpetown. It was all so new and untouched, so empty and dead, like a graveyard waiting. The ground before each house was recently smoothed, like a grave, with the house itself as a headstone. They would kill the village and bury it here.

Ata started back to Taung, and came across in the center of Sharpetown an empty police station behind a high wire fence with coils of barbed wire on top. The buildings inside were red brick, with bars on the windows. There were big garages with metal doors.

She was suddenly afraid and began to run, as the wind rose across the Taung plain, carrying dust. When she reached again the noisy, twisting paths of the village, it did not look at all near death. She saw a tall young woman wearing only a scarlet cloth pinned up at one shoulder, her arms and the side of one breast exposed, feet bare and head erect, walk past with a bowl on her head. She called out a song, offering corn for sale.

Ata did not tell the Jackal she had been to Sharpetown. She gave him her wages, and he began buying appliances. He was right, of course. Each row of Sharpetown houses would carry a different rent. The Jackal looked forward to working his way up through them. He knew how to survive in South Africa, and might even thrive. Ata knew she could do neither. She went to work, cooked, and lay on her back for the Jackal, all the time thinking, waiting.

Sometimes at night, after the Boers had eaten and moved to the bar, Ata walked out from the hotel kitchen. The dining room walls were white and clean, the ceiling high, the floor wooden and glowing with wax. The tables and chairs were wooden with iron legs. Red and white cloths, stained with supper, covered the tables.

Wide windows looked onto the sidewalk, under the long verandah, and village men in good clothes peered in from the night. They were not Boers, so they could not enter. Neither were they English, who never came in but could if they so desired. She would have liked to cook for the men at the window instead of for Boers. She hated South Africa then, Roodie and his hotel, Sharpetown waiting, and even the Jackal.

Sometimes after breakfast Ata walked into the empty bar. There were tables and chairs with short legs and leather circles on every table to keep the glasses and bottles from leaving stains. A mirror covered one wall, behind a high wooden counter, with bottles stacked against the glass. She walked behind to press her face to the mirror. There she saw the stone in her nose, the Indian earrings of brass and glass, the white scarf hiding her hair. Behind her the room was quiet and dark, where men drank beer. It was not at all like the

Diamond Café or the logs around the cookfire in No-Man's-Land.

She met her own eyes in the mirror.

"This is what I will do," she watched herself say. "I will have a place like this."

Walking home through the village, against the lights of the factories, she put together a plan. Armah the Indian would lend her money, she was not sure how much, but enough to start. She would bring Atas to Lorole to work in the shop, and there they would meet men to marry.

Her feet moved faster with each decision. She would have to keep men and babies out of the compound behind the shop. These two things prevented marriage.

She stopped, staring into the lights. There would not be enough men. Lorole was far too small. The Wall-Makers were few and the slaughterhouse workers even fewer. They already had wives. And the miners stepping off the train were only passing through. She needed a growing Lorole, flooded with men in search of jobs and wives.

She arrived at the house, stepped around the Jackal's pile of machines, and began to cook his supper. He was asleep on the bed. Her perfect plan, the solution she had been waiting for, dissolved and mixed with the steam rising from the pot. Vlei often talked like that, about one day running a place of his own. It was the dream of every cook.

She woke the Jackal and washed as he ate. When he finished and lay atop her, she pushed him away.

"Why?" he said.

"I feel lonely," she said.

"But this is the cure."

"I feel tired."

"But I do all the work," he said.

"I feel sad."

"If this happens again," he said, rolling away, "I will give you something to be sad about."

She remained awake, watching him in the dark, so harmless and quiet there beside her. She knew it was almost over.

When at last she fell asleep, it seemed like only a moment before she woke to the sound of metal crashing, screaming, the roar of machines around her.

The Jackal sat up.

"Oh, no!" he said. "They promised to warn me. I am happy to go."

They pulled on clothes and rushed outside to see head-lights of bulldozers cutting the dark. Children wailed, and the people of Taung shouted and pulled from their homes what-ever they could before the bulldozers knocked them down. Police strode among the machines, fingering pistols at their hips.

The Jackal ran off, swearing into the air, and came back with a truck and driver. Ata helped them load up the open back of the truck with the Jackal's electric machines and then everything else they owned.

"Why?" the Jackal hissed. "Why did they fail to tell me?"

Ata watched the Jackal drive off with his load. A bulldozer came behind and flattened their house. Around her the rest of the village packed their belongings onto trucks, donkeys, bicycles, wagons, carts, their own backs and heads. There were far too few vehicles to go around. Women and children sat on piles of furniture, weeping, embracing blankets, framed photographs, and each other.

A streak of gray appeared in the sky. Enormous trucks drove up, green and empty. The police checked passes against their list of English jobs in the factories and Taung city. They marked down the number of each new Sharpetown house on the proper pass. Those without a proper pass, mostly women, the police herded into the trucks. Children went with their mothers. The trucks drove into the countryside to barren pieces of land too rocky and dry for Boers to farm. There they dumped the passless.

Ata showed her pass and the police wrote down the num-ber of the Jackal's new Sharpetown house. She stood watch-ing, frozen with fear, as the bulldozers worked and Taung village vanished to rubble.

The sky brightened and Ata looked into it. She was late for work.

She ran through the dying village, crying, and reached the quiet, straight streets of Taung city, where no one seemed concerned. She found only half the staff in the kitchen. They worked without speaking, wept without chopping onions, sliced cabbage without seeing, and bled.

Vlei came up behind her.

"We are burning our passes," he said. "Tomorrow at the new Sharpetown police station. If everyone does it, how can they arrest us all?"

"I am leaving," said Ata, her voice raw and weak.

"Back to Kalahariland?"

"Yes."

"At least you have somewhere to go."

Vryman Roodie usually ate every meal at the hotel, surrounded by his Boer friends. But today he missed breakfast and lunch, and arrived late for dinner. He sat down among the other Boers and told a story.

It was a long, loud story, and the kitchen staff heard it through the closed door. Sometimes Roodie laughed and slapped the table. Sometimes the other Boers laughed too. Vlei moved to the door to listen, and Ata Four came up behind to ask him to explain. She spoke no Boer. The others lifted their knives and moved up to listen too. Vlei pressed his ear to the door.

"The story is this," he whispered. "It happened today. People came to his farm."

They heard Roodie laugh again, and slap the table.

"They cut a hole in his fence to get in," Vlei said. "They carried everything on their backs. They sat down among the cows. They had nowhere else to go. Roodie saw them. He came with his dogs."

The kitchen staff squeezed their knives.

"He let the dogs go," Ata whispered.

Vlei nodded.

"How many died?" she said.

Vlei squinted, ear to the door. There was no laughing now from the other Boers, just Roodie talking.

"Three," Vlei whispered.

The kitchen staff held their knives pointing through the door. They rocked forward, trembling. They turned away to cut up vegetables instead, into very tiny pieces.

Ata was the last to turn away. She walked to the pantry and came out with one hand in her pocket. No one saw. She brought out the hand and mixed the rat poison into the goat meat, honey, and mustard.

This Boer had killed three, and now she would make him pay. This was South Africa. If she did not, no one else would. She did not know how much poison to use, how many meat pies his friends would eat. If she put in too much, they would taste it and spit it out. She licked the spoon. It tasted all right to her. She rinsed her mouth and spooned the mixture into the circles of dough. When the poison pies came out of the oven, she heaped them on a plate, the waiter took them away, and Ata went out to sit on the back step.

She was very tired. The alley was dark and quiet. She looked up into the sliver of sky above it, empty of stars, moon, or clouds. She feared closing her eyes for the sights she might see within them, but she rested her arms on her knees and her head on her arms, dreaming of sleep, and it came.

Vlei shook her awake.

"They are all gone," he said.

"Dead?" said Ata.

He narrowed his eyes at her, watching her rise to her feet.

"Dead?" he said. "Who?"

"The Boers."

"No," he said, following her into the kitchen. "Why?"

Ata went to the sink and splashed her face with water. The rest of the staff had already left.

"Did they eat?" she said. "Were they sick?"

"They were not sick," said Vlei. "Only Roodie ate. The

other Boers left in a hurry. To see if anyone tore holes in their fences too."

Ata wiped her face with the apron as Vlei fought his way through to the truth.

"How many did he eat?" she said.

Vlei bit one lip, then the other.

"All of them," he said.

Ata raised her hands to his sunken cheeks. She held his face gently, hands still cold from the water, and pulled down his head to kiss its bald top.

"Dani Vlei," she said, "I am sorry. Truly I am. Here is my advice. Do not come back to work tomorrow. Or ever again. Tell everyone else the same thing. Forgive me, please."

They left together, hurrying down the dark streets. He turned off somewhere without a word. Ata entered the flattened village, alone and afraid. She ran, stumbling over shadows, the silent ghost of the village. She passed the shapes of the factories, low and long, far apart in the glare of their lights. She raised one arm to shade her eyes.

As she entered Sharpetown, police stopped her to check her pass. They swung their flashlights onto the pass, onto her face, then waved her on with the beam. Row by row Ata searched through the numbered graves. The numbers grew as the houses shrank, row by row, until she reached the Jackal's.

She lifted a weary fist to the metal door and barely heard the knock herself. She raised the other fist. She hated him then, but thought of sleep and lying against him. She beat the door again, then again, harder, again with all her might. Pain shot up her arms. She hit the door again.

He opened it. There was light behind him and a hammer raised in one hand.

"Ata!" he said.

She fell inside. The Jackal caught her and lifted her into his arms. She wrapped her arms around his neck and pushed her face against it. He laid her on the bed and gently pulled off her clothes. Ata felt the bed, warm with him, and then he lay beside her. This night he let her sleep. Her head lay on his chest throughout the night. His arms held her, strong, safe, still. She breathed him, sleeping. She dreamed of him, hiding in him, escaping, disappearing into him.

He was gone when she awoke. He had let her sleep, but the Jackal never missed a day of work. Even today, the date of Sharpetown's birth. Ata lay on the bed, feeling him there, safe and warm with the smell of him. She dozed again, pushing away all danger, everything but him.

Suddenly Ata sat up.

"Enough," she said aloud.

She looked around the strange, new Sharpetown room, perfectly square, empty, smelling of cement. She rose and went into the other room. His electric machines almost filled it. She touched each one, and in the shiny ones she saw herself, naked and alone, a cloudy stone in her nose. She washed, dressed, and came out again to touch the machines. Her wages had partly paid for them. They were all she had to show for these long South African days and nights.

Outside, far away, she heard a shout. Then another, more, many.

Ata walked into the sunlight, shading her eyes with one arm. Down each street she saw people hurrying, shading their eyes from the sun, toward a distant, gathering crowd. Ata followed, drawn like the others, toward the sound and the sight. She turned down one street, then another, and joined the crowd around the Sharpetown police station. Rising onto her toes, peering over heads, Ata saw the roofs of the brick police buildings, the high fence around them, and the barbed wire, fallen loose in places, dangling, atop the fence.

"Burn them!" voices cried around her.

"Every pass!"

Here and there men and women held up their passes.

"Burn the passes!"

"Every one!"

But no one wanted to start. If everyone burned them, the

9

AN ATA LIFE

Across South Africa, from Kalahariland down to the sea, everyone told the same story. It took many years for the different versions to fight it out, for the victor to stand alone, unchallenged above the rest. When new interpretations sprouted, the victorious version stamped them out.

The story was that a cook had saved a country.

Her name was the same as the Boer she killed. It was an ancient family feud, involving a cloak, a knife, and a bloody chest. The doctor looked at Vryman Roodie's swollen belly, the green in his lifeless face, and gave his verdict.

"It must have been something he ate," said the doctor.

Across South Africa, Boers and English fired their cooks and ate out of cans.

The story continued: in avenging this murder, the police shot sixty dead.

The Sharpetown shooting had nothing to do with passes. They were nothing new. No one remembered a time before passes existed. They had never killed before, and they did not kill at Sharpetown. The police were aiming at the cook. The others were just in the way.

The story ended like this: the English decided to let Kalahariland rule itself.

They ran Kalahariland from Taung, so they knew all about the Sharpetown shooting. The Kalahariland chiefs, still arguing in England, heard about the shooting too.

"See!" the chiefs declared. "They will shoot us all!"

The English, fed up to their stiff upper lips with ruling the world, wanted no more trouble. They began to arrange for

police could never arrest them all. Or could they? If all
Africa burned their passes, the battle would surely be
Everyone wanted to do it, but no one wanted to be the

A policeman came out from the buildings. He held
bullhorn and blared out something in Boer. The crowd
noisy now. Only those right against the fence heard the ho
They turned around to look, pressing their chests and fa
against the fence.

The policeman tried Zulu next, then Sotho, and finally E
glish. The first row of the crowd against the fence watche
and listened. Still they could not make out a word. Thei
fingers and noses pressed through the squares of the wire
fence. The fence swayed. More barbed wire pulled loose
atop it, dangling, swaying with the fence. The policeman
went back inside.

Ata looked around at the waving passes and pulled her
own from her pocket.

"I will be first!" she cried, waving the pass in the air. "I am
leaving this place! Who has a match?"

The first row of the crowd, against the fence, saw uniform
sleeves poke out the barred windows of the station buildings.
There were pistols at the end of the sleeves.

Ata held the pass in her mouth as she lit the match, then
the pass. She waved the flaming pass in the air. It singed her
fingers, and she dropped it. More passes flamed around her,
the crowd cheered and shouted, drowning out the pistol
shots and the screams.

The fence swayed and the first dead fell. The last to see
them fall and hear the shots and screaming, were the first to
have the space to run, far from the fence. The first to hear,
against the fence, were the last to run. They fell, screaming.

The police fired and fired again. The crowd ran until the
street before the station, wide and freshly dug, was empty
except for the sixty dead and two hundred wounded unable
to run away.

Kalahariland to rule itself. They would build a city inside the country, at Lorole Station.

As for the cook, she escaped on the train to Kalahariland. Before her husband came home from work, she hired a truck to load up all his electric machines. At the train station she paid the driver a lamp. For her ticket she paid a radio.

The border police, South African side, demanded to see her pass. She told them she had burned it, and showed them the tips of her fingers, raw and blistered from holding the flaming pass. They took her fingerprints, photograph, and name. Two of the fingerprints came out blank. Then they deported her. Never again could she enter South Africa.

That meant she stayed on the train to Kalahariland, which was just where she wanted to go. The story had not spread fast enough, so the police did not know who she was. Safe in Lorole, she built her own shop with an Indian's money. She gave him all the remaining appliances, except for the freezer, which she kept to cool the beer she would serve in the shop. Men would come from all over Kalahariland to build the new Lorole city. She brought her family to work in the shop and marry the men who would drink there.

The BaNare came to know more of the story than this, and claimed its hero as their own. They sang the song that mentioned her, that mentioned the Atas and No-Man's-Land, adding to them verses to fit their own new knowledge:

> *Jewel in her nose*
> *Jewels in her ears*
> *Jewel of all those Ata years*
> *The Jackal gave her nothing but tears*
> *To last her Ata life*
> *Eater of English*
> *Eater of Boers*
> *Eater of passes and city wars*
> *Who is she who did these chores?*
> *The first Ata wife. . . .*

Lorole

1
KANYE

Ata Four stood on a ladder, painting the name of the shop above the windows. She called it Stardust Café, because Lorole's full name, Lorole-la-Dinaledi, meant "Dust-of-the-Stars" in English, and she wanted the Atas to speak English in the shop. Her belly pressed against the ladder, swollen with the Jackal's second child. As she stretched up her arms for the final stroke of paint, a pain stabbed her back.

She called out to the other Atas, who ran to the ladder, catching her as she missed the last step down. They pulled off her dress and brought blankets and sheets. There on the shop steps, the baby came out.

"A boy!" they cried.

"Impossible!"

"Where did he come from?"

"The first Ata boy!"

They looked twice, three times, between the infant's legs to make sure. Then they laid him against his mother's sweating skin.

"Kanye," she said. "His name."

Kanye meant "Enough," the first word she had ever spoken in Sharpetown. She had had enough then, she had Kanye now.

The Atas passed him from breast to breast, even the girls too young to have them. Ata Four had brought to Lorole Ata girls of various ages to build the shop. She allowed no men or babies, even her own Ata Five.

"Oh, please," they all said to her now.

"Let him stay."

"Please let him stay."

"He is a baby."

"And a man."

"But please let him stay."

At first the Atas had hated the idea of no babies or men in the Stardust compound, but in the end they knew that the rule made sense. Now Kanye arrived, an exception in every way. She pulled him from their dry breasts and pressed him to her own.

"All right," she said. "But only until he can walk and talk. Then he goes to Naring, to be with Jack and Boko Tladi. Boys need men."

Because they were all too busy to look after Kanye, this first Ata boy, Ata Four sent for Ata Five, who was old enough to walk and talk, to come from Naring to take care of him. In No-Man's-Land Ata Five already had a baby to tend: Willoughby, child of Ata Three and Scott. When her grandmother told her the news, Ata Five was carrying Willoughby on her back. She refused to put her down. No one had the heart to pull the baby away from her, so they both went to Lorole.

The shop took a long time to build, and Armah argued over every expense. It stood alone, up the tracks from the station, a short walk from Armah's house and shop. There were two rooms of concrete block painted blue, a front one for men and a back one for bottles, a slanting metal roof, and steps running up the front and down the back of the shop. The front room had big windows and white walls, no shelves or counter, and a cement floor that the Atas waxed shiny red. Ata Four filled the room with metal tables, with four metal chains at each one. They pressed thorn bush branches into the ground and ran a wire atop them, from Armah's shop to the freezer in the back room.

Behind the shop, over a deep dark hole, the Atas built a tin shed with a gleaming enamel toilet inside. Armah cursed each coat of wax or paint and flatly refused to pay for the toilet. Ata persuaded him with numerous platefuls of Indian sweets. Miners from the station, meat cutters from the slaughterhouse, Wall-Makers from the village, came over to investigate. Ata Four chased them away.

Each of the older Ata girls took a turn working in the Indian house. Armah's daughters rubbed ointment in her ears, pierced them through, and hung earrings in the holes. During the first month each Ata learned how to take care of the daughters from the Ata already there. The second month, she herself became the teacher. She left the house with her head held high, smelling of spices and flowers, loving men just a little less.

Every morning, as the Atas rose and washed, Ata Four looked out at Lorole, searching for signs of the city. She expected to see it begin as machines digging earth, or an Englishman with a map. She swept her eyes from the station to the slaughterhouse, to the Wall-Maker village against the hills. Her eye strayed up to the crest, South Africa and the Jackal beyond.

Sometimes at the end of a long day her eyes fell closed as her hands continued to move. She drifted off to the Willoughby kitchen, to the mine office gate and her mother's pots, the Tladi fields, Armah's house and shop, everywhere she had worked. Then she saw the Sharpetown dead and cried out. She opened her eyes to see the Atas turned to her, alarmed and afraid.

"I was dreaming," she said. "Go back to work."

Jack Vanu borrowed the Tladi wagon to deliver meat and corn from Naring. In Taung she had not thought once about him, but once she returned to Lorole she looked forward to seeing him, remembering his parting words to her, that he would wait for her in Naring. But she learned of his nights in the Naring Ata compound, how any Ata sleeping alone rose to visit him in the house with the pot that cooked their beer.

"I thought you were waiting for me," said Ata Four.

"I am," he said.

"I know that you did not wait at all. Not even one night."

"What can I do?" said Jack. "They were all so kind to take me in."

Ata shook her head.

"No one is to blame. I should have warned you."

It was dark and Jack rose to sleep. He took a step toward the compound behind. Ata grabbed his arm.

"You know the rules," she said. "Sleep outside, atop the wagon, underneath it, anywhere but in my compound."

That night, just as Ata fell asleep, Jack crept in to wake her. Ata Five, Kanye, and Willoughby slept silently across the small, dark room.

"What are you doing?" hissed Ata Four. "There are children here."

"Send them to sleep somewhere else," Jack whispered. "Like in No-Man's-Land."

"Never, ever call it that."

Her eyes saw nothing in the dark, but she heard him pulling off his clothes.

"It is you I want," he said. "Believe me, Ata. I mean no harm."

"Put your clothes back on. You are not the man I thought."

"What did you think?"

"Nothing. Everything. I don't know, just go."

At last the shop was ready. The Atas were ready, too, and Armah was ready for Ata Four to pay him back. But still the city did not come. The Atas washed the walls and waxed the floor, again and again. Ata Four stood in the doorway, looking out at Lorole again. Ata Five came through the door with Kanye on her back. He burped into her ear, and she turned her head to lick the milk from his chin. Willoughby toddled behind.

"Those English," said Ata Four. "Where is the town? They raise hopes, then smash them to pieces."

She turned around to face the Atas waxing silently, without looking up.

"I do not smash your hopes for pleasure," she said. "I planned the best I could."

Meanwhile, Alice's turn came to work in the Indian house.

Everyone agreed that she was the loveliest Ata of all, perhaps the most beautiful girl the world had ever seen. Her breasts and hips rose to perfect size and shape, and her face made grown men weep. When she entered the Indian house, she found an Ata bathing the Indian daughters in the sunken tub of white tile. They all looked up at Alice, who unbuttoned her dress and dropped it to the floor. Armah's daughters rose from the tub. Alice stepped in, and the daughters knelt to bathe her. It was the first work they had ever done in their lives.

Each morning, the daughters dressed Alice in silk and jewels, painted her eyes, lips, fingernails, toes, and braided her hair in intricate patterns tight against her head. Each night they took back the silk and jewels. When Ata Four found out about Alice, she marched into the Indian house to drag her out. She found her in the tub, singing in Indian, while the daughters washed her hair with honey and milk. Ata stood at the edge of the tub.

"You are coming with me," said Ata. "This is not the place to find a husband."

Alice closed her eyes as the daughters rinsed her hair. Her skin was very dark, glowing as the milk and honey ran over it. Ata gasped at the beautiful face, turned up, eyes closed, and then Alice rose from the bath. The rest of her was even better. Ata looked away. The Indian daughters dried her with delicate pats of a purple towel, wrapped her in silk, and hung her with jewels.

"Those things do not belong to you," said Ata. "Rich men do not beg at your feet."

Alice moved her eyes, hard and sure, to Ata's own.

"Perhaps someday they will," she said.

Ata saw the knowing smile on Alice's lips, foreign to the Indian daughters themselves. Unlike these daughters Alice knew exactly what she was doing.

"The risk is very great," said Ata.

"I am thinking of copper," said Alice. "Everywhere on me. The color goes well with my skin."

And so Ata Four let Alice stay in the Indian house. She used the last of Armah's loan to send a young Ata to the mission school in the Wall-Maker village. Each afternoon, when the girl came home from school, she tutored Alice in English. The schoolgirl Ata was named Nokana, meaning "Stream." Once she began attending school, everyone called her Gogaisakitso, meaning "Surpassing-Knowledge."

Alice they called "Araba." This was an English name. Missionaries had first used it long ago when they saw the Indians coming and told everyone in South Africa to ignore them, that they fought the true Word with a Word of their own. The missionaries denounced this Word as Arab lies. And so the word for Indian became *Araba.*

Kanye's teeth grew in, with a wide gap in front, just the right size for an Ata nipple. Ata Five carried him on her back around the compound, following their mother. When Willoughby learned to walk, she carried Kanye while Ata Five helped her mother work. Then he learned to walk on his own, and Willoughby went to work. Kanye followed the three of them everywhere, his sister, cousin, and mother.

One morning, as Ata Four rose to wash, she looked out to see a bulldozer far away, and even closer to herself she saw an Englishman with a map. The next day there were more machines, some that Ata could not name, and then even more Englishmen. Then suddenly there were streets, straight and flat, and buildings along the streets.

All at once the best Kalahariland students came back to run the country, and men came from all over the country to build the city. Women came, too, with children. The BaNare among them stopped in to greet the Atas, the only BaNare they knew in Lorole. Ata Four led the arriving women behind the Stardust compound and swept her arm across the empty space between the railway tracks and the rising city.

"Live here," she said. "You can see the advantages of the location."

"Obey your mother," said Ata to the arriving children, pointing out to the city, to the bulldozers, cranes, and nameless masses of moving metal. "Those machines eat children, so stay away."

She led the arriving men to the front of the shop and pointed up to the sign that read STARDUST CAFÉ.

"We open soon," she said. "Beer in bottles is very expensive, so buy one and drink it all night. Men with jobs will be here. Ask them how to find one for yourself."

Ata Four waited for the city to grow large enough to fill the shop every night. More and more men came by, asking when she would open it. And then, at last, she did.

Ata Four kept Kanye in bed all day. When the sun set, she woke him and ordered the younger Atas to bed. She waved a stick in their faces.

"If you come up even to peek," she said, "I will beat you with this stick."

She tossed it onto the woodpile, and the girls ran off to bed.

Ata Four dressed herself and the older Atas in tight blue dresses that left their shoulders and arms exposed. Brass earrings hung from their ears, and on their heads they tied blue scarves with elaborate knots behind. Each Ata took her appointed place, quietly, certain that tonight she would find the perfect man.

The first men came up the steps, in overalls stained with the work of building a city. One of them wore no shoes.

"Ladies!" they cried. "We are here!"

An Ata blocked the door.

"No dirty clothes," she said. "And no bare feet."

The men went away cursing the place. Ata Four came up behind the Ata at the door, who looked to her in worry. Her name was Ipotla, meaning "Lie-Still."

"They will come back," said Ata Four. "With all their friends."

And soon enough they did, and others came behind them. One by one they pushed through the door, each with a hand on the spine of the man before, who stopped still to look up and around as he stepped inside. They stared at the shiny red floor, the neat tables, the shelfless walls, colored lights strung from the ceiling, and Atas everywhere, in sparkling earrings, tight dresses, and bare shoulders.

Men filled the tables, and Atas took orders in English numbers. Other Atas brought out the beer, repeating the order in English. Atas too shy to speak English yet cleared away empty bottles. Ata Four walked from table to table with Kanye at her side. The little boy carried a white cloth. When empty bottles rose from a table, leaving wet circles behind, Kanye stretched his arms to hand the cloth up to his mother. Ata Four wiped the table dry, then handed the cloth back down to her son.

At each table the men pooled their money to buy as many beers as possible, their first in bottles. The price was high but the beer was good, so cold, thin, and gritless against their throats. The place was nice, too, the clean walls, the shiny red floor, and most of all the Atas.

A man stood up, raising his bottle, puffing out his cheeks. "Who am I?" he asked.

Someone else cried, "A Boer!"

Another man rose, raising his bottle, sucking in his cheeks.

Someone else cried, "An English!"

Someone else rose and went out the front door, into the night. He passed Ipotla, descended the steps, and stood against the front wall. Looking in through the lighted window, he opened his trousers.

"No!" cried Ipotla, jumping down to pull him back.

Confused, he fumbled with his trousers, trying to keep the opening pointed away from her.

"Out back," she said, pushing him into the darkness.

He found the metal shed, guarded by another Ata. She opened the door and turned on the light. The glaring bulb and gleaming toilet stung his eyes. He raised his arms against them. When he came out, the Ata looked inside. She grabbed his arm and pointed to brown paper on a shelf.

"You peed all over the seat," she said. "Clean it up."

After he did so, he asked her name.

"Margaret," she said, reaching a hand to touch one earring. "Come back and see me by day."

This is what Ata Four had told them all to say. They said it many times that night. The men watched the bare Ata shoulders, arms, and legs below the knee, the earrings dangling, the lotions smoothing their faces to a dark, shadowy glow. As the Atas leaned close to take orders, to set down or take away bottles, the men smelled something they could not name, sweet, womanly, strange.

Never before had the Atas served beer by night. Never before had they bared their shoulders to men drinking beer or met their gazes so solidly, so daringly, so fearlessly. When a customer touched them, they did not look to the man's friends as the Atas did in Naring. Here in the shop, at night, the Atas looked not to friends but to the man himself. They drilled him with contempt, looking down their noses from far above in a distant, perfect sky.

Kanye, too, helped keep the men calm. When the beer sloshed in their manly heads, when the gleaming Ata shoulders gave them ideas, their roving eyes caught the flash of white, the little boy handing the cloth up to his mother. They looked at the child, each man remembering himself at his own mother's side. Their mouths went dry, and they ordered more beer.

Ata Four watched the boy for signs of weariness. But Kanye had slept all day and loved his mother as no son had ever loved before. He would not let her down. He was tiring fast but stifled every yawn. Ata Four leaned down to whisper into his ear.

"You work so hard," she said. "Mothers dream of sons like you."

When the last man finished his last beer and vanished out the door, Ata Four called all the Atas together and counted them twice. They were all there. She locked the front door, turned out the lights, lifted Kanye into her arms, and led them out the back door. They heard scurrying, giggling in the dark, little girls racing back to bed.

They all went into their houses. Kanye was already asleep. His mother undressed him and wrapped him in blankets, undressed herself and lay down. An Ata came in.

"Please," she whispered to Ata Four. "Just this once. He loves me. Let him stay. He is waiting for me. He is not like other men. He did not try to touch me once. Let me bring him inside. Just for tonight. Please."

There in the dark, sitting up in her blankets, Ata Four scolded the girl severely, meanly, trying her best to smash her hopes at least for tonight, spoiling the feeling inside her Ata chest. The pleading Ata left, confused and sad but ready to sleep.

Another came in. Ata Four berated her, too, and sent her away to sleep. Another came in, and Ata scolded her too. Then another.

At last they all fell asleep, manless, alone, Ata Four last of all. She stared for a long time into the dark, remembering herself at her mother's side when the men came out the gates. She knew she could never send Kanye away to Naring.

She lay in the dark, listening to the soft breath of Kanye fast asleep, wishing this plan to work, that one by one the Lorole Atas would marry. She would bring out more from Naring to replace them, but she could never find them husbands faster than No-Man's-Land produced more Atas. Where would it end, and what of herself? There was always Jack Vanu, devoted and kind, but to him she was just another Ata, one of many to love. She was too busy now to look for a man, with the shop just beginning and the Atas still unmarried.

And the memory of South Africa was still fresh and strong inside her. She sat up in the dark and looked at the shape of her sleeping son. She wondered how it would feel, when Kanye grew older, to look in his face and see in it the Jackal's.

2

LOVERS LEAP

The battle against the hyenas worked both for and against Boko Tladi. On the one hand everyone praised his courage, thanking him for saving the BaNare out in the Kalahari. On the other hand the occasion had called for brutal violence, and Boko had delivered it, coolly, even with glee. All heroes fought the way he had done, aiming at only one foe at a time, ignoring the larger view that would make any other man turn and run. Like all great warriors he was someone both to admire and to fear. One day he almost kills an elder, the next he slays marauding hyenas. Only after his death, when all his deeds were done, could the BaNare give their final judgment of Boko Tladi's life.

As for Jack, the BaNare neither feared nor admired him. The hyena battle quickly won him friends in Naring, but his relations with the Atas lost them just as fast. Whenever a child of unusual size came out of an Ata, the BaNare were sure it was Jack's. They felt sorry for Ata Four, that a man as good as Jack had vowed to wait for her, only to lose himself in a forest of Ata arms. She was working hard to perform the impossible, marrying off Atas, and they thanked her by ruining Jack.

Chief Puo returned from England a hero, sharing with Ata Four and the other Kalahariland chiefs the credit for saving them all from South Africa. Nevertheless, Boko Tladi demanded that Puo repay to Naring the well fees that had paid for the automobile he'd bought for himself and the truck he'd bought for Vincent. Boko complained about Vincent, too, that the miners he wooed with meat and beer were growing wilder and wilder.

But most of all, Boko complained about Vincent's hunting. When game was scarce, Vincent set fire to the brush and came back when the flames had died out. Antelope ran to eat the green shoots of grass that grew up through the fertile ash. Vincent drove his truck among them. They stood very still, stunned by the unknown sound of the motor. He pointed his rifle out the window and shot them.

Hunting with fire was against BaNare law. If trucks had existed in ancient times, hunting from them would certainly have been illegal too. But Vincent's fires never spread very far, and he gave the meat to his many friends, who divided it up among friends of their own, until all Naring had a taste.

Yet Boko's arguing did some good. Puo finally spent some of the Kalahari well fees on pipes to run water throughout Naring. Ko Roodie put the pipes together and hooked up the taps, one for each circle of compounds in the village. Puo personally turned on each tap for the first time, gathering BaNare around him to watch.

"My people," he said, "enjoy this great gift from your chief. When you wash, when you drink, when you boil anything in a pot, lick the thirst from your lips and think of me."

He turned on the tap, and Naring cheered.

After that the BaNare refused even to listen to Boko Tladi's complaints. He just wanted the chiefship for himself. Why else had he attacked the council, shouting out "Twenty-two!" To most BaNare, however, this number did not sound right. They counted again, figuring Boko's place in line to be chief. Some came up with seventeen, others with twenty-six, forty, or eight. While they were at it they counted their own places in line: sixty-one, twelve, two hundred nine, and so on.

These were days when more and more BaNare men left Naring, to herd cattle around the Kalahari wells, to seek work in Lorole, or to sign up for the mines. The Naring plain grew crowded with farms, until there was no land left for married sons to clear new fields. Fathers began to divide existing fields among their sons. Some fields grew so small that sons gave up farming completely. Without fields to plow they needed no wives to tend them. Men took longer and longer to marry, and some never married at all.

And so women, too, began to leave Naring. Some followed their fathers, brothers, or sons to Lorole or the Kalahari wells. Some followed Ata Four and struck out on their own for Lorole. Some married there, but mostly they did not. They had children anyway, in Lorole and the Kalahari, and these children grew up never seeing Naring.

Everything happened so gradually, so quietly and eventlessly. One by one abandoned compounds appeared in Naring. Unattended, they fell apart. Rain wore away the mud walls, roofs collapsed and the poles fell in to point at the ground. Weeds grew up through the floor, and goats wandered in to eat them. Since Ata Four no longer farmed with the Tladis, the Atas stopped attending Maru-a-Kgosi, the harvest dance. Everyone else did too. Even the chief's court met less and less. The famous knife that hung in the tree to announce important meetings grew rusty and silent. The rust blew away in the rain and wind, shrinking the blade to ordinary size.

Naring did notice, but did not know what to make of it, when Chief Puo bought a cattle truck. Again Boko Tladi complained, but no one listened. The truck was enormous, twice the size of the truck that had carried the drilling machine around the Kalahari. The back of the truck was one gigantic cage. Chief Puo drove it himself, grinning and bouncing behind the wheel, from well to well throughout the Kalahari. There he bought BaNare cattle to sell to the Lorole slaughterhouse. He explained the advantages to the owners, how cattle lost weight on the long walk but arrived fat on the back of a truck, how he alone had saved Kalahariland, how he alone was their chief.

Instead of winding along the narrow village paths, Puo drove his cattle truck through the empty compounds, smashing the walls to dust, leaving wide, straight roads. Wagons, cattle, BaNare on foot, and soon more trucks of other

BaNare used these roads as shortcuts through the village. The clearing between the Tladi and Potso compound became a crossroads, until even the mine office bus passed through it to and from Lorole.

Not even the Tladis saw the danger, the changing shape of Naring and its destination. Like everyone else they had cares of their own, children to raise and mouths to feed. The first child of Monosi and Boko married and grandchildren began. Boko mistrusted Puo and Vincent, but not Naring itself. It changed too slowly to see, to comprehend, to stop.

It was the Tladis themselves who first abandoned their fields on the Naring plain, but not because they were too small. With fields so crowded, the BaNare planted the same ones every year, wearing out the soil. The Tladis built a new compound out at Loang, gathered their plentiful cattle into plow teams, and plowed the Kalahari. The crop was very poor, but the fields were so large they yielded enough to feed them.

One day like any other, Monosi went out to their new Kalahari fields to weed a crop of corn. Boko remained at the compound, chopping firewood. As she worked alone at the edge of the field, a man walked out of the brush before her. He was tall, lean, and dressed in rags, the remains of an army uniform. He passed very close, and she saw the scar beneath one eye.

"Timela?" she said.

He turned and saw her.

"Monosi!"

They stood very still, and Monosi let the hoe drop from her hands. She brushed them off and walked to him, extending a hand. He shook it, smiling, warily at first then almost laughing. They sat down on the grass.

"You are well?" she said.

"Yes."

"We have heard no news."

"It travels poorly from well to well," he said. "Only important news reaches them, usually about the Potsos or Tladis."

"So you know what has happened to me all these years."

"Of course. You have four children, one grandchild and another on the way. . . ."

"And how many gray hairs?" she said. "They appeared this very morning, so certainly you cannot know that."

"Not as many as me," said Timela.

He raised his hands to touch the sides of his head. His face was thin and deeply lined. Gray flecked his hair.

"All right," she said. "Now what about you. Children?"

"Three daughters."

"And how is your wife?"

Timela turned his face away.

"She is gone," he said. "To Lorole, with another man."

Monosi raised a hand to touch him, but brought it back to her lap.

"I am so sorry," she said.

"She left me the children," he said, his head still turned and his voice hard. "I thank her at least for that."

Monosi saw him now as on that first day they spoke over the wall of the Potso compound. He leaned against it, facing away from her, across the clearing to Boko Tladi reclaiming his place in Naring, where rich and poor changed places overnight.

"How are your cattle?" Monosi asked.

"Dead."

He turned to face her now, his gaze steady again.

"Do not worry about me," he said. "I am on my way to Naring to find someone else to give me cattle to herd. My luck will change."

"Boko will happily give you some."

She saw him stiffen, then smile.

"No, thank you," he said.

They sat for a while in silence, on the coarse Kalahari grass, in the shade of towering clouds. Timela ran his hands through the sand between the grass.

"You are still beautiful," he said at last.

The memory returned to her now with force, watching Boko come back each morning from No-Man's-Land, from the arms of another. She had never resented it as much as she did now, with a wounded stray before her, his heart open and waiting.

The bushes rustled. They both looked up, searching the brush for movement. Monosi saw and pointed. Timela followed her hand to a tiny antelope nibbling at leaves.

"There," she whispered. "I have seen it before. Every day it comes a little closer. If we catch it, the children can raise it at the end of a rope."

Timela slipped off his shoes, standing up.

"I am hungry," he whispered.

Monosi rose, too, holding out her hands.

"It will fall into these," she said, "and live."

Timela held up his own hands.

"It will fall into these," he said, "and die."

Back at their new compound Boko finished chopping wood, picked up a hoe, and set out to help Monosi weed. When he reached the end of the last field, he saw Monosi and Timela run into the brush.

Boko stopped, swallowing hard. Blood rushed to his face. He dropped the hoe and moved through the brush, crouching, quietly, circling around to follow them.

The antelope skipped along between tufts of grass, over branches, and stopped again to nibble. Timela and Monosi crept through the brush. As they came close they lay flat on the ground, crawling now and close together. Their legs touched, and then their arms. The antelope looked up and they froze, still beside each other on the sand. They looked into each other's eyes.

Boko came up behind and saw them lying together.

They all leapt at once. Timela and Monosi leapt for the antelope. Boko leapt for Timela. The antelope leapt away.

3

THE BATTLE OF THE BOTTLES

Naring behind
Lorole ahead
Last night a cold and empty bed
Lonely visions, safe, instead
Of babies on the way
Queen of the bottle
Queen of the pan
She has him eating out of her hand
The one and only perfect man
To marry me today. . . .

This is the song the Atas sang as they worked by day in the Stardust compound. Men did come to visit, and at sundown Ata Four chased them away. The tables were filled every night, she began to repay Armah and even send money back to her mother, but still no man offered marriage.

As in their Naring compound, no wall divided the Atas from the rest of the world. But every day new houses pressed closer, of mud, brick, tin, and straw, a village that everyone called Stardust, after the shop. The name appeared on no map of Lorole, but everyone knew it, except for the excellent Kalahariland students who came back from England in suits to run the country. They moved into the biggest houses in town, on curved, shady streets leading off from sunny straight ones. Some of the English from Taung moved up to Lorole to work as advisers in the new offices. Young Englishmen came from England too.

Kanye, Ata Five, and Willoughby saw that all the compounds except their own had walls, so they decided to build a wall too. They used the empty bottles around the compound. The Taung Brewery paid less for empty bottles than it cost to ship them back, so they collected in piles higher than Kanye's head.

The other Atas noticed the wall and joined in the work. They mixed cement to hold the bottles together. In one row the necks pointed out, in the next they pointed in, with a dab of cement between. The wall rose, sparkling in the sunlight. After walling in the compound, as high as they could reach, the Atas built interior walls, dividing the shop from the houses, then the houses from each other. Last of all they knocked down the old houses and built up new ones of bottles. Kanye, Ata Five, and Willoughby always laid the bottom rows. When the Atas woke at earliest light, they sighed at the streaks of dawn through the brown glass. They liked moonlight through the bottles, too, and the sound of wind passing over the open necks.

As Lorole reached full height, roofs appeared and shops and offices opened. Ata Four sent some of the older girls to apply for jobs in the city. They were clean, neat, and answered to English commands. Ata by Ata they won the jobs. Ata Four worried about letting them out of her sight, for babies happened by day as well as by night, so she started making surprise visits around the city. In this way she came to know all the offices and shops. When a new job appeared, Ata Four was there to offer an Ata to fill it.

It all turned out so well, except that the Atas remained unmarried. Men wanted to know exactly what they were getting, first, and Ata Four refused to let them stay the night. Lorole was such a new place, so unsettled, that men were wary of settling down too fast.

Each morning as the Atas washed, Ata Four looked out at Lorole growing. Each day she noticed something new, another roof completed, Stardust village reaching the railway tracks, the bulldozers working their way across the city. One morning she woke from dreaming of that day in Taung when the bulldozers had come. She heard crashing, breaking glass,

and a roaring engine. When she heard the Atas cry out, she knew it was more than a dream.

They all rushed out, pulling on dresses, and ran to the front of the compound. Ata Four ran with her eyes closed, seeing before them the sixty dead and two hundred wounded sprawled on the Sharpetown street. When she opened them, she saw a gaping hole in the wall of bottles and a bulldozer in the hole. The blade swung again, glass flew. The Atas shouted and pulled the driver off the machine. The engine died as people ran up from Stardust village.

"They told me no one was home!" the driver explained. "They told me everyone knew."

"Knew what?" demanded Ata Four.

"The road!" said the driver. "Right through here, across the tracks, all the way to Naring. Very wide and black with three white stripes."

The crowd cried out in anger. They turned to run back to their homes, to pull their belongings to safety.

"Wait!" said Ata Four. "Look around!"

Everyone stopped and looked around.

"Do you see police with guns?" she said. "We do not live in South Africa. Our homes are safe. Someone made a mistake and we will make them fix it. The village is safe."

Ata turned to the driver.

"Tell your boss," she said, "whoever he is, he has lost a machine. I found it in my compound. If he wants it back, let him come for it himself."

The driver ran off, fleeing the jeering crowd, as the Atas swept up the broken glass. A man came forward to drive the bulldozer a little bit forward, just inside the wall. The Atas repaired the wall behind. Ata Five, Kanye, and Willoughby laid the bottom row.

The police arrived in six black cars, driving slowly through the silent crowd. They came out of the cars with gold braid looped over their shoulders and pistols at their hips. Last to come out was a young man in a gray suit, a white shirt, red tie, thin black socks, and a black belt. There were gold

squares at the end of his sleeves, a gold bar across his tie, a gold buckle on the belt, and a gold watch around one wrist.

The crowd stared, and Ata Four wondered if his teeth were gold, too, like Ko Roodie's. He smiled at the crowd. No gold. The crowd fell back, leaving Ata Four alone against the patched wall.

"I am Archie Sedile," he said, approaching, "Deputy Minister of Works. Where is it?"

"I am Ata Roodie," said Ata, "owner of this shop. Where is what?"

Archie looked up and down the unbroken wall of bottles. Then he looked down on the ground and saw not a sliver of glass. Then he looked out at the crowd. So many bottles, such a big crowd. This was a popular place.

"Inside?" he said to Ata.

She led him inside. The police moved to follow, but Archie waved them back. He stepped through the narrow gate, saw the bulldozer on the other side, then measured the gate with his arms. Shaking his head, he followed Ata into the café. She sat him down at a table.

"How was England?" she said.

"Cold."

"Beer or tea?"

"Beer," said Archie Sedile.

Ata went out the back door. She was gone a long time. Archie folded his hands on the table and looked around. He had never heard of this place, but perhaps he should have been more careful before ordering it torn down. Ata came back, sat down across from Archie, and folded her hands on the table too.

"One of the girls will bring you beer," she said. "Now tell me why you are tearing down our homes."

"We have the money to build a road," said Archie. "Everyone wants it. And once I have approved it, how would it look if I backed down now?"

Ata watched his face, calm but intent, smiling but somehow fierce. She did not want to beg, to threaten or plead.

This was not the kind of man who came to drink at the Atas', either in Lorole or Naring, and she could not be sure how to fight him.

"I know all about these things," she said. "You will smash the village and then run out of money for the road. Then there will be nothing. At least now there is a village."

"This is not a village," said Archie. "It is a hopeless mess of worthless shacks that break the law. A city must have city houses. When it rains, these shacks will fall down and kill someone. What are they made of? Mud. Concrete blocks stacked without mortar. Flattened cans. Sticks and grass."

"And bottles," said Ata.

"Your houses are bottles too?" said Archie.

He was impressed, and paused to think again.

"And they do not fall down when it rains," said Ata. "The sound of the rain is very nice against the glass."

"Maybe I can find some money," he said, "to resettle you people somewhere else. Not everyone, of course. That would be too expensive. We can start with you. How much do you think you need?"

"What did they teach you in England?" said Ata. "Where do you think you are? People leave their villages, they come here, and when they are ready to buy a suit like yours, they move to a house in the city. I am happy to take your money. You can leave it right here on the table. But we all are staying right where we are."

Archie reached a hand to adjust his tie. Ata's eye moved from gold to gold around his body. He seemed not at all worried, and Ata tried to appear the same.

"Did you see those police outside?" he said. "Did you see their guns? I am sorry no one warned you. We will give you time to move."

Ata leaned toward him, spreading her hands on the table, squinting into his face, making her move.

"You should be ashamed of yourself," she said. "I am talking politely and now you threaten me with policemen and guns. You do not seem to understand. While you were learning nothing in England, I was in Sharpetown running from bullets. They buried a village and sixty people with it. And now you want to bury this one. Go right ahead. But I swear to you now, Deputy Minister of Works, you will have to bury me with it."

Archie saw the tips of Ata's fingers on the table. Two were smooth and printless, from the pass she had burned in Sharpetown.

"You are the cook," he said. "The cook who saved Kalahariland."

"I am the cook," said Ata. "And you know who saved Kalahariland. Those sixty dead. They could not save Taung village. Who will save this one, Archie Sedile?"

He nodded slowly, thinking quickly, setting up a plan in his head. Ata sat back, folding her arms across her chest, glaring, angry now, no longer worried but ready to fight him however she could.

Then suddenly Archie heard singing, sweet and strange, lovely and high. He looked to the back door. Through it came more beauty than Archie had ever seen in any one place, enough to stop hearts, to stop his gold watch. She carried a tray but Archie did not see it. She set it down before him and opened a bottle that Archie did not see. She poured beer into a tall, thin glass. Archie did not even know it was there.

He did see, he did know, the flowing cotton parting to show the dark, fragrant skin, now visible, now gone, as Araba glided to him. Her head was bare, showing the tight braids against her head with copper beads woven in. There were copper bracelets along each arm, copper rings on every finger and toe, copper bands around her ankles and close around her neck. Her nose was softly flared and pierced with a copper disc. The copper was perfect, just the right color for her deep black skin.

Archie looked down at his watch, then held it up to his ear. He lowered his hands and folded them on the table again. Araba spoke in English, pouring his beer.

"You people wear rings when you marry," she said. "Unfold your hands."

Archie spread his fingers flat on the table. There was no gold.

Ata Four rose and left them. This was the chance Araba had trained for, a risk she had worked very hard to take. And now they were all in her hands, she bore upon her magnificent shoulders the fate of Stardust village.

Archie moved very fast. First, he publicly denounced his boss, the Minister of Works, for insisting all houses be built in certain ways that no one could ever afford. After that, Archie married Araba, publicly. She wore copper, he wore gold. Next, in public, Archie accused the Minister of Works of sending a wedding present in the form of bulldozers to tear down the popular shop owned by the family of Archie's wife. This crime was clearly an underhanded, cowardly attack on a popular political rival, Archie. The shop had been founded by the cook who had saved Kalahariland.

All Lorole, and then all Kalahariland, heard the news. The Minister of Works was an enemy of the poor, a vicious, dirty fighter, and a traitor to his country. He resigned in disgrace.

The road to Naring took a different route, crossing the tracks without knocking anything down. Just on the other side, the money ran out.

Stardust village survived. After the wedding other men began marrying Atas. Archie Sedile became Minister of Works.

4

WILLOUGHBY TWO

After the tenth wedding feast at Stardust Café many BaNare thought that the story of Ata Four was over. There were always more Atas waiting in Naring, but not even she could change that. Her plan had worked. She was successful, famous, and the Atas no longer faced husbandless lives.

Other BaNare were not so sure. Ata Four herself remained manless. They suggested that the Jackal invaded her thoughts, that she saw him every day in the face of her son, that she loved him still and always would. Or perhaps she was simply too busy to find a man of her own. There was always Jack, who learned to drive Armah's truck and used it to speed more Atas to Lorole to replace the married. But Ata Four still refused to let him sleep in the compound, let alone in her arms.

A few BaNare guessed the truth, that her calculation in winning husbands for the other Atas spoiled her sense of romance. As she stood at the door of her shop, watching the Atas serving men, she did her best to pair them, to judge the men and their intentions, and during the day she counseled each girl to judge them for herself. No man touched her heart, and perhaps no man ever could again. If she were to meet the Jackal now for the first time, she would laugh in his face and keep him far away from her girls. But he had slipped inside her when she was young and just like them.

And so her son Kanye became for Ata Four the man who stayed. Neither she nor any other Ata ever mentioned again her vow to send him to Naring to learn from Jack and Boko Tladi how to be a man. He grew up working beside her, with Ata Five and Willoughby never far away. Ata Four sent him to school with the youngest Lorole Atas, and Kanye played with the girls. They loved to kiss him and touch the gap in his teeth. At first the boys tried to beat him up, but the girls ganged together and chased them off.

In their Lorole compound the Atas told stories of Naring. Lorole itself, so new and unsettled, offered stories only of strangers, while all the Atas had been born in Naring, except for Kanye himself. Even after they married and came to Stardust to bear their children, the Atas spoke of Naring as home. Jack sometimes drove them back for visits, and Naring Atas visited Stardust, but Kanye stayed close by his mother, who never left Lorole. She dared not leave her Atas so long. By morning the place would be crawling with men.

And also to Ata Four, despite her success in Lorole, Naring remained the place she belonged but did not, where she came from but never returned. She had made something of herself, but not in Naring where it counted. Sometimes a goat wandered through the gate in the bottle wall, of the same size and shape, coloring and eyes, as the goat Monosi had helped her milk in exchange for the secret that won the life of Boko Tladi.

To Kanye Naring was a daily dream, a place of the past where tales had no time, everyone knew everything about everyone else, where no one was ever a stranger for long. He loved the story of Mojamaje, Eater of Rocks, his famous cloak, Vlei's enormous knife, and Roodie's chest. He pictured the knife hanging from the council tree in the clearing between the Tladi and Potso compounds, a gleaming sword the BaNare sounded whenever danger appeared. To him the BaNare were more numerous Atas, living and working as one, and Naring was one big Stardust compound, teeming and familiar.

From the endless stories Kanye came to know Naring better than the Atas who once had lived there. He knew the locations of compounds, the families inside, and the loves and hates inside them. But it was an old Naring, an impossible place untouched by time or Chief Puo's cattle truck knocking down compound walls. And this Naring became his child-hood home, the place to which he would one day return. He missed the BaNare, and imagined they missed him.

In truth, of course, no one missed the Stardust Atas except for the Naring Atas themselves, who anyway saw each other often. And then there was Monosi. She remembered her parting words to Ata Four, that despite how all the BaNare laughed she loved her as her daughter. She knew that Ata Four might never come back, but she asked her at least to remember her.

So now Monosi waited for Ata Four to return to Naring. She was not surprised that Ata did not. They passed on greet-ings and sometimes gifts, and it would have been easy enough for Monosi to ride with Jack to Lorole, but Ata never asked her to come. When Ata was ready, she would return to face the Naring she left behind.

Those early days, when Ata Four was a little girl, when Timela first appeared, came back to Monosi time and again, especially after he and Boko had come to blows. For months and months BaNare stopped her to ask for further details on the event, precisely how she had happened to be in the bushes with Timela tugging at her clothes, the exact color and age of the antelope, which of her suitors won the fight.

"I won," Monosi always replied. "I knocked their empty heads together."

The truth was not very far from that, for Timela and Boko had fought like demons until she threw herself among their moving fists. They stopped for fear of hurting her. As she shouted explanations at Boko, Timela backed away into the brush, with bruises and a laugh rising on his face. And then, once again, he was gone.

Monosi and Boko could only tell the truth about Boko's bloody face. The story made its rounds, yet another chapter in Boko Tladi's reckless, violent life. That night Monosi sat up in bed and spoke her thoughts in the dark.

"If only it were true," she said. "I want a past to match your own, at least that much, a former love. You know of

South Africa, of Egypt, of the Kalahari, of another woman. What do I know? Only you."

Boko lay motionless beside her. Monosi ran her hands along her bare breasts. They were still high and firm, not at all those of a grandmother.

"And someday you will be chief," she said. "When your hair turns white like mine."

"Naring thinks I am hopelessly wild. And your hair is not white."

"Some of them are."

"How many?" he said.

"Enough."

Boko sat up beside her.

"Timela should have stayed on the train. I never should have taken him back to Naring. He fought me as if we were at war."

"You are lucky I stopped him," said Monosi.

"Stopped him?" said Boko. "You stopped me. His very last breath was between his teeth the moment you pulled me away."

Monosi lay back on the bed and turned toward him.

"How does it feel," she said, "to fight over a woman?"

Boko lay back, too, embracing her.

"To tell you the truth," he said, "and for this you will never forgive me, it feels like nothing else on earth."

Timela made his way back to Naring, where another BaNare loaned him cattle for herding; then he vanished again into the Kalahari. Over the years news came back to Naring that his herd refused to grow, he borrowed more, and his daughters grew up lovely, sweet, and devoted to their father. He loved them fiercely, his only possession, and let no boy come near them. But no BaNare believed for a moment the story was over between Timela and Boko Tladi. They had come to blows. Someday they would come to more.

By this time the pastures around the Kalahari wells were crowded with cattle. As fewer and fewer BaNare plowed the Naring plain, as more retreated to graze their cattle around the wells, more and more they bought their food from the Indian shops in Naring. It happened so slowly that no one noticed, until Vincent Potso had an idea.

He still wore his miner's overalls, his orange helmet, and still had never worked in the mines. Waiting for his father to die, to become the chief in his place, was hard and monotonous work. Every time Chief Puo sneezed, Vincent's hopes soared to the sky, only to crash to earth when Puo wiped his nose dry. Vincent hunted, drank, and who knows what else with miners back in Naring between contracts, but nothing could hold back impatience and boredom from closing in around him. This was the tunnel, dark and cramped, that Vincent Potso mined.

So when Vincent decided to do something worthwhile, all Naring took notice. He hired a drilling machine to drill him a well in the deepest Kalahari, and he bought a tractor to plow the land around it. Even with poor rains everyone agreed that the tractor could plow so many fields that Vincent might make a profit after all. As the son of the chief he did not want to clear the land himself, so he made an offer to all the BaNare. Whoever cleared the land around his new well would own half the fields. Vincent's tractor would plow them all.

Once again Boko Tladi complained, about where Vincent had found the money to pay for both a well and a tractor. Once again no one listened. In any event, who on earth would even dream of accepting Vincent's offer? Who could ever be desperate enough to trust him?

The answer came as a rumor, unchallenged by any contrary tale: Timela. It was his last chance to make something of himself before his daughters were old enough to marry. He wanted them to marry well, and for that they needed a father of means. He and his daughters climbed onto the wagon behind Vincent's tractor, and Vincent drove them out to the Kalahari.

Through the years the Atas had followed Timela's story, especially Ata Four. He, too, was less than a full BaNare, and

Ata Four remembered his shadow if not his face, there beside Boko Tladi the night they came out the mine office gate. While she had departed Naring, Timela continued his fight to join the BaNare. Kanye followed the story, too, but it puzzled him, for it fit not at all the Naring he knew and loved. So he explained it as an unfinished tale that would someday come to a fitting end.

When Kanye turned sixteen, old enough to go to the mines, Ata Five fell in love with an Englishman. He worked in Archie's office, and came to the shop at night to practice speaking BaNare and drink with the other men. At first Ata Four refused to let him near her daughter, but gradually she relented. It was true, she admitted, he did not seem at all like Scott, but then at first neither had Scott himself.

Willoughby, Ata Four's sister, married an Indian, the cousin of two fat, rich brothers who courted and finally won the hands of Armah's daughters, who in no time at all were as fat as their husbands. Willoughby's husband was handsome and slim. Their first child came out a rich, pale brown, a girl, and everyone called her Willoughby Two.

Willoughby came back to the Stardust compound to bear the child. She strolled around with her daughter in her arms, stopping Atas in the middle of their work to show off her beautiful infant. The Atas opened their dresses and pressed the child to their breasts. She passed him to Kanye, who held the girl clumsily in his arms. He was almost a man now, and he looked intently at the infant, imagining one of his own. This was a new thought, and he looked up at the Atas around him.

"What will mine look like?" he said.

The Atas fell silent, staring, Ata Four among them. She looked at her son, a boy who had never spent a night away from her, suddenly becoming a man. The Atas were never tall, but his shoulders had formed into muscle, his face was no longer round and smooth, and the baby looked very small and out of place in his arms. She took the child into her own.

"Is there something you want to tell me?" she said. "Some girl with my grandchild warm in her belly?"

The Atas moved closer around him. Kanye looked from face to face, shaking his head.

"There are some men you can trust," he said.

"Name one," said Ata Four.

Kanye ran through a long list in his head, everyone he knew in Lorole and all the BaNare stories. His father, Scott, Jack, Chief Puo, even Boko Tladi, all failed the test. At last he came to the end of the list.

"Kanye Roodie," he said.

The Atas swung their eyes to his mother.

"That remains to be seen," she said.

From that day on, the Ata women watched Kanye more carefully, until something else distracted them. The event came at the end of Willoughby's month in Stardust compound, the night before her return to her husband's house in the city. At the time the event took them all by surprise, but in truth they should have foreseen it. Perhaps they forgot they were Atas and what that meant to men.

It was late afternoon and the shop was empty except for Ata Four, counting coins in the front room. Ata Five, Kanye, and Jack were counting bottles in the back. Ata Four looked up to see an Englishman come through the door. He was not very tall, with creased olive skin, thick gray hair, and round eyeglasses that Ata Four long ago had polished every morning.

She stared at him from behind the counter, coins in both hands, as Scott sat down at a table.

"Is it you?" he said in rusty BaNare. "Ata? Do you remember me?"

She dropped the coins and came around the counter. The memory invaded her, the smell of the wax on the wooden floors and the high, soft English bed where the Jackal changed her life. She sat down at the table and looked at him. They folded their hands and did not smile.

"Willoughby," she said, half to herself, and for the first

time in long, long years she did not mean her younger sister.
"We have missed you," she said, louder this time. "How is
England?"

Scott kept his eyes fixed to her own. She saw in them no
hint of remorse or regret.

"We live in Taung," he said. "And that is fine. We like it
very much."

"How is Madame? Please greet her for me and tell her I
miss her truly."

"She is very well, and I will do it."

"She has friends?" said Ata.

"Many."

"Children?"

"No," said Scott.

And now his eyes moved, down to his hands on the table,
on the very spot where Araba had seen that Archie Sedile
wore no wedding ring. Ata's life here in Lorole was already
long and full, but now she felt herself back in Naring, bringing to Scott warm water for washing, porridge, tea, and his
shirt.

"You remember how to speak BaNare," she said.

"A little. Can you still speak English?"

"Yes," said Ata, switching from BaNare. "We can do that
if you want."

"Please," said Scott, switching too.

They watched each other across the table, unsmiling, remembering.

"Why do you live in South Africa?" said Ata. "I was there
in Taung, soon after you left Naring. I saw them shoot those
people. Why do you live in a place like that?"

Scott shrugged and leaned back in the chair.

"I spent too much time in Kalahariland. There was no job
for me back in England."

"So live here," said Ata. "You can work in Lorole. My
own daughter knows an Englishman who works—"

"We like South Africa," said Scott. "We are both very
happy there."

Ata unfolded her hands and spread them flat on the table.
"You like it?" she said.

"That's right."

"So why are you here?"

"Business," said Scott.

"No, why are you here in my shop?"

"I heard about it in town. I thought it might be you."

"It is," said Ata.

Now she drummed her fingers on the table, debating
whether to tell him. He did not deserve it, but her sister
Willoughby did. At last she decided that every child should
meet her father, if only once.

"Are you going out to visit Naring?" she said.

"I don't have time."

"Do you know you left something behind?"

"Many things," he said. "I remember those years as good
ones, in spite of what you might think."

"This thing you left behind," she said. "It was very important."

Scott leaned back in his chair, folding his arms across his
chest.

"What was it?"

"A child," said Ata.

She watched him take the news without blinking or skipping a breath. But he took his time to speak again.

"Oh?" he said.

"And lucky for you she is here right now. With a child of
her own. I am very close to letting you see her."

Scott waited, his hands still folded, meeting her gaze without flinching.

"Well?" he said at last.

"All right," said Ata, rising. "For her, not for you."

She led him through the back room, past Ata Five, Kanye,
and Jack counting bottles.

"This is Willoughby's father," said Ata Four. "Lucky for
her she looks nothing like him."

She led Scott outside, into the compound behind. The sun

was down but the sky was still blue. An Ata threw wood onto the cookfire. Willoughby sat before it holding Willoughby Two, and looked up at the man approaching.

"This is your father," said Ata Four.

Scott sat down beside his daughter. Willoughby smiled, greeted him in BaNare, and pushed the infant into his arms. Atas came to gather around. They looked into Scott's face, then into Willoughby's, shaking their heads, unable to see the resemblance except for the color of her skin.

"When you did what you did," Willoughby said to her father, "I was not yet there. If you did not do it, I would not be here."

No-Man's-Land rushed back at him, Atas all around, the cookfire flaming, night falling, his wife waiting up at the English house, barren and alone. He looked at his daughter, an Ata, a woman, strange and alive, and then he looked at the child. In the fading light her skin looked very pale, much lighter than her mother's, almost as light as his own.

He stood up with the baby in his arms.

"May I hold her for a while?" he said.

"Of course," said Willoughby.

The Atas watched him stroll around the compound, holding the baby close to his face, whispering into her ear. Ata Five, Kanye, and Jack joined Ata Four and Willoughby around the fire, discussing with low voices this turn of events and those of long ago. Scott and the child moved in and out of the gathering shadows between the bottle houses, the past reappearing and vanishing in the night. And then it was time to open the shop. Ata Four rose and looked around for Scott.

He was gone.

"The child!" she cried. "He took the child!"

5

A KIND OF MAN

Late that night, after the Atas had run through Lorole in search of the stolen baby, spreading the news and their own panic and sorrow, after they had come back empty-handed and cried themselves dry, after Ata Four had cursed Scott and her own careless eye until she was hungry, exhausted, and hoarse, after Willoughby had scraped her fingernails across her cheeks, drawing blood and bits of flesh and the Atas had tied her arms against her sides with torn and twisted sheets—Kanye lay awake. He stared out from his bed in his small bottle house at the moonlight silent through it, and felt himself a man.

It was just like in the tales of Naring, a crisis appearing just as someone came of age to face it. He was old enough to go to the mines, to plow, to herd cattle, or even marry. In his head the alarm sounded, the famous knife ringing, drawing all Naring to the council tree. To keep to the stories he should go there and ring it, announce his attentions to the BaNare, to give them hope through the long months of his quest. He would go to South Africa, as all men did and his mother, and there he would find the child and bring her home.

Kanye stood up and pressed his cheek against the cool glass of the wall of bottles. The thought of South Africa excited him, as he knew it once had excited Mojamaje, Eater of Rocks, the first BaNare to go there. It was he who had come back with the famous knife. Perhaps Kanye should take it with him. That was how stories went, one tale becoming another, on and on without end.

He went outside, into the empty compound, silent except

for Willoughby's weeping. He unlocked the shop and turned on the light. Here he had spent his childhood, and now it was over. He took out pencil and paper and wrote a message to Naring:

DO NOT WORRY FOR ME
I, Kanye Roodie, am going this night to South Africa. You will hear all about it and know why I went. Right now I can say no more. The rest I will have to do. Goodbye. I love you all.

He rolled up the paper and slipped it into an empty bottle. No BaNare had ever done exactly this, but that was part of the challenge, to take new steps in an ancient direction. He turned out the light, locked the shop and went out the front gate of the compound. From far away he heard Jack breathing, asleep in the back of the truck. Kanye quietly climbed on back, felt among Jack's clothes, and pulled out the keys.

He was old enough to drive, old enough to make his way alone to Naring in the dark, along a route he had never traveled except in stories, countless times. He started the truck, looking behind in the mirror. Jack stirred not at all. Kanye drove away to Naring.

The plain was dark but Kanye filled it with fields, cattle, women sowing, swinging their arms as if shooing crows. The mine bus careened along it, with Boko Tladi and Timela Timela alone inside and unaware of the lives awaiting them, intertwining, a world away in Naring. Armah drove past and picked up his mother, she pushed the pot with her name on the bottom between her legs and breathed in the Indian smell, smoky, sweet, and new. And there came Mojamaje, Eater of Rocks, leaving Naring with the cloak on his shoulders that soon he would trade for the knife.

Kanye moved among them, cutting his way through the darkened road with his memory and the lights of the truck. At last the Naring ridge loomed up, and the road swung into the canyon through it. On the other side Kanye caught his first glimpse of Naring, invisible in the dark, but he saw it clearly, the compounds packed tight and the winding paths among them. He knew his way up to the clearing between the Tladi and Potso compounds, the site of great BaNare events, the heart of Naring.

The paths were much wider than he had expected. They cut at unfamiliar angles, and sometimes the headlights caught empty compounds with walls and roofs collapsed. He lost his way. Around and around he drove, searching each tree he passed for the knife hanging. At last he found Chief Puo's cattle truck parked outside a compound gate, and beside it the council tree.

For the first time Kanye suspected that not all the stories were true. He pointed the headlights straight at the tree, but no sword gleamed in their glare. He got out and looked closely. Instead of a solid weapon with history behind it, protection from peril and ominous fate, Kanye saw a rusty scrap of iron, no larger than his hand, hanging from a leather cord.

As he took down the knife and hung the bottle in its place, Kanye tried to think. His disappointment gave way to wonder and even to worry. Perhaps Naring had changed. He held the knife in his palm, scraping off rust with his fingers.

Driving back to Lorole, Kanye felt tired and cold. He would make it back to Lorole just in time for the train at dawn. He would sign onto the mines then and there, and get off the train in Taung, like his father and mother before him. As Naring retreated behind him, the shock of it softened and mixed with the rest of his knowledge. Of course Naring had changed. Old compounds crumble and new ones rise. Iron rusts. The BaNare had changed not at all, only their village.

Lorole reappeared, and then Stardust Café. Kanye pulled up and turned off the engine. Jack slept soundly, and Kanye returned the keys to him. Then he jumped down and hurried away, into the towering night.

He should have known it would not be so simple. He was young and still had much to learn. When he returned from South Africa he would go to Naring and see it by day, to walk its paths and see for himself. He had stayed away too long, all his life. But at least Naring was there, with BaNare in it and past intact. No one could change the past.

He turned around to look back at the compound, visible now beneath the graying sky. The Atas would be rising to wash, among them his mother. This would be his very first morning away from her, and after that his first day, and then his first night. It had to happen sometime. This was something men did—they left their mothers. He was a man now, with work to do, and after all he would soon be back. She would think at first he was gone forever, as all mothers do, but Kanye knew better. There in the dawn, on his way to the station, he vowed to himself he would never become that kind of man, the kind the Atas knew well, the worst, the kind that never came back.

6

WHERE CHILDREN SLEEP

"Why?" the Jackal said to his son. "Why on earth did she leave?"

Kanye sat very still at the table, facing his father, with a plate of food beneath his nose. He was hungry and tired from the journey, but he kept his eyes on the Jackal.

"She must have been lonely for home," said Kanye.

"Home?" The Jackal laughed. "You call that place home? You see Taung, the factories, this house, how could she give it all up?"

Kanye had easily found his father at the Taung brewery, and in the Jackal's Sharpetown house he found another woman. Her name was Marea. She cooked their supper, which now grew cold on the table between them.

"She was a very good cook," the Jackal continued. "Does she still make those English pies with meat inside?"

"She taught my sister to make them instead."

The Jackal raised his plate before him, then dropped it on the table. It hit with a smack, but the heap of food barely quivered.

"No one here knows how to cook," he said. "She poisoned one Boer, but I have been poisoned many times. Every time the factory promotes me I move up a Sharpetown row. I find a new woman to move in with me, hoping she can cook. Maybe next time, eh, Marea?"

Kanye saw Marea at the stove, stiff and intently stirring. The Jackal laughed again. He was still handsome, with a creaseless face and grayless hair. Kanye looked away.

"You are a lucky boy," said his father. "The rule of the house is no children allowed. Marea here has two somewhere but they never sleep under this roof and never will. For you perhaps I will make an exception. How many years of school do you have to go?"

"One," said Kanye, idly picking up his spoon.

The Jackal smiled, baring his teeth.

"Perfect. One year of eating money, and after that you bring it in. It will take you no time at all to pay me back."

"All right," said Kanye, twisting the spoon into the solid mass on his plate.

"I will get you a school pass. But beware. There are children your age who love to complain. They make noise and shake their fists. What do they know? Sixty loudmouths died on the very first day that Sharpetown existed. I arrived in this place with less than nothing, a miner's pass, expired. I did what I had to do. When I finally got something your mother stole it all. Now I am doing better than ever. Along the way I learned two secrets, the secrets of South Africa. And lucky for you I will tell you now."

The Jackal held up one finger.

"First," he said, "work hard."

He held up another finger.

"Second, keep your mouth shut."

Kanye saw Marea glance hopefully at him, at his spoon in the lump of food. There was nothing to do but take a bite.

"Thank you for the information," he said, struggling to swallow.

"Good boy," said the Jackal, leaning back in his chair, smiling at his son.

He never once asked Kanye why he had left Kalahariland for South Africa, and Kanye never told him. To the Jackal it was a natural thing, like fleeing a fire. Kanye signed up for school, and so would have the weekends free to search in Taung for Scott and Willoughby Two.

Sharpetown was nothing at all like his mother's story, empty and dead like a graveyard. Over the years it had filled to overflowing, children sleeping twelve to a room, police sweeping row by row to arrest the passless, all South Africa crushed together, squeezed and squeezed until only this Sharpetown life remained. It was the wild, senseless place of Mojamaje's lifetime, nightly fights with knives and sticks, breathless beauties arm in arm, igniting the deepest desires of men.

Wildest of all were the Imitation Zulu. They came down the street in gangs, waving their clubs at schoolchildren, growling and cursing in broken Zulu:

"Beware!"

"We will eat you!"

"The Zulu are coming to eat you!"

These were the barracksmen, who lived in the long blocks on the last Sharpetown row. The BaNare knew the Imitation Zulu from the mines, especially Boko Tladi, for the very miner who had tried to kill him but had ended up instead with Boko's pick in his chest had been an Imitation. The Sharpetown barracks were just like those in the mines, except that right across a narrow street slept numberless women and children. That made it so much worse.

Very few of them were actually Zulu. Long ago, when Zulu armies roamed the earth, men surviving a Zulu attack banded together to form regiments of their own. These Imitation Zulu chanted Zulu songs, carried Zulu spears under their arms, and marched in Zulu formation, the horns of an ox encircling its prey. It was kill or be killed, and they turned out worse than the Zulu. Instead of fighting other armies, they descended on innocent villages, thus creating more of themselves. The Zulu army traveled alone, without women or children, so the Imitations did the same. It was very much like the barracks. In Sharpetown they carried clubs instead of spears as they drilled in formation up and down the barracks yard. They shaved their heads and filed their teeth to points.

Kanye ran with the other children when the Imitation Zulu appeared. They turned into the school, atop a rise in the Sharpetown land, long concrete blocks with concrete verandahs, seventy students to a room and not a single desk. Children sat on the floor and fell asleep from hunger. Older boys fought with knives behind the buildings, drawing crowds and blood.

On the first day, when the teacher called the roll, he heard his own name and then twelve later, "Claire Vlei." He turned around to see who answered. Schoolgirls wore blue jumpers over white blouses, except for Claire, who had no blouse to wear. Her jumper was tattered and years too small, revealing her thighs and shoulders and much of her breasts and back. When the class was over, Kanye came up to her in the schoolyard.

"You are a Vlei," he said.

"So?"

He was close enough to smell her. He smiled through the gap in his teeth. She could not help smiling back.

"So?" she repeated.

"Did your father work at the Roodie Hotel?"

"My uncle. Before he disappeared."

"My mother worked there too. She is the cook who saved Kalahariland."

"So?" she said again.

"The story," said Kanye. "Roodie's chest, Vlei's knife, Mojamaje's cloak. I brought the knife."

He opened his denim jacket and pulled it out of the inside pocket, over his heart. He had filed the blade to a sharp edge.

Claire thought for a moment, eyeing him cautiously.

"I know nothing about it," she said. "You must be looking for someone else."

Kanye nodded. He liked her already.

"Yes, I am looking for someone else, but I heard your name. You must know the story. It happened here in Taung."

Six thugs, huge and dressed like schoolboys, grinning with menace, came up to surround Kanye. Claire waved them back.

"Leave him alone," she said.

Then she turned back to Kanye and said, "Put that knife away. It excites them."

"Yours?" he said, motioning to the gang.

Claire nodded.

"Want to join?" she said.

Kanye rammed the knife back into his pocket.

"Sure," he said, looking around at the thugs. "Sure."

"You make friends fast," said Claire.

These were the boys who went to school but never entered a classroom. They swaggered, swore, smoked, and imitated the Imitation Zulu. When school ended they refused to look for jobs. Passless, they hid out by day and stole by night, climbing onto buses that left for work before dawn. They collected an extra fare, and everyone paid. The passless toughs used knives and bicycle spokes to make their point.

Kanye did his best to fit in with these future criminals, to do whatever Claire wanted. From that first day he loved her. They all did, and that was why they followed her. He swaggered, smoked, and swore alongside them, but even as he did these things he usually broke into a smile, showing the charming gap in his teeth. He was so glad to be alive, among friends and in love, here beneath the great South African sky.

Kanye decided they needed a name. He suggested Eaters of Rock, after Mojamaje, and everyone liked it, even Claire. He painted the name on the back of each boy's denim jacket, including his own. They met each morning and walked together to pick up Claire, swaggering down the Sharpetown street, waving cigarettes and singing:

They come down to the street like warriors
Look out!
Who knows what damage these rough guys will do
Run!
They look so mean and strong
Who are they?
Look on their manly backs

And the Eaters of Rocks spun around together, showing the name that Kanye had painted on their jackets.

Claire lived in the last row of houses before the barracks,

in one of the blocks that looked like barracks themselves except for the many doors. Each door led to a room, and a family slept in each one. The boys came up to the Vlei room. A canvas sheet hung in the doorway instead of a door. Babies crawled in the dust outside, and two of the boys picked them up. Claire's mother came out, smelling of the beer she brewed and hid from the police in a hole in the floor.

"We will trade you these children for Claire," said Kanye.

Claire's mother pulled the infants away from the boys. She held them on her hip, scowling.

"What do you bums know of babies?" she said.

Claire came out and kissed her mother, the infants, and each of the Eaters of Rocks.

They went off to school, past a wheelless car, long burnt out and stripped. Children slept inside. When the police swept the street for passes, they arrested the family and shipped them out to the countryside, to a rocky piece of nowhere. Another family moved into the car.

The street filled with children on their way to school, men and women off to work, buses coughing thick black smoke. A band of Imitation Zulu appeared, waving clubs.

"Beware!" they growled.

"We will eat you!"

"The Zulu are coming to eat you!"

Children hurried off the street, Eaters of Rocks included, to let the Imitation Zulu pass.

"My brave warriors!" said Claire. "They were just the same number as you."

The Eaters of Rocks looked away.

"They would tear us apart," said Kanye. "Like chickens ready to boil in a pot."

"So who will you fight?" said Claire. "Innocent victims? Will you steal with knives and bicycles spokes like the passless toughs? Will you die in a barracks fight?"

The boys kicked stones in the road.

"Who do you want us to fight?" said Kanye.

She was almost ready to tell them, this morning, right there in the street. Were they ready to hear?

"Soon," she said. "I will tell you soon."

Every weekend, Kanye searched for Scott and Willoughby Two. First he telephoned every Scott in the Taung phone book, and then he set out to knock on every door on every Boer and English street. Cooks and gardeners offered advice on which street to try next, and sometimes dogs chased him up trees. He told the story to Claire, and persuaded her to come along. They took the bus and walked a long way before ending up on an English street. Kanye carried a paper bag filled with newspaper. Claire swept her arm across the wide, clean, quiet street with flowering trees shading the high white walls around each house.

"Look how they live," she said. "It makes you hate them."

"These houses look lonely."

"Better loneliness than Sharpetown."

"Better Kalahariland," he said. "I will take you there when I find the child."

They entered a wide gate, looked and listened for dogs, and then ran to the front door.

"The front door?" said Claire. "They will call the police."

"Watch," said Kanye, ringing the bell.

A maid opened the door, and Kanye talked so fast she could only fall back, calling for the Englishwoman, who came out scowling.

"What do you want?" she snapped.

"Madame," said Kanye in English, "forgive my sister and also myself for disturbing you. It is only a very small thing. Here is a bag of money my father owes to a certain Mr. Scott who once worked in Kalahariland but lives now in Taung."

Kanye held up the paper bag. Claire turned to run.

"My father told me," continued Kanye, "to give one half to the kind person who directs me to Mr. Scott."

The next thing Claire knew she and Kanye were sipping lemonade inside the English house. The woman picked up the telephone and began calling everyone she knew. At last she reached someone Kanye had already visited. She slammed down the phone and chased them out of the house.

Claire and Kanye ran into the street and halfway down it.

"You will never find them like that," she said.

"Then how?"

"Give up," she said. "The kid is better off. Her skin is light, they will raise her like an English girl. Look at these houses. Leave her alone. This Englishman did her a favor."

Kanye kept walking, shaking his head.

"You do not know," he said. "You only know Sharpetown and this. Kalahariland is different, especially Naring. I myself grew up in Lorole but lately I favor Naring."

Meanwhile, across South Africa, the Boers had finally had enough of the English. The countryside still spoke Boer, but most of the Boers now lived in the city. There they refused to learn English. Whenever they could, the English fired a Boer and hired someone else who spoke English, like the Jackal, at less than half the Boer's pay. And so, instead of studying English, the Boers now declared that all schools across South Africa must henceforth teach in Boer.

"No!" the Sharpetown children cried.

"Never!"

"Boer?"

"What kind of language is that?"

English was their last hope for ever finding a job. And now the Boers were taking even that away. First the land, then Taung village, and now they would lose their English.

The children called a meeting. They sent out a leaflet, explaining exactly what they would do. The police read it, and also reporters. The children promised to march from the Sharpetown school to the center of Taung city. There they would stay day and night, until the school spoke English again.

Claire read the leaflet and called together the Eaters of Rocks.

"Stop them," she said. "Right in the schoolyard, before they take a single step."

The boys were very quiet. They had never seen Claire so upset.

"Why?" said Kanye.

"Just do what I say," she snapped. "Afterward I will explain. Hurry. Words will not stop them. Hurt them if you must."

The children met in the schoolyard, shouting slogans. Their number excited them, the whole school assembled, defiant, resolved beyond fear or doubt. The Eaters of Rocks moved through the crowd. Three older boys made speeches from the verandah, predicting success, punching the air with their fists.

All at once, without warning, the Eaters of Rocks attacked. They overpowered the speakers and forced them back, into a classroom. At first the crowd fell silent, watching. Then they joined in the brawl.

Claire watched from across the yard, leaning back against a verandah post, hands to her cheeks, despairing. The Eaters of Rocks fell to the concrete floor. Children broke from the chaos, crying out.

"We march!"

"Nothing can stop us!"

"We march!"

The children turned away, ready for victory, to stream out the schoolyard gate. They filled the Sharpetown street, heading down the rise, clapping and kicking up dust.

Kanye stood up. His jacket was torn, he was sore all over but not at all bloody. The knife was still there. The children were many but none of them hit very hard.

One by one the Eaters of Rocks rose to their feet. Kanye watched the last of the children swarming out the gate. He took a step to follow, and the Eaters of Rocks came up behind him, watching and marching too.

The children began to sing, girls first, high and sweet, and boys joining in, reaching low for the voices of men. Kanye pushed up through the marching, clapping, singing crowd. He looked around, at every face, girls smiling and laughing as they sang, too young for hips or breasts, marching down the Sharpetown street.

The street was wide and straight, lined with box houses, trash cans, paper blown against the fences. Kanye looked down the rise, over the heads of the children. One of the speakers that Kanye had attacked now danced at the front of the crowd, shouting and raising his fist.

The noise of the children erased all other sound. Then Kanye saw far ahead of the crowd, lined up across the street, metal glinting in the sun. He peered down the rise, shading his eyes with one hand. Then he looked to the faces around him, the faces of children, their eyes impossibly hopeful and young, and the houses along the street, filled with impossible lives.

He suddenly saw it all, the impossible Sharpetown around him, whereas up to now Kanye the only Ata son had known nothing but the possible. He saw his mother, her years of work and solitude, his father of the childless house, and now he saw the impossible future in store for these children, the line of police and armored cars blocking the street ahead.

It was a day without weather, a moment of infinite time, step by step to the end of the street. There were no birds. Kanye searched the sky, thinking back. He tried to remember a single one, even a pigeon or crow, but no, birds never came to Sharpetown.

And then the police opened fire. The first shot pierced the dancing leader's open mouth. Others followed, and children screamed and fell. Those in front turned to run but the mass of the crowd held them there against the firing. Children bled and fell. Dust blew into the blood. In rippling waves, shrieking, bleeding, the children at last fell back.

Kanye alone saw the enemy one by one. He looked not at the mass of police and armored cars but at single targets, like Boko Tladi among the hyenas. He stood his ground as the children fell back. The other Eaters of Rocks saw him through the smoke and chaos. He called to them and they all ran to the side of the street to pick up trash-can lids. They filled their pockets with rocks.

When the police began their charge, on foot, carrying rifles, they saw a line of boys emerge from the fleeing crowd. The line stretched across the street and the boys carried shields and now hurled rocks. The police halted their charge and knelt to fire at the boys.

Kanye stood in the middle of the line, aiming, throwing, aiming, forcing himself not to look at the enemy all at once. He saw them one at a time. The Eaters of Rocks fell around him.

Dube hit the ground first, without crying out. Blood gushed out of his chest.

Tengo's shield rang as a bullet passed through it to pierce his belly.

Nelson fell to his knees.

Mbeki fell, then Koos.

Kanye kept his eyes ahead, moving from target to target. Children screamed and ran for their lives behind him.

Diep fell, Sollie dropped to his knees. Kanye stood alone. He looked at Sollie beside him, then back up at the police. He saw them all at once, all rifles swinging to aim at only him, the last boy standing. Baring his teeth, growling with despair, he hurled a final rock. His shield rang with bullets and two struck him, one in the leg and the other in the chest.

The blow knocked him over. His shield flew away. He felt nothing beneath him, saw nothing, not the sky or police or the ground rising to meet him, Kanye Roodie, a BaNare falling alone to earth.

The police stood up to resume their charge. It had taken them only a moment to shoot down the line of boys. The armored cars rolled up the street behind them.

The crowd of children rushed back into the schoolyard and there they gathered, praising the boys who had fallen to save them. The police and armored cars appeared. The children scattered, running down streets, into every house in search of kerosene. They emptied tins, lamps, and cookers, pouring the kerosene into bottles, jars, rubber balls, anything they could throw. They lit them and threw them at the police.

The battle raged all day. Police lost cars, burning with green smoke, but none of themselves. Children fell on every street. Long green vans came through to cart away fallen children. Parents came home from work and saw the smoke and fire from far away. Some joined the battle but others rushed to find the children as they fell.

The police drove up and down the streets. Children ran out, hurled their flaming missiles, then ran back into the houses. The police could only end the battle by entering the houses, a dangerous job they had not planned to do.

So they left.

The last police car out of Sharpetown stopped first at the Imitation Zulu barracks.

"We go," said the police. "We are not here to see what you do."

All Sharpetown stopped to listen. They heard the last police car drive away.

There was only silence.

They held their breaths. Had they won?

They heard singing.

Not children's voices but men's, chanting in Zulu.

The chant rose to fill the Sharpetown air, every street, every house, every room, and every ear. The Imitation Zulu grabbed their clubs and gripped them under their arms, marching out from the barracks in Zulu formation, the horns of an ox encircling its prey.

How dare these children complain? Greedy, spoiled, these children marched to protect their privileges, speaking English, sleeping in houses with women, men, and children mixed together. Now the Imitation Zulu marched, with shaved heads and pointed teeth, to cut these children down to size. Their chant grew louder, louder. They burst through doors, clubbing away the boys and men, forcing themselves on women and girls. Row by row, house by house, room by room, they squeezed the last life out of Sharpetown.

7

ENOUGH

Throughout the world everyone saw the same photograph.

A reporter took it, standing among the police. He had seen a leaflet and came to watch the event. Leaning against an armored car, smoking, talking with the police, he kept his eye on the street rising up to the school. When the children appeared, he threw down his cigarette and saw them fall through the tiny square in the camera. Late that night he developed the film, and there in the dark he watched the battle again.

First the children far away, up the rise. Then he saw them halfway down, then close to the police, faces clear, eyes alert and mouths open, silent, staring up through the liquid in the tray. Then smoke and dust and chaos, and then there were the Eaters of Rocks.

Four frames followed, all shot from the same angle. Smoke clouded the left and right margins but the center was clear. Machine guns poked out from an armored car in the lower right corner. All four photos looked over the shoulders of three policemen kneeling, firing rifles.

In the first of these four frames Diep lay dying, his shield atop him. Kanye and Sollie still stood, shields up, arms cocked to throw. The camera brought them close to the rifles and made the boys look shorter and very young. Just beyond them, frozen, transfixed, two small schoolgirls stared at the police.

In the second photo Diep still lay in the dust on Kanye's left and Sollie knelt on his right, eyes wide and empty. Kanye's head was turned to look at Sollie. The girls behind were turning to run. The angle of Kanye's head made the muscles stand out on his neck. His hands hung by his sides, gripping a rock and the shield. The foreground remained unchanged: police, smoke, guns, the armored car.

In the third picture Sollie and Diep both lay flat and dying, shields atop them, to Kanye's left and right. The girls were almost out of the picture, heads turned away from the sight. Kanye stood alone. One arm held out the shield, the other hurled a rock. His legs were steady, spread far apart for the throw, and his eyes were wide with rage. His teeth were bared, showing a gap that made him look even younger. It was easy to see the boyish charm the gap would give his smile.

In the final photograph the girls were out of the picture except for their ankles and feet, flying to safety off the frame. It looked as if the boys had saved them, especially Kanye, the last to fall. He was caught in midair, toppling to one side, shield flying, eyes already closing.

Some magazines printed the whole roll of film. Newspapers tended to print only the last four frames. They all printed at least the shot of Kanye hurling his final rock, teeth bared, facing the guns and the armored car while the two boys died beside him and the girls ran to safety behind.

In a world of short memory, across the earth, everyone stared at the face of the boy in the picture. Thereafter, for the rest of their lives, they heard the name of the country and remembered the boy.

"South Africa," they recalled. "The place they shoot children."

When the *Kalahariland Daily News* printed the series of four, the Atas recognized Kanye's face. They wept, and the eldest remembered his lips upon their breasts, their nipples pressed into the gap in his teeth. Men consoled them all, stroking their faces and crying too. The Stardust houses filled with men, who spent the night holding husbandless Atas against their chests. No Ata slept alone, except for Ata Four. Jack offered to slip in bed beside her, but even now she refused. She had no strength, no will, no voice to chase away the others.

She would not close the shop for even a night. The Atas collected copies of the newspaper page and pasted them up on the walls. They wept as they worked, as Ata Four herself sat with Ata Five at a table, staring at the pictures. The customers shook their heads, staring into their beer. Now and then Ata Four rose and went to the door, to lean against it, looking out at the lights of the city. This was how Lorole remembered her, a mother watching the night, grieving for her son.

It had all been a grand mistake, leaving Naring in pursuit of the Jackal, opening this shop, marrying off the Atas, trying to live beyond her fate. It was she who had tugged Boko Tladi into No-Man's-Land that very first time, to spend the night with her mother. One thing led to another, on and on until her son had ended up leaving a note in a bottle, hanging it from a tree, throwing rocks at machine guns, and finally falling on page after page across the world.

She turned to look at the wall of photos, willing him alive. If the Scotts had lived in Lorole, she might have given them a child to raise, as long as the girl visited Stardust once or twice a week. But Taung was another story, and now it was over and Kanye with it. She moved from the door and pressed her face to the wall, her nose against the pictures, surrounding herself with the Sharpetown she herself had known.

Suddenly she pulled away from the wall.

"Where is the fifth?" she said aloud.

Atas and men turned to her.

"The fifth picture," she said, facing them now, pointing to the wall. "I see only four. They show him fighting and falling, but where is the fifth, the final proof?"

No one's throat was clear enough to answer, no one knew what to say. She walked among them now, excited and relieved, still pointing to the wall.

"As evidence," she said, "these pictures are no good at all.

Where is the fifth? Until we see it, once and for all, we know he is alive."

Night after night she repeated this prayer, and no one spoke a word against it. They whispered instead, the customers leaning forward across the tables, the Atas bending over the freezer to bring out more beer. They worried now, as each night she seemed more certain, more resolute in her hope. But slowly, against their will, they all began to hope too.

In the compound behind, the Atas too young to work in the shop rose from their blankets and crept up to look in the lighted windows. Ata Four was in no condition to chase them back to bed. They slipped inside and under the tables, then came out to help the older Atas clear away empty bottles. They listened to the men and Atas whispering, to Ata Four repeating her wish. Soon they grew tired and went back to bed.

But on the way past the cookfire, red against the black of night, the youngest Atas stopped to sing. Too sleepy to clap or dance, they circled slowly the cookfire embers, singing softly into the dark:

> *Child of bottles*
> *Child of beer*
> *Child of all we overhear*
> *We sing against our nightly fear*
> *Until another day*
> *Enough! A rock*
> *Enough! A shot*
> *Enough! The children now are not*
> *She waits to see the final spot*
> *Where Kanye Roodie lay. . . .*

Naring

1

FORTUNE

Monosi was young, newly breasted, and Boko wore a loin-cloth and carried a herding stick. Beside them their children danced and sang to the moon, forming a circle with their grandchildren inside. They were all the same age, all three generations, and into the circle came Ata Four as Monosi first saw her, a little girl with a secret. Her son Kanye came up beside her, his fists filled with rocks. One by one they fell, Boko first, the children and grandchildren, Ata Four, and then Kanye, spouting blood without sound, leaving Monosi alone to face the charge of rifles and armored cars. . . .

Monosi sat up, awake, and wrapped herself in her arms. Slowly she shook off the dream. Rising, pulling a blanket over her shoulders, she returned to herself and went out into the night. It was a dream that many BaNare had these days, since Kanye Roodie had fallen.

No one knew exactly when the boy had placed the note in the bottle and hung it from the tree, but after hearing the news of the stolen Ata child the BaNare had been able to piece at least some of the story together. How Kanye had made his way to Naring remained a mystery. He could not have used the Stardust truck, for Jack himself had been sleeping atop it. Neither could anyone guess why Kanye had taken the rusted knife.

Monosi walked out to the clearing between the Tladi and Potso compounds, empty now beneath a quarter moon. She feared returning to bed where the dream waited, ready to seize her again. In the distance she heard an engine, the armored cars advancing, louder, approaching, until a tractor rumbled into the clearing.

It was old and rusty, pulling an even older wooden wagon with barrels of fuel on top. The driver turned the tractor toward her. It rolled to a stop and he switched it off. The world fell silent between them, Monosi and Timela.

"I greet you from Naring," she said.

"I greet you from South Africa," said Timela.

In the moonlight she could not see his scar, the mark of a true BaNare stray, but only the deep, shadowy lines of his face.

"You have a tractor," she said. "Congratulations."

"Yes," he said. "My luck has changed at last."

"The BaNare will be happy for you."

"Which ones? How many?"

"One at least," she said. "Myself."

Timela sat unmoving on the tractor. Monosi turned away, facing across the clearing.

"What happened to Vincent's tractor?" she said.

Timela laughed, half in bitterness, half in scorn.

"It never came," he said. "My daughters and I cleared enormous fields but he never came. At last I realized his trick. The well belonged to him, so I could not borrow cattle to plow. He wanted us to give up, to abandon the fields so he could have them all to himself instead of only half."

Monosi pulled her blanket tighter around her shoulders.

"You should have taken the case to court," she said. "The council would have made Vincent keep his word."

"That was just what he wanted, to see me begging here in Naring."

"He wanted the fields," said Monosi, "and bringing a case is not at all begging."

Timela climbed down from the tractor. He kicked the wheels, slapped the sides of the wagon behind, punched the barrels on top.

"Do you see these things?" he said. "They are mine. I earned them myself, without begging a court or anyone else. Your brother thought he had me, but I left my daughters out at the well to farm with hoes a corner of each field. That way the fields still belonged to them. By the Law of the Kalahari, Vincent could not prevent them from drinking, only cattle. I walked to South Africa, passing through Naring at night."

He paced before the tractor, waving his arms, and Monosi took a step back. His voice was tired, hoarse, and frightened her more than a little.

"So there I found a Boer," he continued, "with a tiny farm and one rusty tractor. I worked for food and nothing else, by day and moonlight, side by side with the Boer. Still the farm lost money. At last the Boer gave up. He sold the farm and gave the tractor to me. He threw in the wagon and three barrels of gas."

"You should have told someone," said Monosi, "to check up on the girls."

"Who?"

"Me, or anyone else."

"You do not understand," said Timela, moving close, his face looming up through the moonlight. "I cannot bear even to think of you. But here I am again, alone with the woman I cannot have, in the village that will not have me. But now my luck has changed, I am on my way to Vincent's well to plow my fields. In no time at all I will come back here with this wagon overloaded with corn. My daughters will marry the men of their dreams, with cattle and fields of their own."

Back in the Tladi compound Boko stirred in his sleep and reached out for Monosi. She came back in, slipped off the blanket and under his arms.

"Where were you?" he murmured.

"Meeting my secret lover," she said.

"Again?"

"He has his own tractor now. His daughters await him at their fields in the Kalahari."

Boko lay still, his arms around her, and then he sat up.

"You are serious," he said.

So Monosi sat up, too, and told him the story, sparing no detail.

"Did he touch you?" said Boko.

"Of course not."

"Where is Vincent?"

"Hunting," she said.

"Someone should have gone out to see them. Everyone knew that Vincent could not be trusted, that Timela could not take care of his daughters himself."

Monosi lay back down against him.

"The BaNare are everywhere now," she said. "Naring is not the same, abandoned compounds everywhere, miners drinking instead of marrying. Not only Timela is on his own."

"His luck has changed."

"Like shy children and debtors," she said, "luck is a thing that flies at the sound of its name."

Long into the night they discussed the matter, finally falling asleep near dawn. Timela drove on, into the Kalahari. Who would have thought that a few short years in South Africa would set everything straight? The morning air was cool and still, the cattle path was wide, and he opened himself to the feeling of triumph, an old soldier relaxing at last.

Long ago, coming back from the war, Boko Tladi had promised to him that before their first grandchildren came Timela would be rich and Boko would come begging at his door. To one man it was a passing remark, but the other guarded it close to his heart, wishing throughout his life for such a thing to come true. Every year Timela lowered his hopes, until he was ready to explode. Success had arrived just in time, saving him from a bitter, unknown end.

On past Loang, past well after well scattered through the brush, the cattle path grew narrower, fainter, and then disappeared. Timela turned off to Vincent's well, making his way through trackless brush from one large tree to another, with branches twisted in memorable shapes. Close now, approaching at last his beloved daughters, he looked up for the next tree, then forward to drive around bushes, and only once glanced down at the sand below.

There were tracks.

2

A GLORIOUS DAY FOR NARING

Chief Puo called a meeting. It was the first since the English had tried to settle the Kalahari. Puo told no one the purpose of the meeting, so everyone tried to guess. There was no obvious event or occasion, and indeed, as years passed less and less ever happened in Naring. In the end the BaNare could only conclude that the meeting would be a ceremony in honor of Kanye Roodie.

They met in the clearing between the Potso and Tladi compounds. Puo stood at the council tree. He reached to strike Mojamaje's knife to call the meeting to order, but then remembered the bottle. They had read Kanye's note and hung the beer bottle back up on the tree. So Puo clapped his hands instead.

"BaNare!" he yelled. "My people!"

Everyone sat down in the clearing and Puo began his speech. The Atas moved through the crowd, serving beer.

"Citizens of Naring," he said, "look at your chief. My hair is white and falling out. The chiefship is a heavy weight upon my shoulders. Think of all that has taken place under my fatherly eye. I brought you wells, a slaughterhouse, good weather, pipes for water, and saved you from South Africa. I am sick and old. Serving my people has worn me out."

The BaNare regarded their chief. He did not look sick at all. He was as fat as ever, his hair was gray but intact.

"And so," continued Puo, "the time has come for a change. My father and his father passed on the chiefship before they died. That was a very good thing. This way the old chief can guide the new one through the difficult early years of his reign."

The truth dawned on the BaNare. Everyone stared at their chief, then at Vincent sitting beside him, and then at Boko Tladi.

"Let this be my final chiefly act," said Puo. "Forget everything else I have done for you. Become ungrateful, forget my name but only remember this, my greatest achievement. I raised him myself. He is nothing but me with a younger face. I give him to you: Vincent, my son."

No one said a word. The Atas stopped serving beer and sat down in the crowd. Boko Tladi stood up.

"My Chief," he said, "we your children thank you for this great gift. Now it is up to us to decide whether or not to accept it."

"I am no longer chief," said Puo. "Talk to Vincent."

And with that Puo walked away from the council tree and into the Potso compound.

Vincent stood up.

"My people," he said. "This is a glorious day for Naring—"

Boko interrupted.

"You are not chief until the council confirms it."

Vincent turned toward him, smiling. They were far apart, with many BaNare sitting on the ground between them.

"You want them to depose me," said Vincent, "and everyone else in line until they get to you."

"If the BaNare so wish it," said Boko.

And now the crowd erupted in comments, some for, some against, all marking this moment when Boko Tladi at last revealed for all to hear his desire to make himself chief. When the noise died down, Boko continued, turning away from Vincent, raising his arms to the crowd.

"You know me," he said. "You know Vincent. Am I wrong to ask you to choose between us? Or perhaps there is someone else more deserving. I only ask you to make the choice yourselves. Do not leave it up to the chief."

There were some BaNare who thought it a good idea, others who dreaded the thought of backing the loser. The winner would never forgive them. And they could not divide the proposal from the proposer, Boko Tladi, who wanted the winner to be himself.

"All right," said Vincent, "let the BaNare choose. Who will stand with this hyena-slayer, who struck an elder, whose own father struck him down in shame, who killed in the mines, killed in the war, and someday will kill in Naring? Who else but his family will stand with him against their chief?"

There was silence. Everyone looked around for someone else to stand up. Many wanted to, but no one dared, except for Ata Three. It meant the ruin of their business selling beer, Vincent would never forgive them, but still she rose to her feet. She was close to Boko, and everyone saw their eyes meet and the look that passed between them. Everyone had a different opinion of what that look contained. One by one the rest of the Atas stood up too.

Vincent laughed. He rolled his head back and showed his teeth and sincerely, viciously laughed.

"Of course!" he said. "I forgot about the Atas. Does my sister know how many children her husband gave them? That is one way to be chief. Soon they will outnumber us and seize the chiefship for Boko Tladi—"

"Stop!" said Monosi, rising to stand beside Boko. "You will do your best to ruin as much as you can. What kind of chief is that?"

Vincent was truly enjoying himself. He had not believed it would be so easy.

"Oh, sister!" he cried. "Look at this Ata, look at your husband. They stand there declaring their love for all to see. You alone remain blind. The wife is always the last to know."

Boko stood there, unable to see a solution. He had made too many mistakes in the past. Vincent was using every single one against him, and now against the Atas and his wife. In his younger days Boko would have turned this meeting into a fight. He was older now, and wiser at last, so instead he just sat down.

The BaNare stared. They could not believe it. Vincent folded his arms in triumph and leaned back against the council tree.

Monosi sat down. The Atas sat down. The crowd rose and drifted away, muttering, shaking their heads in wonder and chagrin.

That night, Boko and Monosi lay in the dark in their house in the Tladi compound.

"She is still very beautiful," she said.

"Yes, she is."

"You did the right thing."

"I know," he said.

"Have you seen her again?"

Boko turned toward her.

"What do you mean?" he said.

"The look. There was more to it than I expected."

"What look? All I saw was a sad and frightened face. Now no one will buy their beer."

Monosi wrapped her arms around him and pressed her face to his.

"Tell me you never think about her," she whispered.

"Never," he said. "I only think about you."

"And becoming chief."

"Not after today."

"They are slow," said Monosi. "They were confused at the meeting, but I promise you they now are discussing the subject and changing their minds. By morning they will have come to their senses. By noon tomorrow you will be chief."

Around the cookfires that night there was very little debate. Most BaNare ate in silence and went to sleep thinking in private. Surely an age had ended. In former times a warrior such as Boko Tladi would never have faced such humiliation without a battle. Losing the chiefship was one thing, losing his pride was another. They could only conclude that Boko Tladi was not the man they had thought. They had made the right decision. Vincent would remain their chief.

3

THE LAW OF THE KALAHARI

It was a bright and windy day in Naring, no different from countless others that had gone before. All BaNare who had ever lived knew days like this, the wind ferocious but warm, bearing no sand or hint of peril. The clear, empty air showed every roof crisp and sharp against the sky. In South Africa, in Lorole, out in the Kalahari, when BaNare woke to such a day they remembered the sight of Naring, the smell of the air and the wind against their skin.

This was the day that the ancient tractor came back, pulling a wagon loaded with barrels of fuel and bundled blankets. The wind blew the noise of the engine one way and then the next, so few BaNare could guess where it was coming from or where it was going. Timela sat atop the tractor. There was murder in his eyes. They both stormed out of the Kalahari, Timela and the wind.

He arrived at a moment when Boko Tladi was down at Ko Roodie's forge, watching the Boer repair a crack in the famous hyena rifle. In the center of Naring miners climbed onto the mine office bus. Vincent was on his way back from hunting, and Former Chief Puo brought back another load of cattle. The rest of the BaNare were in their compounds or walking between them, working and talking, raising their voices to make themselves heard above the wind.

The wind tore at the blankets on the wagon behind Timela's tractor. He pulled into the clearing in the center of Naring and drove through the Potso compound wall. The dried mud crumbled and flew in the wind, the tractor jerked, and the engine died.

Many BaNare looked up, distracted by the distant motor's

sudden quiet. Timela jumped down from the tractor, reached into the wagon behind, and pulled out an ax. It was the same ax he had used to clear his Kalahari fields. Now he would use it on Vincent. He strode through the Potso gate, shouting Vincent's name. The compound was empty, the wind was roaring, no one heard a word.

At the Roodie forge the wind bent the flame of the welding machine. Ko and Boko tried to shield it with their bodies, but to no avail. In such a wind the Boer could not complete the repair. He stood up and yelled in Boko's ear.

"No good!" he said. "Leave it for tomorrow."

Monosi looked up from the Tladi compound, squinting with one hand, to see the tractor and wagon lodged in the Potso wall across the clearing. Timela came out, swinging the ax. His mouth moved but made no sound above the wind. She hurried across the clearing and other BaNare followed, heading for the bundles among the barrels on the back of Timela's wagon.

In the center of Naring, behind the gate of the mine office compound, the driver turned the key to the bus, but the engine refused to catch. The miners turned their faces away from the wind coming through the window bars. The driver shouted to get out and push, and they did. The bus rolled out the gate and the engine rumbled to life. Fighting the wind, the miners climbed back on the bus.

Monosi reached the wagon just as Timela's ax swung into the council tree. More BaNare saw and hurried toward him now. Monosi had told them of Timela's good fortune, but here in the swirling wind he did not look happy at all. Monosi reached up to the blankets atop the wagon, just as the wind pulled them back, revealing three faces, young but no longer lovely, crumpled with shame. BaNare crowded around, staring, leaning into the wind. Monosi called softly and reached out her arms. Timela's daughters stood up, each holding a baby, and their bellies swollen with three more.

All at once, in the rushing wind around them, everyone saw the truth. While Timela was gone, Vincent had gone out many times to visit the girls. He would refuse to let them drink from his well, unless they paid him back. The babies were the result.

Out in the Kalahari, just beyond Naring, Vincent's truck sped along the sandy track. Dead antelope lay piled on back, and two Lorole Indians sat up front. They were very rich, his newest friends, and Vincent had tried his best to impress them. He had lit a fire, drawing antelope to eat the new grass sprouting up through the fertile ash. He shot them through the window of the truck.

Timela chopped away at the council tree, eyes aflame, shouting curses lost in the wind. No one dared come near him. They helped his daughters and grandchildren down, and Monosi led them across the clearing. The daughters trembled against her, hiding their eyes, turning away from their father.

On the edge of Naring, moving swiftly toward its center, Puo grinned and bounced in the seat of his cattle truck. The cage on the back swayed with frightened cattle. Their horns caught in the bars. Puo drove into Naring, through flattened remains of abandoned compounds, past Boko Tladi walking home, unarmed, against the wind.

Boko waved away the dust behind the enormous truck. He felt it against his teeth. Far ahead he saw Timela chopping the council tree, and a crowd forming around him. Boko broke into a run. But the cattle truck reached the clearing first, and then the mine bus, and last of all Vincent's truck.

Vincent drove too fast, as always, and swerved around the bus. He did not see Timela, who ran out from the other side to swing the ax at just the perfect moment. The blade smashed through the windshield, and glass flew into the wind. BaNare jumped back, shouting, as Vincent's truck veered into the bus, which slammed into the cattle truck. Metal tore and twisted. The wind carried the hollow sound to every ear in Naring.

The bus fell over, spilling miners, and dead antelope flew into the air. Cattle rolled out of Chief Puo's truck, lowing in panic. Children screamed at the sight and the sound, and the wind blew sand into their mouths. The ax ended up on the floor of the truck. The Indians sat in the cab, smoking, brushing glass from their laps, unimpressed. Vincent wiped blood from his eyes, grabbed his rifle, and struggled out of the truck. He aimed at the blur approaching, but Timela knocked him down, seized the rifle, and placed the end of the barrel against the side of Vincent's head.

The BaNare stood surrounding Timela and Vincent, amid glass and twisted metal, wheels upended, spinning, cattle staggering, antelope carcasses, and everywhere the terrible wind. Vincent knelt in the sand, eyes closed, feeling the gun at his head.

"Do not touch me," he whispered. "I am now your chief."

Monosi and Boko came up through the crowd from different directions. She caught his arm and told him the story as he moved toward Timela. Everyone knew what he would do. There was no other way. Chaos erupted there in the clearing, but no one yet had died. He would try to keep it that way, to rescue Vincent despite his guilt. They watched Monosi's eyes meet Boko's, pleading, but he turned to face Timela.

"BaNare!" Boko called but addressing Timela, his eyes on the rifle. "It is not just Vincent who broke the law of the Kalahari. How could we leave Timela's daughters alone in the Kalahari for all this time, with no one but Vincent to pay them a single visit?"

The crowd leaned forward, straining to hear him over the wind.

"What?" they said.

"What?"

"Speak up."

But he spoke to Timela, not them, slowly approaching.

"I am the one you want," said Boko. "Blame me for all the abandoned compounds, the roads carving up the ancient circles, the crowded Naring plain where fathers weep for land to divide among their sons, for the landless, cattleless miners who never settle down, for the Kalahari wells spread so far apart that life and death is a private matter. Blame me, who brought you here, who married the woman you still cannot have, blame me and no one else."

"What?" the BaNare said again.

But Timela heard him, and swung his eye between Vincent and Boko, judging which one he hated more. The crowd gasped as the barrel swung to Boko. The BaNare closed their eyes, expecting the sound of the shot and Boko's mortal cry.

Timela looked down the barrel at the face of the man he was not. There was no fear in Boko's eyes, no apology, scorn, or pity. He faced Timela soldier to soldier, as if nothing had happened in all these years and they were just now stepping off the train. Timela looked down at Vincent, still kneeling in the wind, eyes closed and trembling. For all his bad luck, the ruin of his life and his daughters, he was still more like Boko Tladi than Vincent Potso. He would keep it that way. He raised the barrel to point to the sky and fired a single shot.

The BaNare cried out at the noise, and then slowly opened their eyes, expecting the worst. They saw instead Timela throwing down the rifle and Boko picking it up. Timela pushed through the crowd to find his daughters. Vincent still knelt, eyes closed, awaiting his end.

With one voice the BaNare sighed in relief. Things were not so bad after all. They had let Vincent go too far, but Timela, too, should have been more careful. At least no one had died. They had Boko Tladi to thank for that. They did not quite understand his speech, how the abandoned compounds and landless miners were all his fault and had somehow led to the ruin of Timela's daughters. But they were willing to accept his verdict. They knew the fault was not their own.

And so as the BaNare drifted away from the scene, they did their usual best to ignore the worst and pretend that all was well. They fought the wind, which all at once turned into smoke. With one voice the BaNare coughed. A cloud of ash swirled around them, sweeping out of the Kalahari.

Everyone knew how Vincent hunted, setting fires. They

burned for days but never spread far, except in a driving wind, like this one. BaNare turned to face the smoke, and far away they saw the glow of red.

Screaming above the wind, gathering their children, the BaNare had to flee Naring. The air turned hot behind them, around them, filling with ash and now with embers. The first grass roof caught fire. They coughed and ran, spitting out smoke, and then suddenly the animals appeared.

First came the gazelle and impala, bounding and leaping, flying over Naring's mud walls. Their terrified eyes reflected the fire. They lost their way, ran through open doors, and kicked out windows from inside. Wildebeest came, too, with the horns of cows, chests of buffalos, tails of horses, blue and black against the rising flames. Foxes and jackals slithered along between the antelope, hugging the ground, peering left and right. Warthogs ran up behind, grunting and wheezing. Ostriches loped in flocks, the heads in front looking out ahead, the heads in the rear swinging to watch the fire behind.

Birds flew out of the Kalahari, high, higher, beating against the smoky air, tumbling with the wind. At last they broke into the cold clear air above, too tired to go on, so they fell back to earth to land in the dust. Moths came from the other direction, flickering white in the glow of the fire, straining to reach it against the wind. They hung in space, desire suspended, as the BaNare abandoned Naring.

A rumble rose out of the roar of the fire, and hooves thundered over the earth. Hartebeest came in a long red blur, out of the billowing smoke, their horns a crazy thicket above them. Giraffe necks and heads stuck up among the red herd. The fleeing animals turned up and down the paths of Naring, mixing with BaNare. Now they saw lions lost in the swirl and the smoke. Children stumbled over leopard cubs, and reached out to touch the flying fur and the white stripes along the antelope flanks flashing like lightning past in the dark.

Animal and BaNare eyes glowed through the choking haze, as they all headed down to the canyon through the

Naring ridge. When they reached the other side, the Naring plain, the BaNare looked back at the flames towering above the ridge. The crackling roar was deafening now. Children screamed and held their ears. Men fell to their knees and pounded the earth, women turned their backs on the smoke and flames to cry at the eastern sky.

The fire climbed the far side of the ridge, skipping up rocks, from bush to tree to clump of dry, brown grass. There at the top it paused to wait for the last of the flames to burn behind. Then it leapt, flying out into empty air, dying and falling to earth below.

4

UNDERGROUND

The pain was everywhere, sourceless, complete. There was no light, no place for his body to feel. Perhaps he had no body now. And then he smelled beer.

He sniffed the air. Yes, beer, a smell he knew very well.

The ability to sniff meant a nose. He sniffed again and heard the sound of the sniff. That meant ears. All together this argued for a head, and thus a mouth and eyes within it. He tried to speak.

"I am not dead," he said.

He heard his voice, a creaking whisper. He was sure now his eyes were open. He closed them and saw the same thing.

"Blind but alive," he said, feeling his mouth forming the words.

Suddenly light burst above him. His hand moved to shade his eyes, dazzled behind the closed lids.

"So you are awake," a voice said.

He strained to open his eyes.

"Claire?" he said.

A hand touched his face. Slowly he opened his eyes and saw her, a blur above him. He lay in the hole in the concrete floor where Claire's mother hid beer.

"You still have a fever," said Claire.

She kept her hand against his cheek.

"Smile for me," she said.

"It hurts," said Kanye.

But he forced a smile, and then it came by itself. He was so happy to see her, so happy to be alive. She looked at the charming gap in his teeth and smiled down to match it.

Kanye's eyes adjusted to the light. He saw the bruises and lumps on her face, the missing tooth in the front, on top.

"What happened?" said Kanye. "You look like me."

She raised a hand to her missing tooth.

"Visitors," she said. "Imitation Zulu. It was very bad for a while. Now things are calm."

"What did they do to you?"

"Everything they could."

Kanye closed his eyes, fighting the image of what that meant. Claire closed her eyes, too, remembering. Her hand was still against his cheek, and he pulled on her wrist, to bring her down into the hole.

"No," she said, pulling back. "I do not need consolation."

"Then console me," he said. "I cannot get up, so you must come down here."

Claire shook her head, but she did it. Kanye moved over as far as he could. There was just enough room for her. She lay in his arms, looking into his face.

"Did many die?" he said.

"Very many."

"The Eaters of Rocks?"

"All but you."

Kanye raised a hand to her hair.

"Where did they shoot me?" he said. "It feels like everywhere."

Claire rose from the hole, brought back a newspaper page and the old Vlei knife, and climbed back down.

"They shot you once in the chest and once in the knee," she said. "But instead of your chest the bullet hit this."

She showed him the knife, a bullet lodged in the blade. Kanye nodded solemnly.

"And your face is famous," she said, handing him the page.

Kanye stared at the pictures. He brought the page to his nose, surrounding himself again with the sound of rifles crackling, children screaming, the ring of bullets against the shields.

"This is why I keep you in this hole," she said. "If the police find you, they will shoot you again."

Kanye closed his eyes from the pain. Claire kissed him and rose again from the hole. Kanye fell asleep.

Once and sometimes twice a week the police came through every house on the street, but they missed the hole every time. When the raids subsided, Kanye came up to eat and sleep aboveground, with the twenty Vleis crowded into the tiny room. He and Claire slept in the corner, together, under an ancient fur cloak.

They awoke in the dead of night and listened to make sure everyone else was fast asleep, and then they came together, careful not to harm his leg. They made no sound except for their movements under the blanket. Sometimes the final moment raised all their senses and left them crying together for the children who had died. Afterward they lay entwined, and fell asleep still pressed together, safe in each other's arms until another day.

Kanye's knee healed badly. It was months before he took a single step. Sometimes the pain woke him at night, and he lay awake listening to the beating of the Vlei hearts around him. He pulled the cloak over his head but heard them still. They seemed to come from the fur itself. The pelts were silver jackal, the same as Mojamaje's cloak, and according to the story, the jackal hearts still beat. He turned the fur over, feeling the seams along the back to count the pelts. There were thirty, just as the story said.

Kanye lay beside Claire, staring up at the dark, surrounded now by Naring. Vlei's knife, Mojamaje's cloak, Roodie's chest. His own name was Roodie, the Vlei knife had stopped a bullet from piercing his chest, and now he had found the cloak.

The next day, as everyone ate, Kanye told them the story. Even the eldest among them knew nothing about the original Vlei, but they had indeed worked on the Roodie farm until the war, when the farm turned into factories. They moved to

Taung village, and when that died they moved to Sharpetown. That was all they knew.

As Kanye told the tale, they asked for more details, until he told them all about Naring, the Atas, and even about Taung, at least the parts that ended up in BaNare stories. Every morning and every night he told them more, until they carried inside themselves the same idea as his own, of Naring as a true and lasting home. Every night as Kanye spoke, Claire watched the children falling asleep, far away from a crowded Sharpetown room, atop a wagon beneath a moon and countless stars in a Kalahari sky.

Every morning Claire and Kanye woke before light, to wash outside before anyone had a chance to see Kanye's face. They rose in silence, stepping over sleeping children, feeling their way to the door. Outside they raised their arms against the factory lights.

Kanye went for water at the end of the street, limping heavily on a stick, while Claire lit the kerosene ring. When the water was hot, Kanye scooped it over his arms and chest, but mostly he watched Claire. She wore only a blanket around her waist and stretched her arms in a yawn. Kanye saw her straight, smooth back, the fine breasts and the graceful line of her neck. She placed one foot in the basin, drawing water along her leg, parting the blanket up to her hip.

"I will tell you the truth now," she said one morning, pulling on her jumper. "About you and me and the Eaters of Rocks."

She sat him down outside the door and looked in his face.

"It was my job to recruit young toughs, to send away to secret places in the hills of the northern border. There the boys would learn to be men. They would also learn explosives."

Kanye stared into her eyes, seeing there a hardness, resolute, against even him.

"You were almost ready," she said. "Still a bit wild, but ready to listen to orders. You proved me right. I am proud of what you did."

"So you are in danger too," he said. "We can escape together, to Kalahariland."

"No," she said. "My knees are healthy, my face is not famous. I am strong and unknown. I will go on here as long as I can."

One night, as the last of the children fell asleep to Kanye's tale, an unknown voice spoke from outside, through the canvas sheet across the doorway.

"Quick! The police know about the boy!"

Claire leapt up and rushed to the door, but the stranger was gone.

"Hurry," she called to Kanye. "Throw on rags to wear. I should have known this would happen."

Claire herself pulled on a long, faded dress and threw a blanket across her shoulders.

"Who told them?" said Kanye.

"Anyone," said Claire. "Maybe someone next door, afraid the police will blame them too if they find you. Or maybe no one. Maybe the rest of the block wants you out before you bring more trouble and more police."

Claire threw Mojamaje's cloak over his shoulders, and Kanye limped on his stick. Together they rushed out into the night, along the empty Sharpetown street. Perhaps it was all a trap, and the police were waiting at the end of the block. Kanye could not run, and Claire could not carry him far. Up the street they saw the lights of a car waiting, perhaps a police van.

"Go back," Claire hissed. "Back to the room."

"What if the police are already there?" Kanye whispered.

The only way out was through the barracks. They hurried to the gate, moving past the sleeping guard without breathing.

The barracks were windowless, dark, reeking of urine, sweat, and beer. The only sound was the creaking of the metal roofs cooling in the night air and a lone voice chanting in Zulu from somewhere on one of the bunks. There were shapes on the ground, and one of these rose to his feet and reached for Claire. Kanye swung his cane and knocked him down.

Claire and Kanye stood frozen, searching the shadows for signs of others, for Imitation Zulu streaming out of the barracks to tear them apart and worse. They stood for a long time, listening, to the chanting voice, the creaking roofs and a car passing the barracks gate. Then they moved again, and reached the back fence. The barracksmen had torn huge holes in it. Kanye and Claire climbed through and out of Sharpetown.

They crossed a field, stumbling over dried cornstalks, and found a road across the Taung plain. Staying to the shadows alongside, falling to earth when a car passed, they made their way through the dark. A wind rose to tear at Kanye's cloak and Claire's blanket. Rain mixed with the wind, and then came hail. Claire held her blanket over their heads, and Kanye wrapped one arm around her to keep himself from falling. He felt her breath and the side of her breast and hip pressing against him, the warmth and smell of her skin.

At a crossroads they stopped and waited for the sun, sleeping against each other until a bus came by. Claire jumped up and flagged it down. It was huge and blue with bundles and bicycles tied on top, chickens and sacks of grain inside. The passengers saw Kanye's limp and gave him a seat. The woman beside him, holding a baby, rose to give her seat to Claire, who sat down and took the baby.

Claire waited some miles and then moved up to talk to the driver. She whispered to him, and a look of worry spread across his face. He turned around to look at Kanye. But he gave her good directions and demanded no fare. He let them off at another crossroads, to wait for another bus. The sun was high and the plain around them was barren and dry.

They slept again, in the shade of a thorn tree, until the next bus came. The last stop at the end of the day was a jumble of tents, cardboard shacks, and tin huts. Claire helped Kanye off the bus. There was no grass, just yellow weeds with spiny flowers and leaves like thorns. Goats picked among the weeds, their skins pulled tight against their ribs, shifty eyes desperate for something to eat. Women wore rags held together with pins.

When bulldozers had buried Taung village, this was where the trucks had dumped the passless, on the southern edge of the Kalahari, too rocky and dry to farm. Claire led Kanye north, just out of sight of the shacks. He dragged his leg now, weary from the journey. The ground was rocky and red. They crossed a rise, and the soil gave way to yellow sand. Claire stopped and Kanye drew up beside her.

"There," she said, pointing ahead, north across the land. "The Kalahariland border. There is no water after this. It will take you a day, maybe three."

"Come with me," he said.

"Remember," said Claire, turning to face him, "you are a herdboy looking for strays. And never open your mouth."

"Come with me," Kanye repeated. "How can we part after all that has happened?"

"You know I must stay," she said. "But someday when this all is over I will come to Kalahariland to see you and this wonderful place Naring."

Kanye took out the Vlei knife.

"You take this," he said, "as I take the cloak. Just like Vlei and Mojamaje. This way the story continues, this way we meet again. When my knee heals, when my face is no longer famous, I will come back and find you."

Claire took the knife, and Kanye took a step back. They stood in the afternoon sun, silent, staring into each other's eyes. Kanye pulled the cloak tighter around his shoulders, and Claire slipped the knife into the belt of her dress. She turned away, and Kanye turned to the border.

He stared out at the horizon stretching before him. It looked empty and cold. He shivered, his knee ached, and he wanted to turn and shout for Claire. Instead he limped across the sand away from her. Soon he was deep within it, nothing but rolling dunes and thorn.

The sun set and he slept against a thorn bush. He woke in

the dark and walked some more. Soon after dawn an armored car drove up. A soldier stared through binoculars but Kanye limped on, a crippled herdboy looking for strays. The soldier looked for a long time, watching Kanye's knee. Then the car drove on.

Thirst and hunger dazed him, blurred his sight, and multiplied the pain in his knee. On the third day he reached the fence. It was wire, as tall as himself, and he climbed with one leg and two hands. His bad leg hung and slammed against the wire as he fell to earth in Kalahariland.

5

SEBE'S WILD PIG

And so Naring no longer existed. The BaNare silently picked through the rubble of their former homes. The wind was gone, the morning was calm and clear, and they wondered where they would go. It was the end of a long and intricate story, less than unique and more than true. Timela finally had his wish. He was like the BaNare, or they were just like him.

There was nothing left, no roof remained intact, no compound was spared. The mud walls and every bush and tree between were blackened and lifeless. In the center of all lay yesterday's twisted metal, as if Naring had not simply burned, but exploded. Already the day before hung cloudy and dim behind them, and the day before that more distant still. The past dissolved, and they wondered where it would end. Without Naring, could they call themselves BaNare? Would their children ever dance again to a luminous moon, fearful of the years to come and their absolute end, their sole comfort and consolation the circles around them, ring upon strangerless ring?

The Tladis, the Potsos, Timela and his daughters, everyone stood with head down and mind spinning from the blow. The danger had crept so slowly upon them, year after year without warning, without Zulu, Boer, or English horde descending upon them. Instead the battle had broken out inside them, and Naring fell. The first rain of the season, not far in the future, would wash away its last remains.

Before the sun had climbed very high, a truck drove up through the canyon. The BaNare had just seen enough traffic to last a lifetime, so very few looked up. Those who did saw the Stardust truck, a familiar sight, and Jack as always pulled up to the Ata compound. He was not alone. An Ata came out of the truck, and then a young man with a stick. He leaned heavily on it as Jack came around to help him. The Atas came out to surround them.

The BaNare were all in their usual places, among the remains of their former compounds, and so word spread as it always did, along the same route from ear to ear as when Naring existed. Like any unbelievable news, it spread very fast, and soon the whole of the former village descended on the Ata compound.

Suddenly, swiftly, it was like old times, a hero returning, and there amid the ash of Naring there glowed a spark of life. The BaNare surrounded Kanye. Their hands cupped this final ember, and carefully fanned it back to flame. Miners pushed forward to raise him onto their shoulders. Mothers wept, children danced and sang.

And so the Atas revived Naring. They alone had remained as all the BaNare once had been, united in their lives and fate. Unforeseen but true, the Atas were the only rightful BaNare left. The others watched Ata Four embracing her mother and then Monosi, her first time back in twenty years. Despite her success, to them she had always remained the Ata girl who tried to become a full BaNare, and fled from Naring when she failed. Now Naring lay destroyed and Ata Four returned triumphant, famous herself, with a hero for a son. Her arms were thick, her breasts heavy, and gray showed behind her ears.

The miners carried Kanye up to the center of the former village to the charred trunk of the former council tree. Everyone sat on the ground or climbed the wreckage of the previous day, forming a circle around him. They saw Ata Four and Boko Tladi speaking quickly, then Ata stepped into the circle beside her son.

"BaNare!" she said, raising her arms and turning slowly for all the crowd to see.

And now they fell quiet, all eyes upon her.

"BaNare!" Ata said again, looking into the eyes she had turned away from twenty years before. "You may have noticed: my son is no longer dead. But while he was gone and saving children he did some thinking, and maybe you should hear it."

The BaNare moved their eyes to Kanye, who leaned heavily on one leg. He took a step forward, as in the picture, grimacing in pain to show the gap in his teeth, and everyone caught their breath.

"In Sharpetown," he said, surprising them all with the depth of his voice, "they know no such thing as Naring. I told them all about it, and they thought it a fine idea. For them, for me, for BaNare out in the Kalahari, away in the mines, in Lorole, we all must know that such a place exists, that anytime we can come back and call it home."

The BaNare stared at the ground.

"Tell us," someone said at last.

"Tell us the story."

So Kanye did so, sparing no details, of life and death in Sharpetown, his escape to Kalahariland. The tale confirmed their worst suspicions of life without Naring. And so that very morning, the day after Naring burned to the ground and Kanye Roodie came back from the dead, the BaNare at last made Boko Tladi chief.

His hair was not completely gray, but surely the time had come. The chief's council came foward to sit beneath the blackened tree. Their wooden chairs had all burned up, so the Ata brought pots to turn upside down for the elderly bottoms. The pots left round, black smudges on every seat.

They deposed Vincent, and one by one the BaNare rose to endorse the decision. Then the council made Sleeper Sebe chief. One by one the BaNare rose to praise Sleeper, a noble, generous man, but circumstances beyond their control, which everyone knew and lamented, forced the BaNare to depose him too. They gave examples of Sleeper's good works, stories of childhood and pure-hearted deeds. Those who did not know Sleeper himself but knew his son or a distant cousin explained how wise the whole family was, going all the way back to the first Sebe who caught a wild pig and trained it to open cans with its tusks. Someone else rose to say that cans had not yet existed when the first Sebe lived.

When at last they named Boko Tladi chief, the sun was low in the sky. The BaNare were tired. He rose to deliver a speech that everyone strained to follow, but their minds wandered, children squirmed, and afterward no one could quite agree on what their new chief had said. For days they argued over the speech, debating what they themselves would have said in the same situation, the turns of phrase just right for the moment, the proper vows to swear.

The BaNare rebuilt Naring, not exactly in circles but more or less. The tale joined the others they knew and soon they hardly remembered the days before Boko Tladi was chief, or what all the fuss was about. Timela's daughters earned a living plowing fields for hire on the Naring plain, using their father's old South African tractor and Vincent's as well, which the court had given the girls as *mpe* for the six children that Vincent had given to them. Vincent and Timela both disappeared, perhaps to Lorole, perhaps at last to the mines, perhaps even together. No one knows.

Ko Roodie repaired the cattle truck, which the council seized, certain that Puo had bought it with fees from the Kalahari wells. Boko Tladi took the truck around the Kalahari, carrying BaNare to and from the distant wells, holding meetings with BaNare living at each one. Everyone came to hear from Boko news of Naring and other wells and add to it their own. Monosi sometimes rode along on the back, and kept the children quiet by telling them Ata's tale. In time it became their favorite story, of the little girl who grew up to save a country, raise a heroic son, and return to Naring to save the BaNare themselves.

In ancient times heroes died and ages ended, so BaNare stories usually end in just the same way. Not so today, the age of Ata Four. Although more events followed, Monosi ends the tale in the middle of Ata's life. In this way the children learn the point about living heroes, that they, too, in their very own lives, must do their best to find their own way in the world. And if Monosi did add those later parts, the tale would be too long for the journey on the back of the truck.

As for Kanye himself, he worked for his mother, driving the truck, counting money and crates. At night he sat with the customers, discussing the news of the week, awaiting that miraculous day when his knee would heal and his face would no longer be famous. Whenever a stranger mentioned South Africa, Kanye sat down at his table and spoke the words that pained his mother, an echo of her own: echo of herself:

"Did you come from South Africa?" said Kanye. "Did you see Claire Vlei?"

Ata At Night

When the last customer paid and left, when the bottles were cleared away and the tables wiped, Ata Four locked the door and turned out the lights of the shop. Business had never been better since Kanye's return, although his absence had changed everything. Men had spent night after night in the Stardust compound consoling the Atas, and Ata had not the strength to keep them out. They left behind swelling Ata bellies, including Ata Five's. Her English sweetheart never came back. The child was a girl, and everyone called her Ata Six.

As the Atas filed out the back door of the shop, Ata Four took her granddaughter into her arms. The others went off to sleep. She wrapped a blanket around her shoulders, set a chair out on the back step and sat down. The child slept against her breast. She looked out at the dark, quiet compound, her home.

She closed her eyes and summoned back the Willoughby house, cool and dark with the smell of wax, and then looked up at the sky. She followed the stars to the Naring horizon, remembering the first love of her live, handsome and smiling at her from the English tub. She remembered what he felt like against her, his smell, his eyes and voice promising her so much. After all these years she felt no different, thicker, grayer, but inside herself the same. It was like that with all the Atas. Each of them could never forget that moment that changed her life, that morning he woke up distant and cold and she found out her first love no longer loved her back. Her heart was broken forever. After that each Ata made the same vow, committing to it her life and very breath. If she could not love one, then she would love many, all men, and the children they left behind.

There on the steps of her famous shop, holding against her breast the future mother of Ata Seven, who in turn would grow up to bear Ata Eight—Ata Four knew that she would let the men come back. The Stardust compound would fill with babies and men, like the Naring home of her youth.

The truth was clear and cold like the African night around her, the same sky she had danced to as a child. Her life to come had once seemed far away, so fearsome and unknown. She remembered the circle of children, the song they sang out loud and the song she sang to herself. It was a wishing song, a hymn in praise of men. She knew better now, that the earth did not turn around them. She had made a life of her own. Yet sometimes as she fell asleep she found herself dreaming again. Those were the times she had to admit that she loved him still, Elias Bajaki, the Jackal.